I0524706

THE MYSTERY OF LEANDER WELLES

ASHLYN DREWEK

FOX HOLLOW BOOKS

This book is a work of fiction. Names, characters, places, and incidents are either products of the author's imagination or are used fictitiously.

Any resemblance to actual events or locales or persons, living or dead, is entirely coincidental.

Copyright © 2020 by Ashlyn Drewek

All rights reserved.

No part of this book may be reproduced in any form or by any electronic or mechanical means, including information storage and retrieval systems, without written permission from the author, except for the use of brief quotations in a book review.

Cover design by Teresa Conner at Wolf Sparrow Creations

For Amelia,

FOREWORD

2021 Award Winner!

The Mystery of Leander Welles was a finalist in the Suspense category of the 2021 Next Generation Indie Book Awards!

———

Content Warning:

This book contains references to animal abuse, child abuse, self-harm, and suicide. Reader discretion is advised.

CHAPTER 1

he scratches on the side of my neck were still raw and scabby. If I craned my neck too far I ran the risk of splitting them open. I shifted my ponytail over my shoulder, hoping the blonde strands hid them from view. It was the first time someone actually tried to rip out my windpipe. Knowing my luck, I'm sure it wouldn't be the last.

The heavy metal door slammed shut behind me. Try as I might not to jump, I knew I flinched anyway. It was a reflex I had little control over no matter how many times I stepped into this interview room.

I hated the sound. I hated how it scared me every time it closed, a booming reminder I was trapped in a room with violent, deranged people. Not to mention, it made me look weak, made the patients giggle at my discomfort. It was my job to put them on edge, to suss out whether or not they were truly insane or just pretending for the courts.

From now on, I would make sure I was the first one in the room. That would solve the problem. Of course, it also meant I couldn't observe the patient beforehand. I would have to do it another time. There. Yet another problem resolved.

Now, for the man of the hour.

Ray, a fifty-six year old alleged schizophrenic, was drooling on the table. He was practically catatonic by the look of things. How many tranquilizers did the staff give him this morning? I'm sure if I asked them they'd say it was for my benefit, given what happened during our last interaction. At least they'd clipped his nails.

"Hi Ray," I said, slipping into the seat across from him.

He didn't move. Didn't even blink.

"How are you feeling today?"

Another droplet of spit rolled over the edge of his chapped lip, plummeting to the white table between us.

Resisting the urge to wipe it away, I focused on his chart. The notes from his other doctors were less than stellar. His violent outbursts were becoming more and more frequent, regardless of the changes to his medication. "Looks like you've been having nightmares again. Is it because of the trial?"

Ray's lids dropped slowly and lifted even slower. I took it as a yes.

"Has your lawyer been to see you?"

He grunted. A no?

"I'm sure you'll hear from them soon." Or not. The public defender's office was chronically overworked and under-staffed. They weren't exactly falling all over themselves to help their "normal" clients, let alone the "crazies."

I flipped a few more pages, keeping my expression neutral while I read the details of Ray's latest episode. Yesterday during free time, he attacked a fellow patient in the day room. "Do you want to tell me about what happened with Jeremy?"

He grunted again.

"You stabbed him in the eye with a pencil, Ray." I closed his chart and folded my hands on top of it. "They had to surgically remove it."

A smile spread across his lips. The cracks in the thin skin split even further and a speck of blood appeared in the center.

I frowned. This was not how I wanted to start my day.

He kept smiling, despite the stream of drool that slipped from the corner of his mouth.

"Ok. We're done." I stood and swept his file off of the table.

Jumping to his feet, he lunged for me.

I yelped, skipping back a step.

His chains rattled against the table, holding him in place. He snarled and clawed the air, trying to grab me despite the cuffs digging into his wrists. A string of expletives spewed out of him, interspersed with threats about the vile things he would do to me when he got out.

"Guards!" I moved a safer distance away in case he managed to free one of his hands. Again.

A moment later, the heavy, chipped metal door buzzed open. Two corrections officers rushed in. An orderly named Calvin followed close behind.

The guards seized each arm while the orderly snuck a hand into the fray, stabbing a needle into Ray's shoulder and depressing the syringe. The effect was almost instantaneous. By the time I retrieved my upturned chair and righted it, Ray was unconscious. The guards dragged him out of the room, the heels of his soles squeaking on the floor.

"You ok, Doc?" Calvin asked.

I forced a smile to my lips and nodded. "Yes. Just caught me off-guard."

"Head on a swivel, Doc. Head on a swivel."

I nodded again as Calvin disappeared down the hallway to make sure Ray was tucked safely into his room.

He was right. Giving patients the benefit of the doubt would only get me so far in this profession. Once they proved how dangerous they were, I needed to remember it.

Straightening my skirt, I exited the interview room, retreating to the safety of my office. Closing the door behind me, I leaned against it and expelled a breath. Goddamn Ray. I thought we were making progress. I guess I was wrong. Or, I vastly underestimated the thrill he got from hurting people.

Turning a negative into a positive, I sat at my desk and pulled up his case file on the computer. If anything, this little stunt with the pencil and his reaction to it today were all I needed to inform the lawyers in his homicide case he was, indeed, fit for trial. Just because he had extreme outbursts and zero impulse control did not mean he wasn't aware of what he was doing. The majority of schizophrenics made it their entire lives without murdering people or permanently disfiguring them. I wasn't going to let Ray use it to play the system and get away with the insanity plea.

When the clock on the wall ticked five o'clock, I was still hard at work, typing assessments and reading over new case files. Calvin waved goodbye through the window on the side of my door. I lifted a hand and kept working.

At seven, my desk phone rang. Huffing, I picked it up without looking.

"Are you coming, or should I just reschedule? Again." Darren. Shit.

Glancing at my watch, I suppressed a groan. It was later than I thought. I closed the file I was working on and shoved it into the filing cabinet. "I'm coming. I just lost track of time."

"Uh-huh. See you when you get here."

He hung up before I could, which was just as well. I didn't need to hear it. I knew I'd get an earful in person. There was no need to go through it twice.

I logged out of my computer and made sure everything in my office was secure before bolting out the door.

"Leaving kind of early, aren't you, Dr. Clayton?" the desk clerk called out as I rushed by.

"Night!"

Hurrying out to the parking lot, I jumped in my car, slinging my work bag into the passenger seat. I couldn't believe I completely spaced dinner at Darren's. I knew it was soon... I just didn't realize how soon. This dinner had been on the agenda for three weeks, sandwiched between his work schedule and mine. I should have been looking forward to it. Deep down, I wasn't.

⋆⋆⋆

Darren was done eating by the time I walked in. The plate across from him was piled high with food long-since cold. The glass of wine had gone tepid when we both knew it should have been served chilled.

Dropping into the empty chair, I tried to look as apologetic as possible.

Darren downed the rest of his wine and set the empty glass on the table, his expression severe.

I cringed inwardly. He was pissed. The heat was practically rolling off of him in waves. "I'm sorry. I was finishing up an assessment and I—"

He leaned forward and snatched the glass of wine next to my plate, scowling at me. "I know, Lorelei. I've heard it all before."

"Look, I'm sorry I missed dinner. What else do you want me to say?"

"Nothing." He swallowed another mouthful of wine before setting the glass down. "Nothing. Like I said, I've heard it all before. You had to work late. You lost track of time. Last minute eval came in. Just have to finish charting. One more case law and then you're coming."

Drumming my nails on the table while he spoke did nothing to keep my jaw from setting or my molars from grinding together. I didn't question his job. I didn't question how he managed his time. I didn't do any of that because I knew his job was important, yet the same courtesy was never returned. It seemed all of our disagreements centered on my faults, my flaws, my failures — never anything Darren did, or didn't do.

"You prioritize your work over our relationship," Darren continued, probably oblivious to the fact I hadn't even responded. How many bottles did he consume prior to my arrival? It was either that or he had run through this speech a time or two with how easily he spat the words. "I'm tired of fighting with you. I'm tired of fighting to have time with you. Can't see you Tuesday, it's dinner with Mom. Can't do Thursdays or Fridays, those are your nights at the hospital. Can't do anything on the weekend because you're too busy reading case law. When the hell am I supposed to spend time with you? Huh? Why isn't there a night for me? I thought I made my needs pretty clear."

I shook my head, trying not to be baited even though my blood was boiling. Work was exhausting enough, I didn't need to counsel people outside of it either. Especially not a grown man with a litany of his own issues. He spent too much time masquerading as a saint to be the least bit intro-spective. Like any good narcissist, Darren sure was quick to point the finger for all of his problems at everyone and anyone. God forbid he ever look in a mirror.

He plowed on after another gulp of wine. "I know you think you're out there saving these people and championing the mentally ill, but over these last few months I've come to realize that is all you care about. Really. You don't actually want a relationship. You have no room in your life for anything else except twisted fucking people who would just as easily slit your throat than thank you for whatever it is you think you're doing for them. What is it you think you're accomplishing anyway? What are you getting out of this? Because I know what you're *not* getting, not that it seems to matter to you at all."

The final, proverbial straw drifted out of his mouth and landed squarely on my back. Something inside of me snapped. Calmly, quietly, and with a startling finality. It wasn't worth trying to explain, or apologizing, or begging for clarification and understanding. He simply wasn't worth it.

"I don't have to explain myself or my job to anyone, let alone you." I stood slowly and pushed my chair in. "Goodbye Darren."

"Wait, Lorelei. Where are you going?"

I ignored him. I'm sure in all of his dress rehearsals he didn't envision me walking out. No one walked away from Darren Perkins. No one told him no. His ego couldn't handle it.

Yelling my name, he commanded me to return the entire way to the door. He was still yelling when I slammed it shut and walked to my car.

The door on our fledgling relationship was closed, nailed shut, never to be opened again. I tried not to dwell on all of the time and energy I'd wasted despite his complaints to the contrary. I didn't even cry on the way home. It wasn't worth it. If anything, I felt relief, like a pressure had finally been lifted. Until that moment I didn't realize I was drowning all these months.

Darren was right about one thing, though — there was no room in my life for anything other than my job. It was a never-ending battle of thankless, frustrating work, but it was important. If I didn't do it, who would?

CHAPTER 2

"Sorry I'm late," I said, pecking my mother's cheek and dropping into the chair adjacent to her.

"I know you own a watch, Lorelei. I gave you that Cartier last Christmas for this very reason."

Great. It was going to be one of those dinners. "I forgot it today."

"Did you forget your cell phone, too?"

"You know I can't have my phone on me when I'm at work."

"I just don't see what's so hard about remembering a standing dinner reservation. Every Tuesday at seven, it's not like it's an unreasonable—"

"Can we drop it?" I asked through gritted teeth as the waiter set drinks on the table. Wine for her, water for me. Of course.

"I took the liberty of ordering for you," she said when the waiter disappeared again, ignoring my attempt to call him back.

"Great." God only knew what I'd be getting. It better not have kale in it. Or fish. There was only so much I was willing

to do to stay healthy and eating disgusting food for the nutri-
ents was not at the top of my list.

She smoothed my hair away from my face. "You look
stressed, dear. You should really book an appointment with
Celine. She'll add some glow back into that skin of yours. You
don't want to start slacking on basic upkeep. Especially at your
age." Her gaze fell to the remnants of the scratch on the side of
my neck. Her nose wrinkled in obvious disgust. "I can't believe
it's not infected. You should really cover that until it heals."

"I'm fine. It's fine." I swatted her hand away and spread
my napkin across my lap. "Can we please talk about something else other than my skin?"

She sniffed, taking a sip of her wine. "I heard the most
interesting thing at work today."

I could only imagine. Sipping my water, I tried to appear
interested when I was anything but. I really didn't care what
lawyer was sleeping with which clerk, or how someone's re-
election campaign was going. Courthouse intrigue never
interested me. It was like a bad soap opera. After dealing
with violent offenders and people in the midst of psychotic
breaks, I didn't have the energy to care about regular drama.

She fixed me with a knowing stare, oblivious to my disin-
terest. "You broke up with Darren."

I swallowed hard and tried to smile. Maybe I could bluff
my way through dinner and put off this conversation for
another night when I had more patience. "Who told you
that?"

"I'm not stupid, Lorelei. Darren wouldn't even look at me,
let alone talk to me. He thought you were going to get
married, you know. I heard him lording it over one of the
bailiffs just last week."

"We were never getting married. Trust me."

"Why not? He was perfect for you."

I made a face at her. Perfect was a far stretch from reality. Photogenic, maybe. But not compatible in any category that actually mattered. "Not really."

"He's handsome, well-educated, ambitious. The money will come later, you know that. Especially if he goes into politics or becomes a judge."

"He's self-centered, lacks empathy, is domineering—"

"He's a lawyer, Lorelei. What did you expect? A bleeding heart? Then maybe you should go out with that public defender who is always trailing after you. Or better yet, go find another doctor. You can save the world together."

"Can we not talk about this?"

"You're beautiful, I don't understand what the problem is."

"There's more to a relationship than how attractive people are."

"What do you want? Romance? Passion? Someone to sweep you off your feet? You know that only happens in fairytales. You need to be pragmatic."

"I want to eat dinner and go home. I'm tired." To emphasize my point, I tore into a bread roll and chewed viciously, imagining everything I wanted to say going down with each buttery bite.

"Lorelei, you are over thirty now. If you don't marry and have a baby in the next few years, you'll lose your chance forever. Then you'll end up alone, surrounded by nothing but those people in the looney bin."

I gritted my teeth. Why did she insist on bringing up my age, and my uterus, every other week? Thirty-three was not ancient, even by reproductive standards. "You're the one who pushed me to have a career instead of a social life. 'Career first, Lorelei. Boys second.' 'You'll have time to date later, Lorelei.' And now it's all 'Have a baby, Lorelei,' 'I need a

11

ASHLYN DREWEK

grandchild, Lorelei.' Not everything is on your timetable, Mother."

"I just want what's best for you." She gave me a little pout, completely undermining her sincerity. She wanted what was best for her. She always had.

If this was going to end civilly, I needed to stay diplomatic. I took a breath and smiled, my wide, close-lipped doctor smile — the one I used when I wanted to say more but professionalism dictated I keep my mouth shut. "I know. I appreciate that. But, I've got it from here. Ok?"

Thankfully, she returned the smile and patted my hand. "Ok, honey."

Letting out a deep breath, I relaxed the tiniest bit. "Thank you."

The waiter returned with our food, setting a plate in front of each of us.

I tried not to turn up my nose at the white rectangle nestled in a bed of vegetables. "Please tell me this is chicken."

"Tilapia, ma'am. It's our special tonight," the waiter replied.

"The omega-3 is good for you," Mom said brightly.

"Would you like me to get you something else?" the waiter asked with a nervous glance at my mother.

"No, thank you." I offered my best apologetic smile and picked up my fork, hoping it would put him at ease.

He nodded, apparently relieved, and disappeared.

"Do you always have to make a scene?" Mom asked as soon as he was out of earshot.

Round Two, ding ding!

It took every ounce of remaining energy to not roll my eyes at her. "How was that making a scene? I don't like fish. I've never liked fish. And yet you make me eat fish."

"You're a grown woman, Lorelei, as we've discussed. If you don't want the fish, then don't eat the fish."

"I'm eating the fish."

"Well now you're just being spiteful."

"By being agreeable?" I stared at her incredulously. Could she hear herself?

"If you were being agreeable you would have just eaten the fish in the first place instead of saying anything."

"Oh my God…" Dropping my fork with a groan, I held my head in both hands and closed my eyes. Would anyone notice if I stabbed myself in the eye? Maybe then it would stop twitching.

"That's another thing," she continued. "You don't cook. How do you expect to attract a man, at your age, if you don't cook?"

"I'm great in the sack." I snatched her wine glass and drained it. Tonight could be over any minute now.

She sputtered, gaping at me. "Lorelei!"

There wasn't much to say after that. The professional in me wanted to point out her hypocrisy, her obsession with my procreation but horror at the act that preceded it. On the other hand, the teenager in me was equally horrified by the idea of my mother picturing me naked. Maybe she was scarred enough by this conversation that I would get a respite for a while. Wouldn't that be marvelous?

CHAPTER 3

*I*t was late in the afternoon and I was failing in my attempt to catch up on case files. No matter how many I read and charted and re-filed, the pile seemed to grow when my back was turned. Between keeping track of existing patients, evaluating new patients, and keeping up to date on medical and legal cases, it was a wonder I had any time to do anything else. Darren wasn't wrong about that.

A reminder popped up on my computer screen, chiming softly. I swore under my breath, closing the window. I'd completely forgotten. Again. I was scheduled to meet with a lawyer and his client at four-thirty. Despite having the file for the last two days, it sat completely untouched.

Digging around the stack on my desk, I grabbed the folder marked WELLES, L. It was thicker than usual, which was both good and bad — good because I had a lot of information to go off of, but bad precisely because there was so much information readily available. I flipped it open, bracing for what I would find.

According to the notes from his lawyer, Leander Welles currently stood accused of a litany of felonies: intimidation, extortion, blackmail, unlawful restraint, and four counts of homicide. I blinked, trying to place the name and charges in the local headlines. I hadn't heard of any murders outside of Chicago lately, let alone four. Darren and the rest of the State's Attorney's Office would have been in an absolute tizzy. Not to mention my mother... A good murder could keep her gossiping for months.

I kept reading, hoping for clarification.

A few pages later, skimming through the legal jargon, I found my answer — the charges originated from somewhere downstate. As a result of Mr. Welles' apparent notoriety there, his attorney successfully petitioned the case to be transferred well away from a tainted jury pool. It obviously worked. People up here didn't tend to care about anything happening three hours south of them, including me.

Mr. Welles was coming to see me due to an apparent suicide attempt while in the Camden County jail. I suspected his lawyer was angling for a favorable diagnosis, one that would either get his client acquitted or at least given a lighter sentence in a psych facility versus prison time. We'd see about that.

Checking my watch, I cringed and hurried into the inter-view room. I wanted to be seated before Welles and his lawyer arrived. No more bad first impressions for me, thank you.

Not but ten minutes later, the heavy metal door buzzed. A guard stepped through first, holding the door open for the people who followed. Mr. Welles' attorney, a man in a blue suit with slicked-back white hair, entered next. Finally, my new patient walked in. I was glad I was sitting, otherwise I would have probably fallen over.

Leander was tall and lean, dressed in a suit even more expensive than his lawyer's by the look of it. His ensemble was entirely black, a striking contrast to his pale skin. A mop of long, dark curls fell in an effortlessly disheveled way, partially obscuring bedroom eyes that moved about the room furtively. He looked like he belonged on a runway in Milan, not in a psych ward.

"Dr. Clayton?" The lawyer said, extending his hand. "I'm Richard Scheible."

I didn't realize I was holding my breath until it was my turn to speak. Standing, I shook his hand before turning my attention to his client. "Yes, we spoke on the phone. You must be Leander."

Leander's gaze stopped wandering and landed on me. Something fluttered in the middle of my stomach as his eyes locked on mine. Gesturing to the empty chair across from me, I gave him a fleeting smile. "Please, sit."

He did as bade, laying both arms on the table, palms up. He was still handcuffed.

The guard stepped forward and linked the table chain through Leander's handcuffs, tugging to make sure they were locked securely before returning to the door.

"I'll be outside," Scheible said to Leander, patting his shoulder.

Flinching, Leander remained mute.

The guard and the lawyer left, slamming the door behind them.

Leander flinched again. I felt for him.

I resumed my seat and folded my hands on the table. Leander's gaze was on his chains. Or perhaps it was the white gauze peeking out from beneath his black sleeve, secured with a silver and onyx cufflink. So, he was a cutter. I made a mental note of it. It wasn't as common in men as in women, but not entirely rare, either. Maybe it was because his options in jail were limited. Desperate times, desperate measures and all that.

"Do you know why you're here?" I asked.

He nodded, chewing the inside corner of his mouth.

"Do you understand the charges against you?"

Another nod.

"Do you want to talk about that?" I asked, indicating his wrist with one finger.

"No." His voice was soft, almost remorseful. It was hard to imagine he had enough aggression to harm himself, let alone murder four people.

"Do you want to talk about anything?"

"No."

"Ok. Well, that's going to make things difficult." I didn't sense any hostility in his refusal. Hesitation, reluctance, wariness — but not malice.

"This is a mistake." He dragged his gaze away from his wrist, meeting mine with such an intensity it made my chest seize. I'd sat across from murderers before, including serial killers, which was technically what he would be labeled as if the allegations were true. They tended to be arrogant or deranged; he was neither, at least on the surface. His beautiful, sad surface…

Frowning at myself, I remembered my mantra. Ted Bundy, Charles Schmid, and Paul John Knowles were the first three serial killers to spring to mind. Traditionally charming, attractive, and utterly lethal. I recited their names in my head quickly, mentally distancing myself from Leander's magnetism.

"What is?" I asked, after he failed to elaborate. It wasn't hard to guess what he was referring to, but it was always better to have the patient explain than to assume their true meaning.

"All of this." His gaze dropped again, along with his voice. "I shouldn't be here."

I tried not to smirk. Now he sounded like every other pre-trial defendant and convict I'd seen. There was the arrogance I was waiting for, the indignation at being caught by people they perceived as beneath them. And yet, the primary emotion I detected was sadness. It permeated every word, every gesture. He was like a broken doll, a comely relic of a forgotten era.

Leander looked up sharply when I failed to acknowledge him. The flash of anger in his eyes was brief. "I'm telling the truth, Dr. Clayton."

"I suppose you're going to tell me the police planted evidence and framed you?"

"I know what it sounds like. I'm not paranoid. Or delusional. Or any other label you want to saddle me with."

"Are you suicidal?" That was a label he couldn't exactly argue with.

His lips pressed together into a flat line as his gaze fell again. He tugged the black fabric over the gauze, as if it would erase the question. It seemed I struck a nerve. I made another mental note.

"Mr. Welles, are you suicidal?"

He gritted his teeth and looked away, staring at something on the far side of the room. "Not currently."

"So you have been in the past?"

"Hasn't everyone wondered what it would be like to die? Since I am accused of murder, doesn't it follow that I would explore the idea of self-murder as well?"

Self-murder was an interesting way to phrase killing oneself and not one I heard outside of academic texts. "Being curious about death and actual self-harm are two different things. Besides, I don't think you actually meant it. At least not this time."

He fixed me with an unreadable stare. I couldn't decipher what emotion lay behind his eyes, nor hazard a guess as to what he was thinking.

When it was clear he wasn't going to say anything else, I

flipped open the folder and scanned the information tucked away in the back. As with most cases of mental illness, it was all depressingly bleak. I could understand why he would be suicidal, even if he was being dismissive about it. Shame was a powerful silencer, along with regret.

According to the file, his mother died in childbirth only to have his father die in a car crash when Leander was six. He was sent to live with his paternal grandmother who was later found beaten to death with a crowbar when he was eighteen. There weren't any other family members listed.

His lawyer spared no detail in laying out Leander's grim history, probably in a bid to garner more sympathy. Even though the trial was still weeks away, I felt for the jurors who would have to hear all of this. I had a hard time reading it and it was my job — those people would probably need their own therapists after it was all said and done if Scheible leaned this heavily on his client's past.

A warm tingly sensation danced over my skin, as if I could feel Leander's gaze on me. Looking up, I met his eyes without blinking. They were full of curiosity now, a mossy green color illuminated with a liveliness I wasn't used to seeing. Unfortunately most of my patients didn't possess much clarity by the time they came to see me.

"Do you really think you know who I am from bits of paper cobbled together by people who don't know me at all?" he asked. His voice was low but without any sort of edge.

I closed the folder, taking the bait. "If you won't talk to me, these bits of paper are all I have to go on."

"How should I convince you I'm not what that file says I am whilst I am chained in front of you in an asylum? You had a preconceived notion of who I was before I walked through that door, Dr. Clayton."

"Asylum? That's an outdated term, to say the least, not to mention pejorative."

"It speaks to the tragedy of these padded walls and everyone who has suffered here. Would you prefer the word sanitarium?"

Another mental note — he was a Romantic; not in the lovey-dovey sense of the word, but in the gothic one, mired in despair and lost worlds. "Is that how you see yourself? A tragic hero? Suffering from injustice?"

"I am no hero, Dr. Clayton, but I certainly am tragic. Humanity itself is tragic, wouldn't you say?"

"Is that why you tried to kill yourself?"

Silence.

His jaw shifted and he turned his face slightly to the side. I couldn't tell if he was staring at the far side of the room again or just trying to ignore me, like a cat. A muscle twitched beneath his pale skin, drawing attention to the sharpness of his cheekbone. His bone structure couldn't have been any more perfect than if a Renaissance sculptor had a hand in his creation.

Over the years it seemed I'd been exposed to every type of human, every level of education, hygiene, and temperament. But never before had I been so awestruck by a patient. It wasn't just his face — it was his mind that was alluring. The way he carried himself. The way he spoke...

Lorelei, pull it together!

Bundy, Schmid, Knowles. Bundy, Schmid, Knowles. Bundy, Schmid, Knowles.

"Say I believe you," I said, throwing him a little benefit of the doubt. "Say you didn't murder those people. What about the other charges? The extortion and blackmail?" He clearly didn't want to talk about his self-imposed injury, so if I was going to get him interacting again, I needed a way in. Maybe a less antagonistic topic would do the trick.

His eyes returned to mine. Yahtzee! "I assume you didn't get to the part in that file where it says I am well-off?"

"Well-off?"

"Independently wealthy. It is so gauche to discuss exact numbers, don't you agree?"

He sounded like my mother. Did he go to boarding school, too? Most trust-fund babies seemed to, or were at least chauffeured to and from overpriced private schools in outrageously expensive cars. "So why would someone who is independently wealthy bother blackmailing someone? I wouldn't think it's worth your time and effort."

"That is my point. Those people were blackmailing me — not the other way around."

"Why would someone blackmail you?"

"Why does anyone blackmail someone? Money. Power."

"I suppose you're not going to tell me what they had on you?" It was a long shot, I knew, but I wanted to gauge his reaction more than the actual reason.

As predicted, he smirked and gave away nothing else. Great. He played things close to the chest, an unfortunate stumbling block for trying to develop a successful treatment plan.

"You realize if that's your defense, it's going to come out in court anyway? Along with any other skeletons in the closet," I prodded.

"That's presuming this makes it to trial."

"Why? Are you going to have your associates tamper with the witnesses?"

He blinked, a small crease forming between his dark brows. "Associates?"

"Do you not run a syndicate where you're from?" I vaguely recalled skimming something in Scheible's notes about a RICO investigation at his company. Maybe it was just a threat from the prosecution — if their case went belly up, they'd hand him over to the feds to try again under different charges.

A small smile curved his lips. "Do I look like some sort of a mob boss to you?"

At least he agreed it seemed ridiculous. I was pretty sure a strong wind could blow him over. Yes, he was stunning, but his physique didn't inspire much fear. Maybe his money did. "You're the first patient I've seen in a suit that costs more than most people's rent."

"I just came from court."

"You didn't exactly answer the question, though."

"Neither did you."

I shifted in my chair. I wasn't used to such an easy back-and-forth repartee with a patient, or anyone, really. Normally I had to pull teeth to get information, even with so-called friends. Everyone seemed paranoid about being analyzed, as if I had the energy to analyze people in my off-time. Or the desire.

I was used to patients acting crazy because it was what they thought I wanted to see, or what they thought would help them out. Leander was different. His intelligence was refreshing but it was going to bring its own particular challenges.

We needed to get back on track. I couldn't let myself keep getting distracted. "I know you don't want to talk about it, but I have to ask — do you have a history of suicide attempts, apart from this one time in the jail?"

"You're the expert. You tell me."

"Yes," I shot back without much thought toward tact. Asking polite questions wasn't getting me anywhere. He answered questions with his own questions, an evasive technique I'd seen a dozen times before. Maybe it was time to start calling his bluff, to see if he was really malingering or if this was his usual style of conversation.

His shoulders straightened ever so slightly. If the chain on the table hadn't clinked, his movement would have been imperceptible. "Why do you say that?"

"You slit your wrist. Razor, broken mirror? Doesn't matter. Most suicides in the jail are hangings. It's easy. Tie the sheet up and jump. Cutting, on the other hand, hurts. You feel what you're doing every step of the way and you have to resolve yourself to a slow, painful death — if you're successful, which is rare despite what the movies tell us. Only someone desperate, or with a past history, would cut themselves, and you, Mr. Welles, do not seem desperate."

He gave me a tight-lipped smile. "Very astute, Dr. Clayton, but what do you know of desperation?"

"Am I right?" I wanted him to know I wasn't a pushover. But more than that, I wanted him to know he'd met his match. He could be as coy as he wanted; I would get to the truth no matter how long it took.

"Do you need my validation? I should think a woman with both an M.D. and a Ph.D. would be confident enough in her diagnostic abilities." Another small smile, bordering on a smirk. It seemed he'd accepted the challenge.

Even if he was teasing, I couldn't help but bristle. "I don't need anyone's validation — especially not a patient's. I need it for the intake form."

"Intake form?" He looked surprised. Maybe he wasn't angling for a cushy place to kick up his heels until his trial started after all. Or maybe it was the fact I wasn't writing anything down during the conversation. Maybe he thought I was just another dumb blonde who would forget everything he said the moment he walked out of the room.

"Yes, Mr. Welles. You're not going back to jail just yet. Your lawyer has asked me to make a full assessment and seeing that you're not very forthcoming... you'll be staying with us for a while for observation."

A loud buzz split the air before he could say anything and

the heavy door swung open. The same guard from before and an orderly came in, followed by Scheible.

"It was a pleasure, Dr. Clayton. I hope our next conversation is as riveting," Leander said.

The guard unlocked the chain between Leander's handcuffs before wrapping a hand around his bicep. He hauled Leander to his feet, directing him out the door.

Scheible lingered in the doorway, his white eyebrows raised behind his glasses. "Well?"

"Too soon to tell." I rose to my feet, considering Leander's dark form as it moved further and further down the hallway. He threw a glance in my direction before the guard shoved him around the corner.

The lawyer nodded and walked after Leander and the others. I heard him call out to one of the nurses, asking where the nearest phone was before peeling off in the opposite direction.

I ducked into my office to complete the large stack of paperwork related to Leander's case. Once that was done I had a lot of background reading to do if I was going to stay one step ahead of him.

CHAPTER 4

The mystery of Leander Welles was still swirling around in my brain well after I left the office. His file was tucked into my bag, peeking out between a stack of others, screaming at me to be read immediately. Even on paper, he was captivating. Med-school-me would have been terrified by a challenge like him. Now, I relished it. I was determined to ferret out the truth he was so determined to withhold.

I poured myself a bowl of cereal and climbed into bed with the file. Reading through each page, I scrutinized the information, comparing it to what little I'd gleaned from the man himself.

At first glance, he presented with paranoia, but he was rather controlled. Paranoid subjects were usually argumentative when you challenged their beliefs. Leander didn't argue. He was practically pleading with me to believe him, if not with his words, than with his eyes. It was probably beneath a man like him to beg outright.

Depression was an easy box to tick. People who weren't depressed didn't cut themselves, suicide attempt or no. But was it situational or an overall disorder? If he had a history of self-harm, my money was on Major Depression.

I unclipped the documents from the file and shuffled them into chronological order. There was nothing striking about his early childhood, except for the loss of both parents in his key attachment years.

The second red flag was his grandmother's murder. The police arrested him only to turn around and let him go when the prosecution declined to bring charges. Lack of evidence, they said. No one else was ever arrested and the case apparently went cold.

The longer I read, the more red flags leapt off the page. Based on his childhood alone, I'd be surprised if depression was all he suffered from. A handful of other possible diagnoses floated in my head, each more disheartening than the last.

The police reports from his grandmother's murder did not paint a pretty picture. Several of the household staff reported Irene Welles was a cold woman, bordering on cruel. They described a strict perfectionist with impossibly high standards and zero tolerance for mistakes, or children.

A former maid remembered seeing Leander beaten and locked in his room for a week, all for scratching a table with a pen during a tutoring session. When the maid snuck him an apple on the third day of no food, Mrs. Welles fired her.

He was six.

It was a mere three weeks after Leander moved in with her after the death of his father.

"My God..." I turned the page.

The gardener's account wasn't much better.

One night, Leander was late returning home from the library. His grandmother locked him out of the house, despite the freezing temperature. He slept in the garden shed. The next morning, his grandmother beat him for getting his clothes dirty and dragged him into the house, screaming. The gardener didn't know what happened next but a different maid said he was put in a scalding bath and scrubbed until his skin was raw.

He was eight.

Skipping past more accounts of abuse and neglect, I settled on the documents pertaining to his most recent brush with the law.

The people he was accused of murdering seemed incredibly random: a car mechanic, a retired police officer, and most recently, a family physician. I could see the cop, a Keith Starkey, if he was part of the original investigation into Irene Welles' murder, but I didn't see his name as the primary officer on any of the reports. And why was the State charging Leander with his grandmother's murder now, after ten years? What evidence did they find that they didn't have the first time around?

The answer was simple, according to the prosecution: the M.O.

All of the victims were bludgeoned to death with a crowbar — the same crowbar, according to forensics. It was easy to see why police jumped to the conclusion he murdered all of them, especially when they claimed to have found evidence Leander was extorting money from the doctor on top of it. A statement from the doctor's widow was particularly damning, outlining late-night visits from Leander, threats, shouting matches, and a peculiar car ride at midnight — the last time Dr. Van Deveer was seen alive.

There was no clear connection to either the police officer or the mechanic, except for how they died. The murders were spaced years apart and there were no eyewitnesses for any of them. Leander had an alibi for each one, but apparently the police and the State's Attorney thought they could poke enough holes in them to sink his defense.

I set the file down and shifted to my laptop. Googling his first alibi, I searched for a guy named Elijah Westbrook. Several newspaper articles popped up detailing Elijah's arrest for aggravated battery and armed robbery. It seemed the past few years he'd been quiet, at least as far as the crime blotter went.

Leander's second associate, Cole Holliday, had his own series of mugshots for various violent offenses. He too had fallen out of the newspaper in recent years.

I knew, without looking, the third guy, Jake Murray, would have more of the same. A pattern was clearly emerging.

So, Leander didn't have the best choice of friends. That was hardly a reason to condemn a man, though it did make me question what other bad decisions he was capable of making.

Deleting the text in the search bar, I typed in Leander's name. My finger hovered over the keyboard, right above RETURN. I knew better than to Google patients. Collecting collateral data from legitimate sources was one thing — scouring the internet for information was not the same.

I chewed on the end of my index finger before stabbing the enter key. A moment later, Leander's stunning face appeared in little squares all over my screen.

Most of the newspaper articles dealt with his grandmother's murder. A few dove into the untimely death of his father, whispered by some to have been a suicide, while others speculated a six-year-old Leander was the cause. The deaths of the mechanic and the cop all got their own headlines as well.

It wasn't until the more recent articles, after his formal indictment, that the *Easton Sentinel* lambasted Leander as a serial killer. There were pictures of him going to and from the Claiborne County courthouse, always in a black suit and only ever with his lawyer. His three compatriots were not in any of the photos as far as I could tell. It was odd an alleged gang leader, or whatever they thought he was, wouldn't have an entourage of cronies.

In addition to the news sites, a "Free Leander" webpage caught my eye. It didn't take long to see it for what it was — a fan page more than any sort of genuine legal defense. There were pictures of him from his various court appearances, a brief overview of each murder, and the address to Scheible's office in St. Louis to send letters. I shuddered to think what sort of content those letters contained or what the writer was hoping to get out of it. Some jailhouse romance? Notoriety of their own?

I went back to the news sites. The comment section of each article was rife with disagreements. Was he a murderer? Was he innocent? Some said he was a spoiled rich kid who got away with murder the first time, only to be undone by his arrogance in the end. Others said he was dealt a shitty hand and was being targeted by the police. It seemed no one could say for certain.

It all made my head swim. I didn't know what to think. In the end, it didn't really matter as far as I was concerned. I was there to evaluate him as he was, not assess his guilt or innocence. That was for the jury to decide.

Regardless, I stared at his most recent picture, hoping it would bring me some clarity. Leander was looking over his shoulder in the courtroom, dark curls across his forehead, his sharp cheekbone in contrast to his black suit. What was he looking at? Or who was he looking at? What was going on in that head of his?

I would never know.

Closing the laptop with a sigh, I sank into the mountain of pillows.

CHAPTER 5

"**I**s that bergamot?" Leander asked, leaning in uncomfortably close as the guard shackled him to the table.

Despite my self-consciousness, I held my ground. I tried not to breathe as I answered, though he obviously smelled it already. "It's Earl Grey."

The guard, a grizzled man named Russ, clamped a hand over Leander's shoulder and forced him into the chair. Leander's expression was blank, but his eyes held the hint of a glare until they flicked from the guard to me.

As with all patients at Parkview Psychiatric, Leander was dressed in a light blue outfit instead of the black suit from the day before. Underneath the t-shirt, he wore another long-sleeved one, making him look more like a medical professional than a patient. The lump of gauze was gone, but nevertheless he continued to tug at his white sleeves.

"How are you today?" I asked after Russ left the room.

Leander shrugged.

So we were back to that. Tucking my hair behind my ear,

I consulted the file, trying to decide where to start. I was pretty sure he would be reluctant to talk about any aspect of his childhood, let alone the reason for cutting himself in jail. I needed a softer opening, but what?

Surprisingly, Leander threw me a bone.

"You look tired, Doctor. Did you not sleep well?"

"No, actually, I didn't." I'd been plagued with nightmares about a witchy old woman looming over a helpless boy, but he didn't need to know any of that. I knew better than to read case files before bed and yet I did it anyway. There was no one to blame but myself. Or Irene Welles.

"Would you like to talk about it?"

He sounded so sincere I couldn't help but smile. I folded my hands on top of each other on the table. "We're here to talk about you, not me."

"That's not very fair. You know all about me. I know practically nothing about you."

I wasn't keen on sharing personal information, but if it meant keeping the flow of conversation going, I'd give him some leeway. "What do you want to know?"

"Is Earl Grey your favorite?"

Random, but harmless enough. "It is."

"How do you take it?"

"Milk and sugar. Lemon is too…"

"Acidic. I agree." A faint smile ghosted his lips before disappearing. "Forgive me for asking, but wouldn't coffee be preferable to combat fatigue?"

"Who says I didn't have coffee too?"

Leaning forward over the table despite the metal digging into his skin, he closed his eyes for a moment, as if considering the question. "I don't smell it. Just bergamot, muguet and…" He inhaled again, slowly. "Musk."

I wanted to shrink away from him, but I made myself stay

31

where I was. He was still a safe distance away, at any rate, and I wouldn't let him have the satisfaction knowing he'd broken through my protective bubble. The fact he'd described my perfume so accurately was strangely fascinating, especially the part where "muguet" rolled off his tongue. "Quite the sense of smell you have."

"Lily of the valley is my favorite flower. Beautiful, delicate, poisonous. I would recognize it anywhere." He resumed a respectable position in his chair, his shoulders straight. Did his grandmother shove a board down the back of his shirt, like they did a hundred years ago? His posture was perfect.

"I didn't know that. That they're poisonous, I mean. Do you like botany?"

"Not particularly."

"And yet you've latched on to a non-traditional flower to call your favorite. Most people go with roses or daisies."

"I believe you meant floriculture." He canted his head to the side.

Lifting my chin, I blinked slowly, trying to appear as unfazed and unimpressed as possible. I wasn't going to rise to his challenge. Plants are plants and not my area of focus, but clearly significant enough to him that he'd bother correcting me. Unless it was narcissism at work, a need to be the smartest person in the room.

"Is this the part where you psychoanalyze my favorite flower and see into the darkest part of my mind?" Even though he was still being evasive, it seemed he was fighting a smile. It kept quirking the corner of his mouth before disappearing.

I refrained from sighing. Not everything was all Freud and Jung. "Can't we simply have a conversation about flowers without there being a sinister reason?"

"There is no such thing as a simple conversation, especially not like this." He yanked on the chain suddenly, scowling at it. Other than the glare he gave Russ earlier, this was the closest thing to anger I'd seen.

I disguised my startled jump by shifting in my chair, crossing my legs beneath the table. "It's protocol. Until we know you're not a threat."

"A threat to whom?"

"Everyone — the staff, yourself." Me, in particular... Lest he get the idea I was afraid to be alone in a room with him, I figured it was safer to leave that part unspoken. I didn't even realize I'd touched the scratch on my neck until I caught him staring at my hand.

"What happened?" he asked.

"It's nothing."

He frowned, lifting an eyebrow.

I raised a brow back at him, silently challenging him to call me on it. Two could play the avoidance game.

"Is it also policy that dictates I can't have a pen in my cell?"

I nodded, forgoing the urge to correct him. Even though he was a pre-trial defendant and still technically in custody of Camden County, we didn't like to call them cells, though I could see why he would. Bleak was one of the nicer words to use. Austere. Spartan. If you had the artsy type of patient, you could cite Scandi culture for the aesthetic.

"Have you ever been restrained, Doctor?"

"Excuse me?" I didn't blink. I couldn't blink. I couldn't react at all in case that was what he was after, setting me up for some lewd suggestion.

He lifted his hands, rattling the chain. "Fettered? Confined? Bound against your will?"

I shook my head, relieved he kept it on topic instead of diverging into the inappropriate.

"Then in an effort to understand your patients' discomfort, perhaps you should. You say this isn't an asylum and yet

33

here we are, chained and prodded like animals, deprived of nearly everything. What's next? Ice baths and electroshock therapy?"

"I understand your frustration, Mr. Welles. It's for your safety as much as mine." I'm sure repeating the policy wouldn't help convince him, but it was all I had.

He looked at my neck before giving sweeping glances over both of his shoulders. "I don't see a crowbar in here, so one could reasonably argue you've nothing to fear. Unless you think I'm planning to strangle you with my bare hands. Do serial killers often change their preferred method of killing?"

Hoping it was just venting and not any sort of real threat, I ignored him. Still, I couldn't help the vivid image that sprang to mind of his hands on me, on my neck, of being that close to him.

I cleared my throat, dispelling the notion. "Since you mentioned it, what are your thoughts on the charges against you?"

Rolling his eyes, he looked away. He was much more agitated than yesterday. Then again, the first few days were always rough on patients. "I told you — it's a mistake."

"There's a lot of rage behind these killings. Are you angry about something, Mr. Welles?"

His gaze shot back to me. "Wouldn't you be?"

"From all appearances, you had a privileged upbringing." I knew what file said. I wanted to hear it from him.

"Appearances are deceiving."

"Can you tell me about your family?"

"There isn't much to tell, I'm afraid. They're all dead." It came out flatly, indicating another sore subject.

I took it as a cue and plunged ahead. There was only so much dodging I would allow in one conversation — family background was too important to let him dismiss it. "What do you remember about your father?"

He snorted and shook his head, his gaze drifting behind me somewhere. "He drove his car into a tree on my sixth birthday because he hated me that much. I killed the love of his life, you see, so he couldn't even bear to look at me. I remember the smell of vodka martinis and the sound of him crying her name. Sometimes I'd wake up and see him at the foot of my bed. I thought he was going to kill me, but instead, he killed himself so he could be with her."

My heart cracked with each word. I wished I could go back and un-ask the question. There was no point in telling him he wasn't responsible for either of his parents' deaths. He'd internalized the blame for so long at this point it would only fall on deaf ears.

"What about extended family? What kind of support system do you have?"

"I never knew my mother's family. Grandmother didn't approve, therefore they ceased to exist."

"What about friends? A significant other?"

"Not worth the effort. Is this really relevant?"

Leaning forward, I tried to appear as earnest as I could. "I'm here to help you, Mr. Welles. The sooner you realize that, the sooner we can get you out of here."

He leaned forward as well, the chain clanking against the table with his movement. If I wanted to, I could have reached out and held his hand. If he wanted to, he could have head-butted me.

"As you can imagine, Doctor, my trust is not easily won. That's not paranoia speaking — it is the sad result of a harrowing childhood, of which you are well aware." His gaze shifted pointedly to the file under my hands. "These questions are redundant and far from a productive use of our limited time."

"Spoken like someone who has been in therapy."

"I've never done anything of the sort." He leaned back, as if in disgust. "That doesn't mean I am incapable of studying the subject."

"You studied psychology?" I didn't see any formal schooling in his records but all of the intelligence tests he took his first day showed a remarkably high IQ. I was almost envious. I'd spent so much of my life in school it was strange to encounter someone who didn't. Other than the fact he was, you know, under arrest for heinous crimes, he didn't seem to be at any sort of social disadvantage.

"I suppose that wasn't in your precious file?"

"No. Would you like to read it? Maybe then you can start filling in some of the blanks for me." Arching an eyebrow at him, I slid the folder across the table. I pulled my hand back the moment the chains clinked.

He shifted forward, his long, slender fingers working the folder closer until he could open it for himself. His dark curls obscured his eyes as he hovered over the documents, but I could see his mouth. It twitched now and again, mostly remaining in a flat, unimpressed line. At last, he sat back and mirrored my defiant expression. "Like I said — life is tragic."

"This isn't a tragedy, Leander. This is horror." I pointed at the file, like he needed reminding of what he endured. How could he be so flippant? So casual? Maybe he'd detached so much from the situation it didn't bother him anymore.

He gave me a withering smile and spread his hands. "If everyone had a happy childhood, I'm afraid there would be no need for your services, Doctor."

"You can see how someone would easily conclude you murdered your grandmother?"

"Just because it's the easy conclusion doesn't mean it's the correct one."

"These murders are virtual copies of her murder. Same

weapon, same M.O. All the prosecution has to do is draw a line from A to B and you're in prison. Juries are swayed by sensationalism, not nuances."

"The problem with the simple conclusion is it leads to lazy police work. Once they latch on to a suspect they develop tunnel vision. They never looked for anyone else in any of these cases. Never investigated anything or anyone, except me. And yet, no one can tell me what my motive would be. For example, why would I bludgeon a car mechanic to death?"

He had a point. I couldn't see a clear motive for killing anyone other than his wretched grandmother. "If you didn't murder them then who did?"

He lifted one shoulder in a shrug.

"You don't care who killed your grandmother?" I suspected there wasn't any love lost for the woman, but she was still family. Societal norms stated you had to at least pretend to care. Then again, Leander was anything but conventional.

"Would you care who slayed the monster of your nightmares?"

"Yes. If only so I could clear my own name."

He leaned forward, bracing his forearms against the edge of the table. "Is your name that important to you?"

"A name is all you have in this life. How you're remembered is all you have."

"I assure you the name Leander Welles will far outlive any legacy Irene Welles thinks she left behind. But what about you, Doctor? What will history say about your name?"

"That I cared. And I tried to help those who need it most — broken minds, lost in a broken system." My spine stiffened with each word. A moment too late I realized I shouldn't have confessed that thought to anyone, let alone a patient I

37

was supposed to be assessing. How had he gotten into my head when I was trying to get into his?

"A fine goal... May I ask for your first name?"

"Lorelei." There was no point in hiding it. He could just as easily get my full name from his attorney. In fact, I was surprised he didn't already know it. Unless it was some sort of a test, a measure of how personal I was willing to be.

"Lorelei," he repeated, almost in a murmur.

My stomach fluttered the way he said it. I silently reprimanded myself, cycling through some more serial killers' names. He wasn't the first patient to try and flatter me and he wouldn't be the last. Although, nothing in his demeanor indicated he was actually trying to flirt. Or if he was, he was being incredibly subtle. God. Is this what society has come to? When a man is being polite you automatically think he's flirting? Get a grip, Lorelei.

"Tell me, Doctor," Leander broke through my chastising. "Do you have the time?"

My brows furrowed and I glanced at my watch. "It's nine. Why?"

Before he could answer, the door buzzed and opened. It was Calvin. "Sorry Doc, his lawyer is on the line."

"Take a message," I said, trying to mask my irritation at the interruption.

"It's for him," Calvin nodded to Leander.

Nodding, I got to my feet. Calvin handed me the portable phone from the doorway. I ferried it to Leander before rejoining Calvin in the hallway. He pulled the heavy door shut behind me.

We stood on opposite sides of the hall, exchanging looks while I shuffled from one foot to the other.

I'd kill for some sneakers. My heels were unbearably constricting today but the thought of taking them off was too scandalous to fathom. Even as a grown woman, I was afraid my mother would sense a disturbance in the footwear-force and have to check in to make sure I was maintaining a perfectly polished image at all costs. The Clayton family name apparently rested on how sleek my hair was or that my Louboutins weren't scuffed. Work ethic had nothing to do with it.

"How's it going?" Calvin asked.

"Eh." I shrugged. I didn't know if he was asking about me or Leander, but I didn't have a good answer either way. Stretching up on my tiptoes, I peered through the glass to see how Mr. Welles was doing.

Leander was still seated — obviously. The phone was cradled against his ear, his head tilted to one side. He seemed to be listening to Scheible, nodding every now and again. When he finally spoke, he appeared more animated than before. An unreasonable twinge of jealousy shot through me. I'd been trying to get him to talk, really talk, all morning. I thought maybe he was incapable of much expression due to his upbringing, but now I saw he was simply withholding.

"You hear Ray bit a guard over at county?" Calvin asked.

I looked away from the window, eyes wide. "He what?"

"Yeah. Right in the calf. Guess it took, like, eight of them to get him out of his cell. Better them than us, right?"

All I could do was nod, discreetly sweeping my hair over the scratches again. Good luck to whoever had to deal with Ray in DOC. There was no doubt he was mentally ill, but it didn't excuse taking a reciprocating saw to your neighbor's head because they told you to keep your dog in your own yard.

A loud crash sounded inside the interview room. Calvin pushed me out of the way and swiped his card, hurrying in first. I followed after him, surveying the room.

At first glance, everything appeared in order. Then I saw the phone shattered on the floor.

"It slipped. I tried to catch it, but..." Leander lifted his chained hands.

"Don't worry about it. Happens more than you'd think." Calvin knelt down and began retrieving pieces of the phone. Mindful not to split a seam in my pencil skirt, I squatted next to him to help gather the fragments, depositing them in his large palm.

Leander cleared his throat softly before speaking. "Doctor?"

Glancing up, I almost fell over when I realized how close we were.

He gestured to his lap. Against my better judgement, I looked down. There was a piece of the phone caught in the fold of his shirt, dangerously close to an area I shouldn't be looking at. I bit my lips and started to reach for it but pulled back.

Leander's eyes crinkled and he saved me the trouble. Picking up the piece between two fingers, he leaned forward as far as he could, holding it out for me.

"Thank you," I said quickly, plucking the antenna out of his fingers. Standing again, I smoothed down my skirt and backed away from him.

"May I go back to my cell now?"

Calvin waited for me to nod before he reached for the chain, unlocking Leander's cuffs from the table.

It wasn't until I was back in my office that I realized I was still holding the piece of white plastic. What did Scheible say to make Leander drop the phone? And why did Leander want to go back to his room so soon? My company couldn't have been that unbearable.

A sudden horrifying vision of Leander bleeding out in his jail cell struck me. Oh God. He wasn't going to try again, was he?

Shooting out of my chair, I sprinted down the hallway as

fast as my heels would go on the slippery linoleum. Swiping my card through the first security door and again through the second, I racked my brain for his room assignment, mentally flipping through the paperwork I'd signed off on. Three! He was in room three!

I slid to a halt in front of the metal door, bracing against either side of the window and peering inside.

Leander was laying on his cot, eyes closed, both hands folded on his stomach. If he was aware of my gaping presence outside his door, he didn't show it. He didn't stir at all. I held my breath, steadying myself, and stared at his hands in order to make sure his chest rose and fell.

"Is everything ok, Dr. Clayton?"

Nora, one of the nurses, stood behind me, frowning. That wasn't out of the ordinary, since she frowned at everyone. In my time at Parkview, I couldn't recall ever seeing her smile.

"Keep an eye on this one," I said after a moment, stumbling over the words in my head before spitting them out. "I'm afraid he might try harming himself."

Nodding, she jotted something down in the chart hanging on the side of his door. I thought I saw her roll her eyes as she walked away, but I couldn't be sure.

I gave Leander one last look to confirm he was fine, at least for the moment.

He hadn't moved.

As I pushed away from his door, I tried to shake the feeling that is what he would look like in a casket. Folding my arms over my chest, I trudged back to my office.

After failing for ten minutes to type my notes, I pulled up the security feed for the interview room and played the footage from Leander's phone call.

Sure enough, he was in the middle of speaking and trying to shift his position when the phone shot out of his hand. It bounced off of the edge of the table and shattered on the floor, as he said. He didn't move, other than to lean forward and swipe the hair away from his forehead. There was nothing hidden in the phone. He didn't squirrel away any parts. It was just an accident.

I closed my eyes and sighed.

CHAPTER 6

*T*he next morning time moved erratically. Everything seemed to pass by in a blur until I stood on the front sidewalk of Parkview, staring up at the looming gray building. Another night of fitful sleep left me even groggier than the day before. Yawning, I gripped my tea and pushed onward.

My phone was on all night but I didn't get a single call, message, or email about any of my patients, Leander included. Still, I dreaded what I would find when I exited the elevator onto the third floor. I wouldn't believe everything was alright until I saw it firsthand.

When I came on the floor, Nora was at the nurse's station, pecking away on the computer.

"How did it go?" I asked.

She didn't look up. "How did what go?"

My jaw clenched, hidden behind a smile. I'd only made one request. Was it that difficult to remember? "Mr. Welles."

"Oh." She waved a hand at me. I couldn't tell if it was at my concern or her idiocy. "He's fine. He's in the dayroom."

"Can I see his chart?"

She handed it to me, still without looking up.

I skimmed through the notes, frowning at each new line of observations by the staff. "He's not eating?"

Nora stopped typing, looking up with a blank face.

I rolled my eyes and thrust the chart at her. "Try to get him to eat, for God's sake. And search his room while he's gone." I knew what I saw on the video, but I also couldn't get over the feeling he was hiding something.

"Do you really—"

"Yes." It was either my tone or the glare that silenced her. I didn't care which as long as she did as instructed.

Like a moody teenager, she stood and circled the desk, practically stomping down the hall. I had half a mind to tell Calvin to go with her, but he was needed in the dayroom in case all hell broke loose.

Sitting at my computer, I sent off a quick inquiry to Scheible before sorting the rest of my email. I checked my schedule about availability for some upcoming trials, declined a few others. When the last of my tea was gone, I decided it was time to make my rounds.

Nora was still tossing Leander's room when I walked by. I paused in the doorway, waiting to see if she found anything. She shook her head in the negative. Even if I knew she'd ultimately hold it against me, I was relieved. Unlike most people, I was ok being wrong about a situation; I wasn't ok standing by and doing nothing. She could think whatever she wanted about me as long as my patients were safe.

Reassured, I made my way into the dayroom.

"Hey Doc." Calvin greeted me with a grin before he went back to posing for Martha, one of our long-term residents. She was doing a terrible job painting his portrait. I'm pretty sure even Picasso would have cringed at the disjointed representation, but it made her happy so Calvin obliged. Daily. He had a stack of paintings featuring brown blobs on the top shelf of his locker.

I checked in on a few others before winding my way through the room to where Leander stood.

He leaned against the window, staring at the gray skies beyond, oblivious to the people behind him. Thunder rumbled in the distance. I hoped the downpour held off until people were able to get outside for fresh air.

"You look tired. Still losing sleep, Doctor?" Leander asked, never moving from his place.

I met his gaze in the reflection of the glass. "It's rude to tell a woman she looks tired, especially when you're the reason she's not sleeping." It was a bold reply, bordering on unprofessional. My cheeks burned a moment after I said it, but it was the truth after all. Another night of tossing and turning must have switched the filter off on my mouth.

He turned away from the window, one hand lingering on the ledge. "How is it that am I the one keeping you awake?"

"I'm worried about you, Mr. Welles."

"You needn't be."

"Maybe I wouldn't worry so much if I knew you were eating."

He grimaced. "Perhaps if you knew what they were serving, you wouldn't fault me for not eating."

Raising an eyebrow at him, I tossed my head toward the seating area. "Come sit with me." I took one of the chairs on the end; he chose the edge of the couch, sitting so close our knees nearly touched. "I have something for you."

His brows lifted. "Oh?"

I slipped a hand into my coat pocket and retrieved the items, a bound notebook and a pen, and held them out with a small smile. "It's not much, but… It's something."

"Thank you." He took them reverently and set them next to him on the couch, as if they were too precious to hold. On maybe he didn't want me worrying I was going to get stabbed with a black InkJoy.

A few more moments passed. It was hard to tell if he was waiting for me to speak or if he was lost in his own thoughts again. I decided it was easier to sit with the silence than try to force something.

"You look perturbed," he said after a while.

I looked up at him, trying to read between the lines. His eyes were soft, almost sleepy. In this light they were a brilliant chartreuse, ringed in an equally stunning emerald. They were mesmerizing. Every time I saw him, I discovered something new to enthrall me, whether it was a physical feature or another facet of his incredibly complex mind.

"I am." Honesty had been the best policy so far with him, probably because he was too smart for anything less.

"Would you like to talk about it?" His half-smile was back, teasing.

"Not until we talk about this." I pointed at his wrist, covered by another long-sleeve shirt. I didn't want to undo the progress with the pen and paper, but I needed to know I wouldn't regret the decision to give him more privileges.

Those beautiful eyes rolled away and he sank back into the couch. "You're obsessive."

"And you're in denial if you think I'm not going to get what I need to do an accurate assessment."

"Do people find this trait endearing in you? This annoyingly dogged persistence?"

I smirked at him. "It's one of my better qualities. Unfortunately for you."

Sitting forward again, his eyes narrowed on mine. He opened his mouth and closed it just as quickly, his lips pursing. There was so much emotion behind his eyes. I could see it. He just needed to stop resisting.

I decided to press my advantage. "Tell me what happened. Please..."

Leander's jaw shifted to the side before he clenched his teeth, looking away from me. In the blink of an eye he seized my wrist, yanking me forward until my forearm rested across his knee. We came face to face again, his nose nearly touching mine.

Calvin moved in my periphery. I shook my head at him before turning my full attention back to Leander, hoping he couldn't feel the uptick in my pulse through my wrist.

"The first time, I took a razor and did it like this," Leander said, slicing a fingertip across my wrist. "It hurt and I bled, but I didn't die. The second time I wizened up and did it this way but it hurt too much. I didn't press hard enough, so again, I didn't die." He dragged his finger down the length of my forearm. I suppressed a shiver at the images it conjured.

He let go of my wrist and pushed his sleeve back, brandishing the long, jagged line on his arm beneath my nose. My stomach churned at the closeness, the proximity to such self-inflicted pain, but I didn't let myself look away.

Beneath the fresh scab were dozens of other white lines running up and down his pale skin, the blueness of his veins standing out like the veining in marble. I couldn't even count them all, nor did I want to.

"But this time..." Leander's thumb caressed the dark red mark as he tugged his sleeve down, covering the wound again. "This time I didn't want to die. I needed someone to listen."

His head dropped into his hands, his long fingers tangling in the mess of dark hair. A droplet splashed onto the tile floor at his feet. Another followed, and another. Each one slow and steady, like a heartbeat. Even his crying controlled, reserved, reluctant — and silent.

I bit my lips and reached out for him, not knowing how

would he react, given he flinched for his lawyer, someone he'd known far longer. My hand hovered above his shoulder before landing gently.

Holding my breath, I hoped I didn't make the wrong move.

He didn't flinch, nor did he look up. Except for the slow, hitched breathing, he was motionless beneath my hand.

"I'm listening, Leander," I said quietly. "I promise you I'm listening."

He sniffed and sat up straighter, wiping his face with the edge of his sleeve. His eyes were a deeper shade of green, rimmed in red.

This was no murderer. This was no crime boss. This was the effect of an awful, abusive childhood. This was a man with too much money and poor decision-making skills as a result of his trauma. At that moment, I had no doubt the charges against him were all a mistake. A horrible, horrible mistake.

Nora appeared, huffing, a phone in her hand. "It's for you, Dr. Clayton."

"Are you going to be ok?" I asked Leander.

With Nora's arrival, he resumed his stony-faced study of the clouds. The only remnants of his emotion were the droplets evaporating on the floor and the fact his eyes hadn't returned to their pale green color. He didn't even look at me when he replied. "You needn't worry, Dr. Clayton."

I withdrew my hand slowly, afraid he might suddenly crumble if I wasn't there to hold him up. He was as indifferent to my departure as he was to my arrival, his expression unreadable, even after the brief display of vulnerability.

Nora waved the phone at me, as if I could forget she was there, breathing down the back of my neck. I snatched it away from her, waiting until I was out of the dayroom before speaking. "This is Dr. Clayton, can I help you?"

"Dr. Clayton, this is Richard Scheible. I was calling to set up that appointment you requested."

I checked my watch, trying to remember my schedule for the rest of the day. "Yes, I was wondering if you had time to discuss Mr. Welles. I'd like to get a little more background on him before I make my assessment."

"Of course. Anything you need. I have an opening after lunch on Thursday."

"Perfect. I'll see you then."

Disconnecting, I looked back into the dayroom.

Calvin had moved on to help another patient pick up the stack of books they'd knocked over, leaving Martha free to wander around. She shuffled closer to Leander, who otherwise seemed oblivious to her presence. His head hung low again, his face obscured by his hair. After a moment, I realized he was writing. Meanwhile, Martha pulled out her sketchbook, her hand fluttering like mad over the paper.

I hoped Leander was a fan of modern art, otherwise he was going to be shocked by Martha's depiction of him. I couldn't wait to see what she came up with.

CHAPTER 7

The next morning I arrived at work well before my usual hour. There was a staff meeting scheduled, but more importantly, breakfast was being served in the dining room. Not that I didn't believe him, per se, but I wanted to see what Leander was talking about, if the food was as terrible as he claimed. I stood in the back corner of the dining room, out of the way, watching the patients file in and select their tables.

Martha bounced in and stomped to a table near the window. She chased away anyone else who dared come near her with a literal snarl and bared teeth.

When Leander appeared, looking like he'd rather be anywhere else except a noisy dining room with a mixture of questionable smells and erratic people, Martha charged at him. I took a step forward to intervene but held myself back. I wanted to see how this interaction played out.

Leander gave her a small smile and said something to her, too far away for me to hear. She grabbed his sleeve and jerked him along behind her, dragging him to the table she'd selected. He'd bristled at Russ's manhandling but didn't seem the least bit bothered by Martha's.

That was... unexpected.

The wait staff appeared, unceremoniously setting trays in front of both of them. Martha wasted no time diving into her food. Leander, on the other hand, pushed his tray closer to Martha. When she reached for his bottle of orange juice, he nodded. She snatched it away, downing it in the blink of an eye.

That was my cue. I wound my way through the tables to reach them on the opposite side. "Good morning. Martha. Leander."

Martha didn't look up from her plate. She was too busy piling eggs and hash browns onto the toast making a messy sandwich, topped with gobs of ketchup. When she reached for Leander's plate with her fork, my hand shot forward, intercepting the theft.

"Give him a chance, Martha," I said gently.

She didn't seem all that put out.

"I'm not eating that," Leander said matter-of-factly. It wasn't outright hostility but it was clear he wasn't going to be persuaded easily.

"If you eat, you can have this lovely cup of Earl Grey." I held up the paper cup in my hand, shaking it temptingly.

He shot me a dirty look. "I am not a toddler."

"Mmm, caffeine. How long has it been since you've had any? The buzz, the wakeful feeling..." I inhaled the tea and closed my eyes.

He folded his arms over his chest, clearly not as amused with me as I was with myself. "This is bordering on abuse, Doctor."

Sliding into the chair next to him, I crossed my legs and carefully peeled the lid off of the tea so it would cool faster. Bringing the cup to my lips, I pulled it away at the last second to give him a puzzled look. "What was it you said yesterday? Dogged persistence?"

"Annoyingly so."

I beamed at him.

He slid the tray toward me and gestured to the plate. "By all means, Doctor, help yourself. I apologize for the plastic cutlery and styrofoam. Apparently no one around here is concerned with the environment, or giving the mentally ill cancer on top of their deranged minds."

"I didn't realize you're so eco-conscious, Mr. Welles."

He held up the spork. "This is an affront to dining." To demonstrate his contempt, he threw it on the tray with a look of utter disdain.

I tried not to laugh, but I couldn't help it. He wasn't wrong, I'd just never met anyone so personally insulted by plastic, hybrid utensils. "Martha found a work-around."

Martha shoveled the rest of her sloppy sandwich into her mouth and guzzled the remainder of her own orange juice.

"I'm not—" He bit his lips, shaking his head. "It is too early for such a circuitous conversation."

"Not a morning person?"

He glared at me.

I picked up the poor spork and stabbed a blob of scrambled eggs, scooping up a bit of potato for good measure. My expression remained neutral while I ate, but inside I gagged. Aside from being cold, it was bland and left a film of grease on my tongue. I could certainly see why someone from Leander's background would resent mass-produced meals, but even I was not happy with the quality and that came from someone who lived on ramen noodles and popcorn for an entire semester.

He raised his eyebrows at me, waiting.

"It's fine," I said, resisting the urge to chug the tea.

"If you're going to lie, you might as well try to be convincing."

"Fine. At least eat the toast, please. They can't screw that up, can they?"

Heaving a sigh, he grabbed a brown triangle and took an irritated bite. "Happy?"

"Ecstatic." I slid the cup of tea across the table, smiling victoriously. "Will you please finish that?"

"Only because you asked me to." He swallowed another dry bite and took ownership of the tea. He eyed it for a minute and sniffed before taking a tentative sip.

I gave him a wry smile. "It's not poisoned."

Coughing, he covered his mouth with a fist. He recovered quickly but not before I saw a dark flash in his eyes, accompanied by a tight smile. "Imagine my disappointment."

"Funny. I don't tend to off my patients, though." I checked my watch, cringing. "Whoops. I have to go."

"Thank you for the tea and the lively conversation. Come back at midnight. It's when I'm at my finest." He dutifully ate another bite of the toast while pushing the tray back in Martha's direction. The second triangle was on a napkin in front of him.

Smiling to myself, I ducked out of the dining room. I was late for the staff meeting and for once I actually wanted to be at this one.

⚜

Barreling through the door of the conference room, I dropped into the first open chair I found. Thankfully it was next to Dennis, who wordlessly slid a copy of the agenda to me. I pretended to busy myself with the list of topics, avoiding the disapproving look from our boss.

"I need volunteers for the suicide prevention conference

in September," Kim said, her pen poised over her copy of the agenda.

My hand shot up, followed by Dennis'. We exchanged a sly smile.

"Lorelei, you're already guest lecturing at Braeburn University that week."

"I can do both."

"Suit yourself." She scribbled our names down and moved on. "Patient updates?"

The doctors and social workers around the table rattled off the basics about each of their patients, how each one was doing, who needed a med increase or decrease, and who was set to be discharged. When it came time for the criminal and court-ordered patients, all eyes were on Dennis and I.

Dennis went first. "Todd is back on restricted status. In group, he told the counselor he wanted to slit Renee's throat. She became hysterical and Todd wouldn't stop laughing. So... there's that."

There was a collective sigh around the table, prompting us to rattle through the rest of our patients quickly. Even the bleeding hearts, as Mom called us, grew weary of patients having repeated setbacks and not responding to treatment. Despite what they taught us in med school, it was not an exact science. Treatment was usually long, with lots of trial and error along the way.

Before Kim could dismiss us, I cleared my throat. "Can we talk about food for a minute?"

Since there was no audible objection, Kim shrugged, gesturing for me to continue.

"I think some improvements could be made on that front," I said, making sure to accompany it with a smile. Criticism always went over better when you were nice about it. "We have the budget for it. It's not like we're state-run. Is it a lack of training in the kitchen, or can someone explain to me why prisoners get better food in the county jail than they do here?"

"We've never had any complaints before," Kim replied.

"Have you ever asked the patients for an opinion?"

A flurry of whispers and giggles shot around the room. Even Dennis kicked me under the table.

I brushed my hair behind my ear and offered an apologetic smile. "All I mean is, we're trying to take a holistic approach to mental illness and recovery. We all know nutrition is a large part of a person's overall health. If the patients aren't eating, then it'll be that much harder for us to treat them. Not to mention the effect it could have on their medication, their sleep, any other underlying health iss—"

Kim held up a hand, silencing me. She surveyed the faces around the table. "Thoughts?"

"I agree. Wholeheartedly," Dennis said quickly, winking at me out of the corner of his eye.

The rest of the table nodded, murmuring their agreement.

Kim scribbled a note on her paper. "I'll talk to food services about what can be done to make improvements. Anything else?"

Shaking my head, I decided to leave the eco-battle for another day. Food was my primary concern. Leander would just have to deal with the spork situation if it meant he could eat something palatable.

"Good," Kim said. "That's it for today. Oh, Lorelei. My office."

"We've got a meeting at St. Mary's," Dennis interjected.

"It'll only take a second," Kim said before breezing out the door.

I made a face and pushed my chair out. "I'll meet you in the car," I said to Dennis, following after Kim like a student being called to the principal's office. She couldn't have been that mad about the food comments, could she?

She met me at the threshold of her office with a box and shoved it into my hands. "I don't know how people know Leander Welles is here, but I'm tired of going through his mail. From now on, your patient, your problem."

I juggled the box until I got a better grip on it. It was disconcertingly heavy. "Is it from his lawyer? Or family?"

"I don't know. After smelling a dozen different perfumes and looking at an obscene number of hearts, I stopped opening them."

"I'll get it sorted." I turned to go, pausing for a moment. "Oh, and I'm sorry if I came across too strongly back there."

She smiled. "I'll never be offended by staff trying to do better by the patients. The delivery could have been a little less blunt, but the intention is all I really care about."

I nodded, relieved not to have gotten on her bad side.

On the way back to my office with the disgustingly sweet and glittery box of mail, Amanda, one of the receptionists, intercepted me with a bouquet of red roses.

"These just arrived for you, Dr. Clayton!"

"Great." Propping the box against my hip, I keyed us into my office. "There's fine. Thanks," I said, tossing the box onto a chair while Amanda set the vase on the desk. I plucked the little white card out of the center and got as far as "Lor — Please call" before I crumpled it and tossed it in the trash. Nice try, Darren. Roses didn't equal an actual apology.

I swept the vase off the desk and carted it down to the nurse's station, smiling at Jeannette as I approached. "Got a place for these?"

"They're beautiful!" Jeannette gushed, shoving a file rack out of the way to make room for the vase. "You don't want them?"

"No room," I feigned a sad expression before hurrying

away. Dennis was probably cursing me, loudly. We were definitely going to be late now.

As I guessed, his car was idling at the curb when I ran out the front door.

"For Christ's sake. Where were you? What did Kim want?" Dennis asked as I buckled my seat belt for the race across town to yet another meeting.

"Ugh. Leander's fan mail."

"What is it with these crazy women and serial killers?" He shook his head.

"He's pre-trial, Dennis."

He ignored me. "I mean, do they really think they're going to have a relationship with some guy they don't know? And why the hell would they want a guy accused of murdering people, of all crimes? What does that say about the woman?"

"They like danger. Murderers are arguably the most dangerous people in our society, but the woman in the relationship is still 'safe' because he's incarcerated so she gets her thrill with none of the actual risk."

Chuckling, Dennis glanced at me with a smirk. "Of course you have a real answer to a hypothetical question."

I grinned at him. "You taught me well."

CHAPTER 8

Leander, you are the most beautiful soul I've ever seen.
Everyone thinks I'm crazy, but from the moment I saw you, I just
knew.
I'm worried about you.
I want to make you happy.
Leander, I love you. Please don't be distant.

*G*agging, I rolled my eyes and chucked yet another love letter into the box. No wonder Kim delegated this task to me. All the perfume and syrupy professions of love were giving me a headache.

I moved onto the next one in the pile. It was a neatly typed envelope versus the ultra feminine ones I'd already sorted. The letter inside was also typed, on a typewriter of all things. But it was the wording that made me sit up and pay attention.

It's true! Yes, I have been ill, very ill. But why do you say that I have lost control of my mind, why do you say that I am mad? Can you not see that I have full control of my mind? Is it not clear that I am not mad? Indeed, the illness only made my mind, my feelings, my senses stronger, more powerful...

Yes! Yes, I killed him. Pull up the boards and you shall see! I killed him. But why does his heart not stop beating!! Why does it not stop!!

My mouth went dry and I had to force a swallow. I double checked the outside of the envelope. There was no return address. No signature. Nothing. Just that disturbing message.

Questions zipped around in my head at rapid fire. Who would send such a weird letter? Was it a confession? Was this the real killer reaching out to torture Leander while he languished here, awaiting trial for a crime he didn't commit? Was this a threat? Was Leander next?

There was only one way to know.

Scooping up the box of letters, I went to find Leander.

He was in the dayroom, more or less posing for one of Martha's paintings. Hunched over a table, his chin propped in his hands, he stared out the window while Martha's paintbrush whisked over the paper in frenzied slaps.

Martha waved me over with a jerk of her arm and flapped a hand at the picture. It was vaguely human shaped with giant black blotches protruding from the back.

I looked over the top of her easel, trying to put two and two together.

The sunlight streaming in the window backlit Leander in a warm glow, adding to his otherworldly appearance. She was portraying Leander as an angel — with black wings.

"It's beautiful," I said, patting her arm before moving on to Leander. Setting the box on the table next to him, I cleared my throat to draw his attention.

He looked up at me with a small smile. "Dr. Clayton. I am graced once more by your loveliness. To what do I owe the pleasure this time? More poisoned tea?"

Any other time I might have been flattered he considered me lovely, even if he was being sarcastic. Right now, with the creepy letter staring up at me from the box, was not one of those times. "Hilarious. May I sit?"

"By all means." He gestured to the chair next to him, his face turning serious. "Is everything alright?"

"I was just going through your mail." I pulled out the typed letter, handing it to him. "And I came across this."

His gaze didn't leave me as he unfolded the paper, not until it was fully open and I looked pointedly at the words in front of him. When I glanced up, he was reading, his brows drawn together.

"I was hoping you might have an idea as to who sent it." I handed him the envelope, though I doubted he'd glean anything from it I couldn't.

Frowning at the envelope, he set it on the table, along with the letter. "I'm afraid I can't answer that."

"I'm giving it to Scheible." We reached for the letter at the same time. Leander jerked his hand back a second before our hands collided.

"No, don't."

"Why not?"

"He doesn't need the distraction."

"Leander, this sounds like a confession. It could help your case."

He averted his gaze, staring out the window again. "It's not a confession. Not a real one."

"How do you know?"

"It's Poe. *The Tell-Tale Heart.* Or, pieces of it, rather."

Looking at the letter again, I was even more confused than before. "This is a poem? Why would someone send you this?"

"It's a short story," he said before chewing his lower lip.

"I don't care what kind of literary format it is. I don't like it. I don't like what it implies."

"What do you think it implies?" His gaze drifted back to mine, the pensive look replaced by a curious one.

It was my turn to look away. I huffed out an exasperated breath, searching for the right thing to say. "I don't know." I did know. I just couldn't tell him without sounding as paranoid as Martha.

He tipped the box forward to peer over the edge. His nose wrinkled almost immediately. "What is all of this?"

"Fan mail," I replied with as sincere of a smile as I could manage.

"Please have someone dispose of it for me." He slid the box further away from him without another word. Even after resuming his position for Martha, he kept glancing at me out of the corner of his eye, as if he wanted to say something but was unsure how to proceed.

"Are you sure? There's some women in there offering all sorts of things. Some men, too, if that's your thing." I watched him for any sort of reaction. So far the relationship section of his background was blank; maybe this would provide some insight.

"I have no interest in whatever is in that box." He was as reserved as ever, so I didn't doubt it.

"You never know. Your soulmate could be in there."

He slid another sullen look in my direction, holding my amused gaze while giving an unimpressed stare in return. "Tell me, Doctor, do you believe in soulmates?"

"No." I smiled wider when he raised his brows in question. It was not the typical answer for a female, as I was well aware, but it was the truth. "Love is nothing more than a mixture of chemicals in the brain. But I also believe it's a choice."

"Poets the world over would disagree."

"They didn't know about oxytocin."

"No, I meant the part where you said love is a choice. I cannot argue against the scientific explanation for the sensation of love, but sometimes there is no choice — not a conscious one. I don't believe you can help it when someone stirs something within you. I don't know anyone who would willingly choose to torment themselves the way the love-sick do."

"Speaking from experience?"

"I have no use for love." He drew further into himself, folding an arm across his chest and holding his opposite bicep. On the surface, I didn't doubt that either. If his childhood was any indication, love was not to be trusted. When the people who were biologically programmed to love you shunned you, it could leave a deeper scar than physical abuse.

"So there's no girlfriend in here, missing you? Waiting for you?" I tapped the side of the box.

"I told you before, they're not worth the time or effort. If I didn't know better, I'd think you were driving at something."

"You caught me. I am desperate, Leander." I leaned forward, propping my elbows on the table and leaning into my hands like a moon-faced girl. "Desperate to know if you've ever been in a serious relationship and if you can form meaningful attachments."

He turned away, shaking his head. I thought I saw a glimpse of a smile but when he faced me again, only a faint crinkle remained at the corners of his eyes. "Isn't it exhausting? Analyzing and assessing every moment, every word spoken, every word not spoken. Do you ever turn it all off and just... experience life?"

Straightening again, I folded my arms on the table. Honestly, no. No I didn't. My mind raced at a hundred miles an hour, twenty-four/seven. My form of relaxation was reading case studies. I tried yoga once. I hated it. I couldn't just sit and do nothing. "It's my job."

"'The busy bee has no time for sorrow.' But I'm sure you're well aware of the signs of high-functioning depression, right, Doctor?"

I made a face at him, ignoring the intimation. "More Poe?"

"Blake." He smiled softly.

"Do you just memorize random quotes to sprinkle in conversations?"

"If someone has already expressed a feeling or thought with such eloquence, it seems fitting to use their words instead of mine. Take our discussion of love. I could say to you, 'Love seeketh not itself to please, Nor for itself hath any care, But for another gives its ease, And builds a Heaven in Hell's despair.' You would think I loved love and subscribed to the belief that love makes us a better person."

Unfolding himself from his position, he turned to face me straight-on, his knee resting against mine. He didn't even seem fazed, full of an energy I hadn't experienced before. It thrilled me. I made a mental note of his progress, pleased a dreadful letter could lead to an illuminating conversation.

"Now, imagine I tell you 'Love seeketh only self to please, To bind another to its delight, Joys in another's loss of ease, And builds a Hell in Heaven's despite.' It sounds as if I despise love, or that I see it as a means of manipulating another for my own benefit. Same author, same poem. Two very different sentiments."

"I don't suppose you're ever going to give me a straight

answer to a serious question." I smiled nonetheless. I was going to have to read up on some of these authors to see if I could suss out any more meaning to what he was saying.

He stalled, licking his lips before finally answering. "I form meaningful relationships with people who are meaningful. Sadly, most of those whom I encounter are not worth the endeavor. I will not waste my time or debase myself keeping up pretenses in order to fulfill some trivial expectation set for me by a society that does not align with my principles."

I marveled at him. It was almost as if he pulled the swirling thoughts from my brain and put them into words — far more eloquently than I could have. That was exactly how I felt about Darren, about dating in general.

"You seem shocked, Doctor. Did I offend you?"

Snapping myself out of it, I gave him an apologetic smile. "No. Not at all. It was very well put. As always."

He was about to say more when Nora thundered down the hallway with the drug cart. A second later, another nurse dashed after her.

Leaping out of the chair, I sprinted out of the room after them without a second thought or backward glance.

It wasn't long before I knew whose room we were going to — Todd's.

He was sprawled on the floor when I rounded the doorway. Tiny red dots covered his face and his fingers were blue.

Staff members were already working on him, tag-teaming CPR. I couldn't see past the nurse giving him chest compressions, but I knew his throat would be mangled by whatever he used to asphyxiate himself.

The AED's robotic voice advised no shock was needed.

Nora wrestled with Todd's arm, cramped between him and the bed. She finally got an IV started and pushed meds into the line.

The AED cycled again. No shock advised.

Kneeling at Todd's side, I swapped out with the nurse doing compressions.

After twenty minutes, the nurses rocked back on their heels, staring at the body in front of them. I blew a lock of hair out of my face and stopped as well. My arms ached and my knees throbbed, despite the cold tile beneath them. There was no point in continuing except pride.

"How long was he down?" I asked, focusing my attention on the gray-flecked tile floor. There was a stream of thin, brownish liquid seeping out of Todd's slack mouth. His eyelids were open, red dots speckling the whites of his eyes. I didn't want to see any of it.

"I don't know," Nora, as the senior nurse, replied for the group.

"Did someone start an ambulance?" I asked. I already knew the answer. If someone called, the ambulance would have been here by now.

There was a circle of shaking heads.

Biting back a sarcastic reply, I looked at my watch. "Time of death, 1636 hours. Nora, call the transport team. And for God's sake, don't let the other patients see what happened."

"What are you going to do?" Nora asked, getting to her feet along with me.

"First, I'm going to tell Kim and Dennis what happened. Then, I'm going to notify Todd's family. And lastly, I'll be talking to Gene in legal so he can get ahead of the lawsuit that's coming due to the apparent disregard for policy."

"We followed policy."

"You're telling me he was checked on every fifteen minutes?"

Glances shot around the room like a twisted game of ping pong. I wanted to scream at them. Maybe then they'd appreciate the seriousness of their profession, understand what happened when they skirted the rules.

Without another word, I closed the door behind me, leaving them to clean up their mess while I dealt with the mountain of paperwork following any incident with a patient.

Leander was standing just inside the dayroom when I walked down the hallway. Calvin had a hand on his chest and appeared to be keeping him from going out the door.

When Leander caught sight of me, he shifted away from Calvin and followed along on the other side of the window. There was no denying the concern on his face. If I wasn't so angry, I might have been touched.

The concern melted into a look of confusion as I continued on.

I shook my head in answer to the un-asked question. No, everything was not alright. And no, I would not be returning to continue our conversation.

Quickening my pace, I swiped my key card across the sensor on the door lock, disappearing around the bend before the first tear spilled onto my cheek. I made it to my office before the rest of them came.

I gave myself five minutes to sit and wallow in the unfairness of it all. Yes, Todd was a pain in the ass patient. Yes, he was difficult to deal with, but that didn't mean he deserved to die.

When the time was up, I wiped my eyes, careful not to smear my makeup. I sniffed back the frustration and picked up the phone, expelling a calming breath as it rang.

"Hey, Dennis. Sorry to wake you... There was an incident today."

CHAPTER 9

"*S*he should be fired, Kim." I crossed my arms over my chest.

Kim held her hands up. "I know you two don't get along."

"Get along? She's incompetent! And she's teaching the next generation of nurses to not give a shit about their patients either!"

"Gene's already been over it. There's no cause for ter—"

"No cause? No cause!" I nearly shot out of my chair and across her desk. "How about the fact she's going to cost us hundreds of thousands of dollars, maybe even millions, in a lawsuit? Is the board ready to fork out that kind of money to keep covering for a useless employee?"

"I know you're upset, Lorelei."

"You think?"

"Patient safety is always our priority. You know that."

My cell phone buzzed in my pocket, keeping me from saying something I might regret. A meeting reminder flashed across the screen and I stood abruptly, shoving it back in my pocket. "I don't want her anywhere near my patients."

"You know we don't have the staff to accommodate that request."

"Move her to another floor! Problem solved."

"I'll see what can be done."

Somehow I refrained from snorting and headed out the door to my next meeting. I may have been young, all things considered, but I wasn't stupid. I knew when I was being pacified and it did not sit well with me.

∙✿∙

The morning had been so busy with paperwork and damage control, I didn't have time to check on any of my patients. I trusted Calvin to tell me if something was amiss, since the nurses and I were not exactly on speaking terms.

Leander was the only patient to cross my mind more than once. It was hard not to think of him while I was seated across from his attorney in an ostentatiously decorated room. With the amount of dark-paneled wood and rows of law volumes, we should have been in an Oxford library instead of a borrowed office inside one of the local law firms.

"Can I get you anything?" Scheible's perky young assistant asked, with the faintest hint of a Southern accent. Did she actually come up with him from St. Louis for this case?

"Just water, thank you."

Smiling, she disappeared, returning momentarily with a silver tray. She set it on the desk between us and ducked out again, closing the door behind her.

I poured my own water from the glass carafe and took a sip before Scheible launched into the heart of the meeting. "How is Leander holding up?"

"It's really hard to say, Mr. Scheible. He seems convinced

this is all a mistake." As much as I agreed, I couldn't vocalize it. Ever. My neutrality would be sunk.

"What do you think?"

"It doesn't matter what I think. You're the lawyer. I just have to assess whether or not he's fit to stand trial and if he's a risk to himself or others when he returns to a regular jail."

"Well, is he?"

"Again, Mr. Scheible, it's hard to say. I haven't been able to garner much useful information during our sessions thus far. Is he fit to stand trial? Yes. Undoubtedly. Is he a risk to himself or others? That I can't say. He'll wax poetically about whatever — literally quoting poetry — and then shut down if it gets too personal. His written evaluations are all over the place. One test says he's a risk, the other says he's fine." I had a growing feeling Leander purposely gave contradicting answers simply because he could, not because they were an actual reflection of his mental status. Boredom and a keen mind were never a good combination.

Scheible rifled through the papers on his desk and slid a thick, tri-folded document across the table. Another petition for the court. "Well, while you're at it, can you do an assessment from the night of the murders? Even the grandmother's?"

I blinked, not sure if I heard him correctly. "You want me to do what now?"

"A forensic opin—"

"Yes, I am well aware of what it is. Why are you asking me to do one? Or, four, rather?"

"Just covering all of my bases, Doc."

I exhaled a breath and set the glass on the tray. "I don't think you fully appreciate how long it takes to do a thorough forensic opinion, especially dating back ten years ago. The best reconstructions are done right after an event — not years later. It's a lengthy process with the amount of data I have to collect. Some would say at this point it's even impossible."

He steepled his fingers. "That's what I'm counting on."

I frowned at him, catching on to his scheme. "We're not a daycare facility, Mr. Scheible."

"I understand that. And please, call me Richard."

"Richard... if at some point Leander is determined to be stable and not a threat, he'll have to return jail. He can't stay at Parkview indefinitely."

"He doesn't belong in jail. The judge is holding him without bond because they say he's a flight risk. So either he stays at Parkview, under assessment, until this whole nonsense is brought to an end, or he gets tossed back in county with the real criminals. We both know he won't make it in there."

"Why not just surrender his passport?"

He chuckled. "And what should he do with his plane? Sign the title over?"

"He has a plane?" I didn't realize "well-off" translated to having a personal plane.

"His company does, which means he does. And with the amount he's stashed away in off-shore holdings, the judge doesn't want to risk him not returning for trial, passport or no passport."

"That still doesn't mean you can use a private facility to house your client."

Scheible grunted, pulling out a stack of folders. Fingering through the tabs, he pulled one out from the bottom and pushed it across the desk. "His assets. So if you're worried about payment for his treatment, don't be. Send my office the bill and we'll make sure it's paid on time and in full. That's more than the county is willing to do, I'm sure."

"Money is not my concern, Mist — Richard." I pushed the

folder back without looking at it. "I want what's best for my patients."

"So do I. Leander has gotten the raw end of the deal in pretty much every aspect of his life. Money doesn't make up for that, which is what I think this all boils down to."

"Someone is doing this just to get his money?"

"To crush the Welles Corporation, yes. You don't know the people in Easton — the Welles family built that town. They made a lot of money and a lot of enemies. It's finally reached a boiling point and Leander is the scapegoat."

"You're trying to tell me an entire town is against this man? Just because of his last name?"

"Like I said, you don't know the people in Easton. It's like the land that time forgot. The cops down there, they've had it out for him for years. Grudges are personal, Doctor. It doesn't matter how much money you have."

If Leander was the one telling me this, I would have labeled him paranoid. But this was his lawyer and his non-verbal cues were telling me he believed every word he was saying.

The creepy Poe letter from the other day was further evidence this wasn't a cut-and-dry murder case. I didn't agree with Leander about not mentioning it, but I kept my mouth shut all the same.

"On the surface, the SA's case looks good," Scheible continued. "But it's not. I just need some more time to prove it. So you tell me what you need to keep Leander safe until this is over with."

I sat for a moment, drumming my fingers on the carved arms of my chair. "I need everything you have. Not just what you gave the prosecutor in discovery. Everything. And I will give my opinion, regardless of what it says about your client."

"I'd expect nothing less." Scheible smiled.

An hour later, my office was stacked with so many boxes I could barely move around the room. I schlepped them down the hall to one of the smaller conference rooms and stacked them in a corner in an attempt at organization.

There was no way I could continue with my other caseload now. Scheible gave me enough work to keep me busy for weeks, especially at the glacial pace Leander and I were going. We'd made some progress into his psychosocial background, but not enough.

Sometimes it was easier when the patients were stark-raving mad. It was easier for the assessment, anyway. But a forensic opinion? I'd have to dig even further into Leander's past than I already did for the standard evaluation. I had the unmistakable feeling he didn't want anyone going there, let alone a shrink.

I grabbed the box with the oldest date on the side and sat down. As much as I didn't want to revisit Irene Welles and what a terrible human being she was, it seemed I had no choice.

Hours later, with visions of Irene's crushed face dancing in front of me, I pushed away from the stack of reports and mashed my fingers over my closed eyes, trying to re-lubricate my contacts. I vaguely registered the sound of footsteps next to me while the black and white fuzzies in my eyes dissipated.

"Hey Doc. What are you doing in here? Something wrong with your office?" Calvin asked, picking up one of the autopsy photos and visibly blanching.

"A forensic opinion on Leander." I took the photograph away and turned it face-down on the table before he lost his lunch over everything. "There's not enough room for all of this." I gestured to the stack of boxes as tall as he was.

THE MYSTERY OF LEANDER WELLES

Calvin made a disgusted noise and turned his attention to the stack of newly-arrived books on the table. He fanned them out, making faces at each subsequent title before picking up one with a skull and a raven on the cover — a copy of Edgar Allan Poe. "Just some light reading, huh? What's with all this creepy ass stuff?"

"Just trying to understand Leander." I took the pins out of my hair and shook it out, rubbing my relieved scalp in small circles. "What's up, anyway?"

He pushed the stack of books out of the way and dropped into a chair. "On break, saw the light on. Thought I'd see what's new. You haven't been around much lately."

I gestured to the table with a half-hearted smile.

"Busy bee." Calvin chuckled, scratching his ear.

I slid a side-ways glance at him. "What'd you say?"

"Busy bee. That's what Leander calls you and I guess I see it now. You're always buzzing around, working hard. I don't know. It's cute. Nicer than calling you a workaholic, I guess."

"I'm not a—" I couldn't finish my weak defense, surrounded as I was by proof to the contrary.

Laughing, he nudged my arm. "Yeah. See. You can't even say it!"

"I'm dedicated. What can I say?"

"Mhmm. Patients have been asking for you the last couple of days, too."

"I know. I'm sorry. First there was the whole Todd thing and now I've got this." I held my head in my hands, groaning. "There are not enough hours in the day sometimes."

"I hear that. Just don't work too hard. You gotta live, too."

"Did Leander tell you to tell me that?"

He chuckled. "No. But dude's got a point." His watch beeped and he stood slowly, stretching his long limbs. "Break's over. Remember. Don't work too hard, Doc."

"Oh, wait, Cal. Can you do me a favor?" I grabbed the

73

copy of Poe and handed it to him. "Can you give this to Leander for me? Tell him to mark his favorite passages. Please?"

"Sure thing." He gave me a wide smile and disappeared, whistling a peppy tune.

I sank back into the chair and stared at the reams of paper scattered around the table. Sighing, I slumped forward until my forehead rested on the table. I was going to be here all night. Again.

A streak of black ink crossed out another name on my paper. The long list of people Irene Welles employed over the years was dwindling with little to show for it. Although she churned through staff rather quickly, most of them were reluctant to talk to me. Of the few who did, most did not speak highly of their former boss.

The maids were mostly terrified. The longest any of them lasted was six months. The drivers stayed on a little longer than most because, according to one, they lived above the garage and rarely had contact with the miserable woman.

Gardeners were another group who tended to stick around longer than average, except for the one who'd left the shed unlocked and unwittingly gave Leander shelter. He was fired that day for his "carelessness" and had to move to find work again after Irene slandered him all over southern Illinois.

Each successive phone call was brief. People didn't reveal too many details, if they spoke at all. Some of them just swore at me and hung up as soon as they heard the name

"Welles." Scheible was right — people did hold grudges down there.

The only employee who lasted the entire length of Leander's time with his grandmother was a cook — Florence Strand. I dialed her number next, tapping my pen on the yellow pad next to me.

When someone finally picked up, I introduced myself and explained the purpose of my call.

"The best thing to ever happen to this town," Florence wheezed in my ear.

"What was?"

"When that monster was locked up."

"You mean Leander?"

"The Devil's in that child. His poor grandmother did everything she could to set him on the right path but it never took. And look what he's gone and done."

"What can you tell me about your time with the Welles family?"

She huffed. "I worked for Mrs. Welles for thirty-three years, right up until the day that son of a bitch bashed her head in with a crowbar. Hit her so many times, he caved her skull in. She had to have a closed casket because of him. And now he's gone and done it again."

"What do you remember about Leander? Before the murder?"

She made a disgusted noise. "Should have died with his mother and saved us all the trouble. That's what happens when you breed with a river rat — you get diseases."

I tried not to be offended on his behalf, but my blood simmered with every word she spewed. "He was just a boy when he moved in. What trouble could a six year old have been?"

She snorted. "You didn't know his mother. Trash. Pure trash. She corrupted Julian and her son was just like her."

"Julian was Leander's father, right?"

"Irene's only son, God rest his soul. If it weren't for that slut and her spawn, he'd still be alive and so would Irene."

"So, I take it Leander didn't see his mother's family?"

She snorted again. "No. Irene wouldn't let those people set foot on the property. She would have tossed that creature out on his ear, but he was Julian's son after all. She thought she could save him and turn him around."

"Turn him around from what? I still don't understand what a six year old could be guilty of."

"He's sick in the head. He's a disgrace to the Welles name. Obsessed with his dead mother and constantly pestering Irene about her. It's unnatural."

I bit my tongue. There was nothing unnatural about a child wanting to know about their deceased parent. The fact both of his parents died when he was so young must have wreaked havoc on his development. Ignorant hag.

Clearing my throat, I moved on. "Do you recall if there was any violence in the home?"

"If he didn't get his way, he'd throw fits. Break whatever he could, attack his grandmother, and then he started in on himself. She had to lock him up after he sliced his arm to shreds."

That was news to me, considering all of the other staff members portrayed Leander in a more sympathetic, or at least indifferent, light. "Did she ever consider counseling for him?"

"That might be how you handle children up north, Doctor, but down here we keep to our own. Maybe you should give it a try." She hung up abruptly.

I stared at the receiver in my hand long after the phone began beeping at me. If Leander was guilty of murder, it's a wonder he didn't off the dear old Florence too, considering the choice things she had to say about him and his mother.

Based on the quality of the phone calls so far, it was clear I was going to have to go to Easton myself. In addition to interviewing a few other people, I could retrieve the rest of the documents I needed that Scheible didn't possess copies of. Plus it would give me a better sense of Leander's actual environment to go along with the depressing background.

Speaking of Leander... I wanted to give him one more chance to open up on his own before I shone a giant spotlight on the darkest parts of his past.

⁂

The patients from the third floor were outside for a change, safely, if discreetly, contained within the inner courtyard of the building. It was as tranquil of a place as Parkview had to offer with lush gardens, shade trees, and stone benches. One could almost forget they were here against their will.

Leander was speaking with Martha when I approached. She jerked her hand at me in an awkward wave. I smiled, happy she appeared to have found a friend other than Calvin. I hoped she didn't ruin it by biting him.

"Hello, Martha. How are you today?"

Her mouth twisted into her version of a smile. She turned to Leander, wringing her hands in front of her excitedly.

"Martha darling," Leander said, bending closer to her good ear. "Would you excuse us for a moment? The doctor has something urgent to discuss."

Martha nodded and shuffled off, waving again.

After she was out of earshot, he produced a book from behind his back, smiling softly as he presented it to me. "Thank you for the book. It was comforting, even if it was for a homework assignment."

I took the copy of Poe back with a mock glare. "It was not

meant as a homework assignment. I was curious. And who better to direct my course of study?"

He cocked an eyebrow. "So I'm to be your version of CliffsNotes?"

"Something like that." I conceded the point with a smile.

"Is everything alright? The mood here has been quite different since Todd's passing. We've seldom seen you." He canted his head to the side, studying me.

Sometimes it was alarming how perceptive he was. If he had a white coat he could have passed for one of the doctors. Hell, he could probably talk his way out of the facility if he was given half a chance. "I've just been busy. Busy bee."

The edges of his mouth twitched as he fought a smile. He scuffed the heel of his shoe on the ground and looked away, his cheeks a shade pinker than before. Suddenly, he looked up again, his brows raised expectantly. "Well? I cannot stand the suspense. What is it you need to tell me?"

I tucked a lock of hair behind my ear as the breeze picked up. "What are you talking about?"

"I can see it in your eyes. You want to say something but you're afraid it will displease me."

I frowned at him. I wasn't afraid to displease him. What was I, a servant? "I wouldn't phrase it like that, exactly."

"By all means, how would you phrase it, Doctor?" His coy little smirk was back. He enjoyed getting a rise out of me, putting me on the defensive instead of the other way around.

I gave myself a mental slap, hoping to regain my focus. I was the one in charge here. I was the one with a job to do. "I have to be away for a few days, so in the meantime you'll continue your sessions with Dr. Atwell."

His smirk vanished. "Is that necessary?"

"Yes. It's part of the reason you're still here. He's a fantastic man. I think you'll like him."

"But he's not you."

"He mentored me, so he knows all of my tricks." I smiled, hoping it would lighten the mood.

"He's not you," he said again, speaking each word slowly to drive his point home. There was no teasing in his tone this time. He seemed genuinely apprehensive about the change to our routine. I took it as a good sign, a testament to the rapport I'd spent so much time building.

"It'll be fine. I'll be back before you know it."

"Might I inquire where you're going?"

"Easton."

He winced, a crack in his perfect facade. I don't know why, but his reaction took me by surprise. I suppressed the urge to reach out, to soothe away whatever fear or memory gripped him.

"I need to interview some people. Get some more infor-mation that wasn't in the case file. That sort of thing," I continued. Why was I explaining myself to him? He didn't need to know the particulars of what I was doing. I was the doctor, he was the patient. He didn't get to be privy to my methodology or my schedule.

"What if I tell you everything you want to know? Would you still go?" Something in his eyes shifted, but I couldn't pinpoint what it was. Anger? Fear? Hope, even? The sunlight illuminated a light spattering of freckles across his nose, adding a boyish element to his appearance. The urge to hug him swelled, especially as the horrible conversation with the cook replayed in my mind.

"I would love that, but yes. I still have to go," I said sadly.

He stared past me, chewing on his lower lip. The breeze tousled his curls and enveloped me in a sudden chill. It was as if he were rebuilding the wall between us, brick by invis-ible brick.

"So if there's anything you'd like to tell me, Leander, now

is the time." I watched him closely, looking for any sort of sign as to what he was thinking. He remained frustratingly inscrutable.

"'Believe nothing you hear, and only one half that you see.'"

I furrowed my brows at him. "What does that mean?"

His chin dropped, his gaze falling with it. He swayed on his feet for a moment before shifting forward, striding past me.

"Leander." I turned and followed him.

Stopping all of a sudden, he dropped to one knee, reaching into the sea of greenery that ringed the inside of the building. He was on his feet again in a flash, a sprig of Lily of the valley between his fingers. "Safe travels."

I took it gently, careful not to crush the tiny white bells. My fingers grazed his in the exchange, sending a spark of warmth straight through me.

He gave me a fleeting, sorrowful smile and walked away again, his hands clasped behind his back. Rejoining Martha across the yard, he sat beside her on one of the benches. She pointed to something in the distance and he nodded. They were too far away to hear what he said, but she laughed, her silent, animated laugh. She pointed to something else and his reply sent her into another fit of hysterics. How was he so at ease with Martha, yet remained guarded with me?

It was a question best left for another day. I checked my watch with a groan. If I was going to get anything accomplished I needed to be on the road soon. It was at least a three-hour drive and who knew what the state of construction would be like. Before I left I made sure to give Leander unrestricted library access. Hopefully it would make the days somewhat more tolerable for him.

With his marked copy of Poe tucked under my arm, I

headed out the front door. Stepping out into the sunshine, I inhaled the soft floral scent of the Lily, wondering what, exactly, I was going to find in Leander's hometown.

CHAPTER 11

*E*aston was every bit the small, sleepy town Scheible described. Bisected by a river and surrounded by limestone bluffs and rolling hills, it was old and beautiful. Yet a sense of unease blanketed me the minute I crossed the town line. There was no obvious reason for it, but it was there all the same, trailing my every move.

My first stop was the police department. I was fairly certain Scheible included all of the police reports but I wanted to double check for myself. Plus, it would be as good a spot as any to get information on the retired police officer Leander was accused of murdering.

As expected in a town this size, the police department was hardly bustling when I walked through the door. How many officers did they even have? Five? Were they even a full-time department?

An older woman sat behind the front desk, sipping coffee and diligently working on a crossword puzzle. A soft chiming announced my entrance. The door had time to swing shut behind me before she set her newspaper to the side and looked up. "Can I help you?"

"I'm Dr. Lorelei Clayton. Mr. Scheible should have sent word I was coming, in reference to the Leander Welles case."

The woman stiffened and nodded. "Wait here." She disappeared down the hallway and came back with a man I could only presume was the chief thanks in large part to the crisp white shirt and array of golden accessories. The woman didn't retake her seat. Instead, she ambled away, leaving me alone with the man.

I tried to introduce myself but he cut me off with a wave of his hand. "I know who you are. I don't have anything to say that isn't in any of the reports."

"I'm not here to question the veracity of the reports. I'm here to gather some additional information about Mr. Welles and the victims."

"What more could you want to know? He did it. He did all of it. These are the only four we could pin on him. Moron used the same goddamn weapon."

Apparently neither Leander nor Scheible were exaggerating the police's dislike of him. While I strove for neutrality in every case I evaluated, I was still taken aback by the chief's assertion of Leander's guilt. It seemed highly unlikely Leander would be dumb enough to use the same weapon on four separate occasions, but that wasn't the part that caught my attention. "What do you mean, these are the only four?"

"People been dying around here for ten years because of that psychopath but the worthless lawyers up at the courthouse don't want to do anything about it. Got 'em all in his pocket. If it weren't for Vera Van Deveer coming forward about the kidnapping, he'd have gotten away with it this time too."

"How many people do you think he's killed?"

The chief blew out a breath, scratching his chin. "At least a dozen."

I blinked, trying to process what he said without gaping.

"A dozen people have been bludgeoned to death and they're only prosecuting him for four?"

"No. Four people were bludgeoned to death — the others were poisoned. People were perfectly healthy one day and dead the next."

"Poison? That's a simple matter to solve with some tests."

"Only if someone orders the toxicology. Either these people don't have family to care or the coroner won't do it."

"I see." I didn't see, but I needed the chief to think I was on his side. Or at least not on Leander's. "Do you know what kind of poison?"

He made a face at me, as if I was the dumbest blonde to ever stand in his presence. "Lady, if I knew that he'd be charged with three times the murders. Does it matter?"

So much for that tactic. I decided to switch topics before he ended the conversation entirely. "I was wondering what, if anything, you could tell me about Mr. Starkey? Do you know what sort of interactions he had with Mr. Welles?"

The chief shook his head. "Keith was as good a cop as any. He did what he could to help that rich brat and look how he repays him."

"What do you mean help him? Help him how?"

"He'd talk to him, you know? Check in. Saved his little ass one time from jumping off the bluff by his house. Took him home a dozen different times when he caught him out after dark. He could have clued in family services about him being a runaway, but he didn't." He snorted. "No good deed and all that."

"Why would Mr. Welles kill someone who helped him in the past?" The lack of motive was concerning. The State's Attorney better have something else to go off of other than citing Leander's alleged psychopathy.

"Why would he kill his poor old grandmother? She took

him in, raised him, gave him everything. She didn't deserve the abuse he heaped on her."

"Abuse?" I raised my eyebrows at him. Florence said Leander had "fits" and would "attack" Irene, which I interpreted as a temper tantrum, if anything. Was there more to it? Was Irene really trying to help an out-of-control child?

"He beat her senseless. She tried to hide it, of course, but I saw the marks, the scratches. He terrorized her, especially as he got older."

I tried to picture Leander abusing a frail old woman. No matter how I rearranged the scenario, it didn't compute. I couldn't picture them in a role-reversal no matter how convincing the chief seemed. "Why wasn't he arrested then, or at least referred to the juvenile court?"

"Irene didn't want to make his life any harder. Can you believe that?" The chief scoffed and shook his head.

He was right — I couldn't believe it. Just hearing Irene's name made the bile rise in my throat, but here was a peace officer adamantly portraying Leander as the violent offender. Nothing about Leander's relationship with his grandmother seemed to make sense, the same as nothing about the murders made sense.

"In your opinion, why would he poison some people and bludgeon others? Those are two very different methods of killing."

"He's psycho, Doctor. You figure it out. Ain't that your job? I'm done talking about this kid. The sooner they throw him in prison, the sooner this whole town will be put out of their goddamn misery." With that, the chief turned and strode back down the hallway. A door slammed shut and that was that.

I was about to leave when I heard the old woman shuffling behind me. The secretary reappeared with a file box and set it on the edge of her desk. "Everything you asked for."

"Is there anything else you can tell me about Mr. Starkey? I understand he worked for this department for his whole career?"

She shook her head. "The chief said we're not allowed to talk to you. Good day, Doctor."

Taking the box with a nod, I walked out. I had the feeling my time in Easton would be as short-lived as the phone calls.

꙳

My growling stomach dictated my next move — to the first convenience store I stumbled across. I picked up a protein bar and a bottle of water and headed to the cashier. It was either that or the questionable hotdogs rolling around in a steamy plexiglass box.

The newsstand next to the register featured a blaring headline: DELAYED AGAIN! Beneath it was a picture of Leander on the steps of the Camden County courthouse. The byline appeared to be detailing the latest in his case — or lack thereof.

I skimmed the rest, looking for any sign of a rat at Parkview that may have revealed his whereabouts or his condition. Thankfully, there was nothing in the article about the cause for the delay, only that the defense successfully petitioned for one.

"Shame," the clerk said as he rang up my items. "That boy had it all."

"Oh?"

"Sometimes I wonder what would have happened if his mother lived."

"Did you know her?"

"Eleanor? Sure. Everyone knew her. She was just as pretty as a picture. Smart, too. Boy was she smart. Got a scholarship to one of them ivy-league schools. Yale. Harvard. I can't remember."

"So she was from here?"

"Yes ma'am, just down the river. Her and Julian was like a fairytale. Til it weren't." Shaking his head, he handed me the receipt.

"Is her family still around?"

He shook his head again. "'Fraid not. Her daddy ran off when she was little. It was just her and her mama. Her mama died about twelve, thirteen years ago, I think."

"Do you know Leander Welles?"

He gave me a wide smile, a flash of tobacco-stained teeth under his white whiskers. "Used to come in here from time to time. Always had his nose in a book. Quiet boy. Polite. Never made trouble, unlike some others. Guess trouble found him anyway."

"Do you think Leander killed those people?" I asked, not because it mattered what an elderly clerk thought, but because I was genuinely curious.

"I can't say for sure one way or the other. I hope not."

"Thank you." I scooped up my snacks and left quickly, avoiding the glaring eyes of a woman and a small child waiting in line.

❧

The Van Deveer house was the next closest address on my list. I finished off my protein bar as I headed up the front steps of a beautiful lilac-colored Victorian. Stuffing the wrapper in my bag, I rang the bell and dusted my hand off on my skirt.

Nothing.

On the off-chance the doorbell was broken, I knocked.

The house remained quiet. There was no movement beyond the lacy curtains. I scribbled a note on the back of my business card and shoved it between the front door and the doorframe, hoping the doctor's widow would find it before it blew away.

As I turned to go, I found a gray-haired woman blocking the front gate. She wore an apron over her yellow sundress and no shoes, just pink fuzzy slippers. "What are you doing here?"

"Are you Vera Van Deveer?"

"You leave that poor woman alone! Goddamn vultures. She's been through enough!"

"I'm not a reporter, but I do need to talk—"

"I don't care what you need! Vera's not home. So get!" She flapped a kitchen towel at me like I was a stray cat in her garden.

Dodging the towel, I pointed at my car. "Can I get through?"

Scowling at me, she muttered something under her breath before marching off and hobbling up the steps of the white Queen Anne next door. The screen door banged shut behind her.

I didn't stick around to see if she was going to fetch a broom. Or worse. Easton seemed like the type of town where everyone kept a shotgun by the door.

The scent of Lily of the valley greeted me as I climbed back into the car. The tiny bells started to yellow and curl at the edges, but the fragrance remained as alluring as ever. I picked it up from the cup holder and smelled it, allowing my thoughts to wander. It didn't take long before I wound up on a dark, twisted path through my mind, replaying snippets of conversations over and over and fitting them together like a puzzle.

The chief believed Leander poisoned people.

Leander admitted Lily of the valley was his favorite flower, in part because of its unexpected lethality.

Dropping the sprig in the cup holder, I shook my head, scattering the thought before it could fully take hold.

I needed a different perspective.

CHAPTER 12

The Welles Corporation was not what I expected. I pictured soaring glass walls and exposed steel beams, sleek and modern and oozing money. What I found was an old brick building downtown, sandwiched between a coffee shop and a clothing store. It looked like it had been there since the town's founding, or close to it, and overlooked the river on a low, flat stretch of the roadway. If it wasn't for the fact WELLES 1857 was carved into the stone beneath the roofline, I might have missed it entirely.

After the less than warm reception pretty much everywhere, I was hoping Leander's own company would be different.

It wasn't.

The receptionist was polite enough and quickly phoned someone, whispering, "She's here," before hanging up and gesturing to a chair in the lobby. "Olivia will be right with you."

I nodded and took a seat.

Ten minutes later, Olivia appeared. She wore a black pinstripe suit reminiscent of Leander's. Her brunette hair was twisted off her neck, held in place with a wicked looking hair pin. She gave me an unimpressed once-over before introducing herself as Olivia Harlow, Leander's personal assistant.

"We can speak in my office." She led the way down a hallway, expertly navigating the hand-hewn floors despite her staggering stilettos. Every aspect of her was sharp and pointy, from her eyeliner to her less-than-amused smirk.

She sat behind a large glass desk and waited for me to sit before leaping over the usual social conventions. "I'll save you the trouble of asking questions. I've worked for Leander for the past six years. No, he's never been violent. Yes, this town is full of liars. No, I don't think he killed all those people. Yes, I'm sure. No, I'm not sleeping with him. No, he's not a drug addict or an alcoholic. And no, he doesn't lie. Not to me."

I blinked. "Well, that is quite the introduction. Thank you."

She smiled, a dazzling white smile that was anything but friendly. "Leander appreciates people who are thorough and efficient."

"Yes, I can see that. Can we go back to the part about lying? What do you mean he doesn't lie, at least not to you? Are you implying he lies to other people?"

"It's exactly what I said. He doesn't lie. He abhors liars as much as he abhors idiots and hypocrites. If he says he's going to do something, he's going to do it. If he said he didn't do something, then he didn't do it. How is that complicated?"

"Because everyone lies. Little lies, white lies, half-truths, omissions. It's human."

"Not Leander. He's different."

"How so?"

Snorting, she rolled her eyes. "Have you even talked to him?"

"I know he's intelligent, if that's what you mean."

She leaned forward, staring daggers at me. "It's more than his intelligence. It's his whole essence. He commands a room simply by walking into it. He knows what he wants and he takes it, no apologies. He's magnificent."

"You seem to admire him very much." That was putting it lightly. She reminded me of a lapdog, snarling at anyone who so much as looked at her master.

Olivia reclined again, tilting her chin upward. "He gave me an opportunity when no one else would. He saw something in me. I wouldn't be where I am without him." Fair enough. I felt similarly grateful to Dennis showing me the ropes, though I was far less protective of him.

"Why do you think people here don't like him?" I asked.

"Because they're vindictive little sheep? He's done more for this town than any of them want to admit. It was his money that renovated the library. His money that started the community garden. His money that funds the breakfast and lunch programs for all of the kids at school, regardless of parental income. So what if he doesn't do all the things his grandmother did? He doesn't host fundraisers or galas or rub elbows with people. He doesn't care. He hates politics. He just wants to be left alone."

Interesting. I didn't peg him as a philanthropist, but given how passionate he was about certain things, it wasn't entirely shocking, either.

"Is there anything else you can tell me? Anything about his personality or the nights of the murders? Interactions he's had with people?"

Her upper lip curled. "Leander's one requirement for anyone in his life is absolute loyalty. If you can't give him your word then you're not worth his time. And God help you if you give it and then break it. So, no, I won't betray his trust or his confidence."

There was the guard dog again... "I'm not asking you to. I

just want to know what he was like around the time of the murders. Was he happy? Sad? Angry? Making plans for the future?"

"Ask Elijah. He's Leander's right-hand man." She handed me one of the Welles Corporation business cards with the name Elijah Westbrook on it. No title, no address. Just a phone number in raised, black ink. "I have work to do."

"Well, thank you for your time."

❧

I was nearly to my car when a group of men a block up caught my eye. They were talking loudly to each other and came to a sudden stop when they saw me. One pointed, elbowing another. A rumbling erupted among the group. The designated leader stepped forward, a scowl etched deep in his face.

"Hey! You the doctor?"

A flutter of panic shot through me. I swallowed and nodded, glancing around. We were in the middle of downtown Easton. Surely a mob like this would draw someone's attention. Right?

"Can I help you with something?" I asked, hoping I sounded polite and unaffected by their size or smoldering anger. How did they know I was here? Did Scheible take out an ad in the paper, or had word really spread that quickly?

"Yeah, take a message to that fuckin—" The man stopped short.

Another man rushed in out of nowhere, settling himself between me and the group of angry townsfolk. My rescuer looked young from the backside, but the mob in front of him took a visible step back. The only other thing I could make out about him was a thick, black tattoo on the side of his neck.

"What were you saying?" the younger one asked, cupping a hand around his ear and leaning forward.

"Nothing." The leader backed into the guy next to him and so on down the line. The throng dispersed, grousing to one another and throwing contemptuous glares in our direction.

"That's what I thought. Take care now. Yep. Bye bye." Once the crowd meandered away, the young man turned and smiled, his blue eyes bright and warm. He looked familiar, wearing a black pin-stripe suit similar to Olivia's, but a far less severe expression.

"Cole Holliday," he said, extending his hand. More tattoos peeked out beneath his cuff. "You must be Dr. Clayton."

I shook his hand with a grateful smile. "I am. Thank you for... whatever that was."

"Everyone's a little on edge lately with a serial killer out there. Of course, these morons think Leander did it, but we both know that's not possible."

"Isn't it?" I arched an eyebrow at him.

Cole shook his head, not the least bit annoyed the way Olivia had been. "Why would Leander murder four random people? His grandma, ok. Fine. I can see the argument for that. But the other three? What's his motive?"

"That's a very good question. I was hoping you could tell me."

"Elijah and I were with him the night Dr. Van Deveer was murdered. So if he's guilty of murder, what does that make us?"

"Accomplices," I replied with a straight face.

He laughed, oblivious to the seriousness of my reply. "Yeah. Right. See how it doesn't add up?"

I didn't, but there was no point in dwelling on it. "What were you guys doing?"

"We were at Bellavia's, the Italian place downtown. It's

really good. You should try the pasta Capone. If you like spicy marinara, it's—"

I spoke up over him, trying to steer him back in a useful direction. "Any reason they don't believe your alibi?"

Cole snorted. "Yeah. We paid in cash because their credit card machine was down. Leander and I don't really like crowds, so we always sit in the back. The police said there's no record of us there. Then the doctor's wife starts crying about how we showed up and kidnapped her husband and suddenly the whole town gets amnesia."

"If she saw all three of you, why is only Leander being charged?" I wasn't a lawyer by any stretch, but it seemed odd the police wouldn't arrest the accomplices of a murderer. Even if the charges didn't stick, they could always use Cole and Elijah to turn on Leander. Or try to, at any rate. Like Olivia, I got the sense from Cole he would do anything Leander asked.

Cole's outrage was palpable, flicking on like a light switch. "Because it's a goddamn joke! A witch hunt. I don't think her or the other families give a shit about any criminal case — they want to stick it to him in civil court and get a huge payout."

"Do you think he's being framed?" I kept my voice calm and quiet, hoping Cole took the hint and brought it down a notch.

"Like, do I think someone is doing this to him on purpose instead of being judgy, incompetent assholes?"

I fished the typed letter out of my bag and handed it to him. I'd saved it from the box of glitter and body spray on the off chance more of them came in. I knew Leander didn't put any stock in it, but something about it was off. "Someone sent this to him. Any ideas?"

Cole skimmed it before handing it back with a shrug. "Sounds like something Leander would write."

"He said it's from an Edgar Allan Poe story. Does that mean anything to you?"

He shook his head. "No. Did you try asking Elijah? Or Jake? Jake is super into literature too."

"Jake Murray? I've been trying to reach him. Do you know where he is?"

He shook his head again. "He's been dodging me. Got his nose out of whack about what's going on with Leander and took off a couple weeks ago."

That was... odd. I set the information to the side and carried on. "Is there anything else you think I should know? Something not in any report anywhere?"

He started to shake his head and then stopped, giving me a side-eyed glance. "Did he tell you about the bunny?"

"No. What bunny?" A tendril of cold dread wrapped around my insides.

"Don't say anything to him!" Cole ran a hand through his sandy hair and looked around. There was no one in our immediate vicinity. There were hardly any cars on the road either. We were as alone as we were going to be.

"What is it?" I took a step closer anyway. If he was this distressed re-telling a story that wasn't even his, I was both intrigued and terrified. This was the sort of salacious information that would inevitably come up in court.

"He told me a story one time about this bunny. He found it in the yard and kept it, like a pet, but he couldn't bring it in the house because of his grandmother. So anyway, he would go check on this bunny day and night, feed it and whatever. His grandmother caught him and she..." He sighed and put his hands on his hips, shaking his head again. "Oh, man. I shouldn't be telling you this. He will kill me."

"Please go on. I won't say anything." The dread crept up into my throat.

"She made him fucking kill it."

"What?" I closed my mouth quickly to keep from gawping unprofessionally.

Cole, the convicted felon who, according to the newspaper, slashed open another man's face with a broken beer bottle, looked equally horrified. "Sick shit, right?"

"Do you know what happened? Exactly?" I didn't want details. I didn't want to know any of it. I didn't want to picture a pint-sized Leander killing a poor, innocent rabbit. But I needed to know. Other than the lasting trauma, the method of execution mattered, not only for his psych profile but for the case as well.

"He, uh, used a shovel, I think."

I tried not to appear as crestfallen as I felt. Bludgeoning. Perfect. "Do you know how old he was?"

"No. He was just a kid." Cole cleared his throat and threw a thumb over his shoulder at the brick building. "Anyway, I gotta go. I've got a conference call in a few minutes. I thought you should know in case someone else brings it up. Let me know if you have any other questions." He pressed his business card into my hand, identical to the one I had for Elijah.

"Thank you, Mr. Holliday. You've been very helpful."

He waited until I was safely in my car before he turned to leave. I locked the doors and stared in horror at the nothingness in front of me. What kind of a person makes a child kill an animal? Sick shit was right.

CHAPTER 13

*E*lijah called me back later that afternoon. He was at Leander's house, of all places, and invited me for dinner. After my experiences in town, I was happy to oblige rather than try to find food downtown and run the risk of encountering another mob.

The Welles' house was a massive red-brick Italianate perched on one of the limestone bluffs overlooking the river. Surrounded by woods, it was nearly invisible behind the greenery except for the tower peering out over the trees.

I drove through the wrought-iron gate and gaped at the mansion at the top of the hill. It was stunning, but the black-painted trim and dark, soaring windows gave it a sinister feel.

Swallowing thickly, I parked and climbed the steps to the sprawling front porch. A pair of gaslight lamps flickered on either side of the imposing front door, an ornate W etched into the glass in the center. I didn't even have to ring the bell before it swung open.

A man stood on the other side of the door with a welcoming smile. Tall and trim, he wore a white t-shirt and a pair of jeans. Maybe he was exempt from the black-suit rule? Even still, his hair was neatly combed and he had a shadow of stubble that suited his dark features. I recognized him immediately from his booking photos in the paper.

"You must be Elijah," I said, extending my hand. "I'm Dr. Clayton."

He shook my hand and ushered me inside. "Please, come in. Dinner is almost ready."

Marveling at the foyer and each subsequent room we passed, I followed him to the dining room. The interior was as dark and moody as one would expect from the exterior, filled with antique furniture and dark-stained wood. It had a severe, masculine feel, completely unlike any other house I'd been in.

"I went by your house earlier," I said, sliding into the chair Elijah indicated. "After I ran into Cole."

"Oh, yeah. He told me you had a little run-in with the locals outside of the office. Don't worry. They won't bother you again." He disappeared into the kitchen and returned with two plates. Steak and potatoes. How manly.

"That's reassuring. I didn't expect so much..." I fumbled for the right word. I still didn't know what the hell that little demonstration was or how they knew where to find me.

"Hatred? Hostility? Vile contempt? There are so many to choose from." He sat and grinned, tucking into his food.

"Yes, all of that." I cut into my steak as well, thrilled it wasn't fish. "Are you, um, house sitting?" Was that the right word when your friend was in jail?

"Just keeping an eye on things. Don't want anyone getting any ideas while he's gone. So how is Leander? I tried calling a couple times, but they said he can't talk to anyone."

That wasn't entirely true, but I wasn't about to get into policies right then and there. "He's adjusting," I replied with a brief smile.

Elijah shrugged. "He's adaptable. I'm sure he'll be fine. God knows he's been through worse. This is just a blip on the radar for him."

A blip? Facing a lifetime in prison was just a blip? Dear Lord. What else had Leander gone through that I didn't know about?

"How long have you two known each other?"

Elijah made a face, chewing on a piece of steak. "Forever? At least that's what it feels like."

"Did you know him before his grandmother died?"

"Yeah. Best thing to ever happen to him. That bitch got what was coming, you know what I mean?" He pointed his fork at me before tearing another cube of steak off and chewing forcefully.

"Care to elaborate?" I bit into a piece of the baked potato, waiting for his take on the situation.

He set his utensils down and held my gaze, his words laced with a combination of seriousness and revulsion. "She was evil. Pure fucking evil. Some kids deserve a smack or two, I get it, but that woman took it to the extreme. And no one did anything. Ever."

"Did you ever see her hit him?" Listening to people's recollections was like watching a ping-pong match of he-said/she-said. The conflicting information made my head spin and my job that much harder.

"No. I never met her. I saw the aftermath of her handi-work. I'm amazed he made it. I told him she was going to kill him one of these days. I mean, you've seen him. Fucking skin and bones. He's still paranoid to eat even though that bitch has been dead for ten years."

"He's paranoid about eating?" I glanced at my steak. I knew he hated the food at Parkview, but I didn't realize there was a deeper reason to it other than preference. I'd merely chalked up his thinness to a combination of depression and years of malnourishment and neglect.

Elijah nodded and took a swig of beer. "She tried to poison him. At least once, probably more. Sick bitch. He told me he was in the hospital for a week. So now he's really picky about what he eats. Plus side is that he's an amazing cook because of it. You should try his beef wellington. Amazing. Bastard won't give me the recipe."

My heart dropped to my stomach, remembering the look in Leander's eyes when I joked about not poisoning the tea I gave him. I'm such an idiot! What other triggers did I unknowingly set off over the course of our interactions? I took his intelligence and dry humor for granted when I should have been more sensitive.

"Do you know if she took him to the doctor a lot?"

"Fuck no. The only reason he went that time was because the maid found him and called an ambulance while the bitch was at bridge club."

Maybe Irene had Munchausen syndrome by proxy? But if she did, she should have been seeking more attention from Leander's suffering. It seemed she kept him hidden away as much as she could, even going so far as firing the staff who had any sort of interaction with him.

I tried to move things in a slightly happier direction. "Was he a social kid?"

Elijah shook his head, slicing off a chunk of potato and skewering a piece of steak beneath it. "Nope. No one was allowed into the house and he wasn't allowed to go to town very often. So, he read. And wrote. Anything that was quiet and didn't draw attention to himself. He's still that way."

"Did he ever talk to you about suicide?" Might as well throw it out there, since I doubted the conversation was going to get any better.

Elijah wiped his mouth with a napkin and shook his head

slowly. It was the first time in the conversation he looked reluctant to talk. "He doesn't talk to anyone about his scars."

"But you know about them."

"Yeah, I've seen them. He usually has them covered. It was a long time ago. He hasn't done anything like that since he was eighteen. No reason to anymore."

So, Leander didn't tell Elijah about his most recent incident. "Have you ever seen him lose his temper? Destroy things, that sort of thing?"

"Nah. That's not his style. He's the quiet type — deadly quiet. Yeah, he gets angry, I mean, he's human, but he's not out there setting puppies on fire, if that's what you're getting at." He stabbed at another piece of steak. "But he's not a pushover. He gets his revenge in the end. Which is why these people better fucking run when he gets out."

Goosebumps erupted on my skin. "Why do you say that?"

"He owns half the town. Ever since he took over the company, he's been buying up properties and businesses left and right. Some people work for him, some are just his tenants. But if you fuck with him, forget it. You lose your job. You lose your house. He calls in all your loans at once. He fucking ruins you overnight with an army of lawyers. That's how he gets his revenge."

I silently agreed. That seemed more like Leander's approach than outright violence. "Did you know the people? The victims?"

"It's a small town. Everyone knows everyone."

Of course. I walked right into that one. "Can you tell me anything about them? Anything that might not be in the police reports or the newspapers?"

He thought for a minute, chewing. "Dave, the mechanic, was alright. Dr. Van Deveer was an asshole. He was cut from the same cloth as Irene — old money, looked down on everyone. They were real tight, him and Irene."

"What about the officer? Keith Starkey?"

"He was the first cop to arrest me. Come to think of it, I think he was the last cop to arrest me too."

"Yes, I saw some pictures in the paper." The versions of Elijah and Cole I met looked nothing like their grainy booking photos, but I couldn't let myself forget the crimes they were arrested for — just like Leander. However, it didn't stop a thought from worming into my brain. If the police were wrong about Leander, maybe they were wrong about his friends, too?

Elijah grinned, dispelling my benefit of the doubt. "Disgruntled youth. What can I say? I've turned it around, though. We all have, thanks to Leander. I'd do anything for him."

"I'm glad to hear it. He seemed reluctant to talk about any sort of support system, so I'm happy to hear he has people he can rely on. He never mentioned a girlfriend, though. Has he ever been in a relationship?"

Laughing, Elijah shook his head. "Hell no. He doesn't have time for that. Besides, I don't know if you've noticed, but he's got a lot of quirks. No one has stuck around very long. Even when they try, he doesn't let them. He likes being alone."

"No one likes being alone. It's a maladaptive coping mechanism from years of trauma." I set my utensils down and sighed. Was it even possible to undo a lifetime of damage? It seemed insurmountable and that was excluding whatever happened as a result of his trial. If they stuffed him away in prison for the rest of his life, the damage would be irreversible.

"Are you ok? You look a little queasy. Was the steak not cooked the way you like?"

"I'm fine. It was fine. Thank you. Is it possible to take a look around? Get a sense of the house?" I dabbed my mouth with the napkin.

"Yeah, sure. Have at it. Let me know if you need anything."

Slipping away from the table, I steeled myself for a self-guided tour through the grand house of horrors.

Aside from modern conveniences, it looked like the house was a time capsule from the 1800s. I felt compelled to pull on white gloves before touching anything, lest some curator burst out of a closet and scold me for touching priceless antiques.

There were no personal mementos anywhere. No photographs or portraits. Nothing that spoke of Leander's personality — unless this was his personality. Somber and moody and timeless were certainly all elements I associated with him.

I wandered the rooms aimlessly, searching for anything to clue me in to what happened in this house all those years ago.

I found a breadcrumb in the library.

The floor-to-ceiling shelves were stacked with books, double-stacked in some sections. Too numerous to count, they were organized by subject and then alphabetically. It appeared once they ran out of room in the built-in shelves, Leander, or someone, added standing shelves in the middle of the room.

The middle shelves featured a collection of familiar writers — Poe, Shelley, Bronte, Byron, among others. Romantics, of course, and apparently Leander's favorites. Unlike the books on the outer shelves, some of these titles were so used they were on the verge of falling to pieces.

Sliding out a tattered copy of Poe, I flipped through it carefully. There were two sets of handwriting in the margins, a delicate cursive and a sharp, neat print. It was almost as if the two writers were engaged in a conversation in the side-lines of the book — the cursive would pose a question or make a remark and the print would challenge the thought or offer another question in return.

Both readers were preoccupied with Poe's short stories and poetry, focusing on the aspects of love, death, and beauty. Only the second writer — a younger Leander, if I had to wager, based on the penmanship — was concerned with the question of madness.

Placing the Poe book back in its place, I pulled out another.

Mary Shelley's *Frankenstein* was equally worn and featured the same dueling commentary in the margins. Again, the readers debated. This time it was the meaning of love, hate, and what it meant to be a monster. When my skimming neared the end of the book, a photograph emerged, tucked in the back.

The picture was of a young woman, beautiful and smiling. She was sitting on the ground surrounded by a sea of Lilies of the valley, a book in her lap. I knew immediately it was Leander's mother, Eleanor. The hair, the eyes, and especially the envious bone structure. Not that I agreed with him, but at least now I could understand why Julian Welles wanted nothing to do with his son. It must have been painful to see his dead wife reflected so clearly in their son's face.

I tucked the photograph back inside and returned the book to the shelf.

Elijah met me in the hallway outside the library. "Find what you're looking for?"

"I don't know yet. Can you show me Leander's room?"

"Right this way." He led me up the wide staircase and down the hall, gesturing to a closed door on the west end.

The room was much smaller than I expected. It was as dark and impersonal as the rest of the house. While it had plenty of space for a bed, an armoire, and a writing table, it certainly wasn't the master bedroom. The only real surprise was the choice of the paint color — dark purple. At first glance I thought it was black, until I compared the black furniture and bedding to the slightly lighter walls. Even the fireplace was black marble.

The armoire housed a selection of suits — all black — and little else.

I turned to the writing table next. The top was devoid of any paperwork, decor, or anything. At the right angle, you could see grooves in the dark wooden surface from years of use. The center drawer was locked, much to my annoyance.

"Does he keep a journal?" I asked, moving to the bed and sliding my hands under his mattress.

Elijah shrugged. "No idea."

There was nothing under the mattress, nothing underneath the bed itself, nothing stuffed in the pillows. Smoothing the comforter back into place, I laid down, staring up at the ceiling for a moment. I closed my eyes and tried to look past everything I'd read, everything I'd heard, and visualize Leander's point of view.

"Do you know if this is the same room he's always had?" I asked, keeping my eyes closed.

"Yeah, I think so. Why?"

"Just wondering. He could have any room in the house and yet he chooses to stay in this one." I stood and walked to the single window. It overlooked the river. There was a small, wooded island in the very center of the water. The edge of town was visible if you craned your neck enough.

"Well, I mean." Elijah scratched the back of his neck. "Would you want to stay in the other room?"

"Can I see it?" Say no. Please say no...

"Yeah sure."

Elijah led me down the hallway again, across the top of the stairs to the opposite end of the house. Like all of the other doors on the second floor, the door to Irene's old room was also closed.

Please be locked. Please be swollen shut with age and humidity.

A draft of cold air washed over me as I pushed the door open. I wanted Elijah to go first, but I knew I was being ridiculous. Ghosts didn't exist any more than aliens or the boogeyman. Besides, if I had the chance to speak with Irene's ghost, I had a few choice words for her.

The master bedroom was far, far more spacious than Leander's. It appeared he left things the way Irene had them. The furniture was covered in sheets, but I got a sense of the layout from the giant white blobs.

"And this was where she...?" I looked over my shoulder at Elijah. He was still in the doorway, leaning against the frame. At a glance he may have looked casual, but his spine was far too rigid. He was as uncomfortable in this room as I was.

"Yep. Right there in the bed."

"He doesn't come in here?" I touched the edge of a sheet covering a pair of chairs in front of a beautiful green marble fireplace. I didn't want to look at the bed. Memories of Irene's mangled skull were burned into my mind.

"No. I'm pretty sure if he could demolish this part of the house, he would. Except, it's over the library, so, it's not going anywhere."

"I think I've seen enough. Thank you." Resisting the urge to bolt and never look back, I tried to maintain a normal pace exiting the room. I was halfway to the staircase when Elijah whistled at me.

"This way, Doc. It's faster."

Following the sound of his voice, I made my way down the other side of the hall and ducked into a smaller, narrower staircase.

"Servant stairs," he said, jogging down them with an easy

familiarity. I wondered how many times he'd gone up and down them, how many times he'd wandered Leander's house to know the ins and outs as well as he seemed to.

Visions of twisting an ankle and landing at the bottom in a heap haunted my every step. I tried not to clomp down after Elijah like a clydesdale on the steeper, rougher wood. I was grateful when we hit tiled floor, emerging into a fully renovated kitchen. It was easy see why Leander liked to cook — aside from the whole fear of being poisoned again. If I had my own gourmet kitchen, maybe I'd be less inclined to order takeout.

"Well, thank you for dinner and the tour. I should probably get out of your hair and let you enjoy the evening." I shook Elijah's hand again with a smile.

"The next time you see Leander, can you give him a message? Tell him mind over matter. He's got this."

"Of course."

CHAPTER 14

 $\mathcal{M}$ y cell phone rang as I was pulling up to Jake Murray's address. A soft-spoken older woman identified herself as Vera Van Deveer, the late doctor's widow.

"I'm sorry I missed your visit," she said. "I'm staying with my daughter for a while. My neighbor found your card in the door."

"Do you have a moment to talk about Leander Welles, Mrs. Van Deveer?"

She sighed. "That poor boy."

That was not the reaction I was expecting. I pressed the phone closer to my ear in case I misunderstood her. "Why do you say that?"

"He's had such a rough go of it. First his parents up and die, leaving him with that vile woman. And now this."

I pulled the phone away to stare at it before shoving it against my ear again. "You're talking about Irene Welles? You two didn't get along?"

She made a disgusted noise. "No. Awful woman. She and Reggie were thick as thieves but I never got on with her. I kept up appearances, you know, but she was a terrible person. She used to call Reggie all the time, at all hours, to come patch up her grandson. She said he was clumsy but you can't be a doctor's wife all these years and not learn a thing or two. I knew better."

"Did Reggie ever say anything about it?"

"No. He'd get a call and go over there and come back muttering about the boy. He believed everything Irene said." God, did Scheible know any of this? I knew she was the only witness for the prosecution but she was giving enough information to actually help Leander too.

"Did Reggie get along with Leander?"

"As much as any child gets along with their doctor, I suppose."

"What about as an adult?"

"They didn't socialize if that's what you're asking. Medically speaking, I think Leander goes across the river to another doctor these days."

"Yes, a Dr. Williams. We've been in touch. Mrs. Van Deveer, can you tell me what happened the night Reggie died?"

She sighed softly. She sounded tired. I felt bad asking her the same questions she must have already answered a hundred times but I had a feeling the police may have left out some key details. "It was late. There was a knock at the door. Reggie went to answer it. I heard him say 'Leander' and then the door closed. By the time I got to the front room, he was gone."

"So you didn't actually see Leander?" My pulse quickened.

"Well, no, but I saw his car."

"If they didn't speak, why would Leander be at your house so late at night?"

"I can only assume it was some sort of medical emergency. Reggie still did house calls for certain patients."

"Do you honestly think Leander killed Reggie?" I chewed on one of my cuticles, waiting for her answer.

"I don't know, dear. The police said he did and they would know better than I would. Wouldn't they? That poor boy. I hope he finally finds some peace."

"You're not angry?" How was it the one woman in Easton who was responsible for Leander being arrested and charged with murder could turn around and be so... civil? Saddened, even, by the turn of events? It was mind boggling.

"If Jesus can forgive, then so can I. It's not my place to punish him — that's between him and his maker."

"Thank you for your time Mrs. Van Deveer. And my condolences for your loss."

Shaking my head, I hung up, awed by the conversation as it replayed in my head.

At last, I remembered what I was in the middle of doing before she called. I got out of the car and made my way up the front steps of a small, rundown house. Jake Murray's house, at least according to Scheible's office. He was the fourth element of Leander's inner circle and the only one I hadn't talked to yet.

I hoped Jake was home, but at the same time, I didn't know if I could handle any more horror stories.

The door opened after the second knock. An older woman in a thin bathrobe leaned against the frame, blowing a stream of cigarette smoke into the air between us. "Yeah?"

"Is this Jake Murray's house?"

"Who's asking?"

"I'm Dr. Lorelei Clayton. I was hoping to speak with him about Leander Welles. Is he around?"

She took another drag off of her cigarette. "He ain't been around for weeks. What kind of doctor goes around interviewing people? Heard about you. Getting folks all riled up."

I smiled politely and handed her my card. "If you see him, can you have him give me a call?"

She took the card without looking at it and slipped it into her pocket. "Don't be fooled by that Welles boy." She pointed at me with two fingers, still holding her cigarette.

"What do you mean?"

"Evil as they come. The whole family."

I blinked to keep from rolling my eyes. It was a refrain I'd grown accustomed to hearing from the Eastonians.

She kept talking, tapping the ash off with a flick of a hot pink nail. "Anything bad ever happens in this town, it's because of them. Now the old woman is gone, it's just that boy and his lost souls."

"Lost souls?"

She nodded, expelling another stream of smoke. "Mmhmm. He collects them — lost souls. Like a moth to a flame. Jake's one of them. Started running with his crew when he was just a kid. Thought it was good for him at first, maybe get a job with the family, be protected. But now I don't even recognize my own son. Leander says jump, Jake asks how high. They all do."

Clearing my throat, I forced another smile. "Well, I won't keep you. Thank you for your time."

"How's your soul, Doctor?"

"Pardon?"

"If there's darkness there, he'll find it and use it. Don't say you weren't warned." She flicked her cigarette into the gravel by the front step and raised a penciled-on eyebrow at me before closing the door.

I stared at it for a full minute before shaking off her bizarre question and walking back to the car.

Easton gave me a lot to think about on my drive north. I didn't know if that was necessarily a good thing.

CHAPTER 15

*T*he green highway sign indicated I was roughly an hour away from home when I started getting antsy. Chewing my nails down to the quick, I ran through every possible scenario that could have happened at Parkview in my absence. I knew Dennis had a handle on things. I knew Leander was fine — Dennis' emails said as much. And yet, I wouldn't be convinced until I was there, in person.

Leander, however, wasn't there. According to the schedule posted outside his room, he and Scheible were off doing lawyerly things.

Annoyed, I made my way into Dennis' office and flopped in the chair across from his desk. I'd asked him to form his own opinion on Leander's mental health and he'd yet to share one with me. "So?"

"What are you doing here? You're not supposed to be back until tomorrow," Dennis said without even looking up.

"I'm just checking in. So…?"

He sighed, taking off his glasses and pinching the bridge of his nose. "I gotta tell you, Lorelei. I just don't know."

"What do you mean?" That did not sound good. At all. His emails said everything was fine but his face said everything was not fine. Dennis didn't get ruffled by patients anymore — he'd been doing this job for far too long.

"At this point, I think you could throw darts at the DSM-5 and you'd get an accurate diagnosis with this guy. He's all over the place."

"So far I've only seen symptoms of depression, anxiety, more than likely some PTSD. Is there something I'm missing?"

He ticked them off on his fingers. "Bipolar, Dissociative, Antisocial, ODD, IED, Anorex—"

I held up a hand to cut him off. "Let's unpack those for a minute, shall we? Bipolar, maybe. Except I haven't witnessed any mania."

"Oh, he's manic, alright. He didn't sleep the entire time you were gone. Go look at his room. You'll see what he's been up to. He didn't even eat. Three days, Lorelei! I get hungry after three hours."

"He's got a thing about eating."

"I figured — that's why I think he qualifies for anorexia. Oh. We hired Antonio while you were gone. You know, the cook from St. Mary's? So you know the food is better now. Didn't matter. He still didn't eat."

Trying to decide how much I should share from my trip down south, I chewed on a torn piece of my cuticle before forcing my hand into my lap. "It's not a body-image thing. I think his grandmother poisoned him when he was little. So now he's overly cautious."

"Fine, not anorexic. But you shouldn't rule out bipolar."

"Ok…" I nodded and moved on to the rest of his list. "Maybe Dissociative, given the trauma, but he's very attached to his sense of identity. Even if he won't really talk about it, I know he remembers what happened during his childhood.

There's no amnesia or split personality. When he does talk about it, he doesn't tell it from a bird's eye view or anything."

Lacing his fingers together, Dennis leaned forward, fixing me with his fatherly stare. "Lorelei."

I ignored him and what he was trying to say by my name alone. "I didn't find any characteristics in his background to support anything else. No destruction of property, no torturing animals, no fires. Nothing." In my mind, the bunny didn't count. It wasn't exactly his choice to kill it.

Dennis rubbed his eyes and sighed again. "Like I said, at this point I don't think it matters what you call him. Stick with whatever diagnosis you feel comfortable using in court and move on. He's fucked either way."

"You think he did it?" I picked at the ragged bits of skin around my nail I wasn't able to chew off. It would end up bleeding, but I couldn't help it.

"It doesn't matter if he did or didn't. That boy — man, sorry — isn't ever going to have a normal life. Whether he's sitting in prison or on a beach, he's his own worst enemy. You can't escape what's up here." He tapped his temple for effect. "And you can't save 'em all, kiddo. Don't kill yourself by trying." His watch beeped, prompting him to stand and swat my arm with the folder in his hand. "Go home. Get some sleep. We'll talk tomorrow."

"Yep. Will do."

I didn't.

I retreated to my office and pulled up the notes Dennis scanned into the computer. There were a lot of question marks. A lot. Each day he'd theorized a new diagnosis. Leander hadn't presented any of these conditions so strongly to me. Was he messing with Dennis? It was hard to tell from the written word alone, just like the standardized tests.

The camera system was down for maintenance, so I didn't have access to the videos from Leander's latest sessions. Frustration crept up into my shoulders, knotting them with tension until I remembered what Dennis said. Leander was supposedly manic for the past three days. With the room unoccupied, now was the best time to see what he was talking about.

It didn't take long to figure it out.

Stacks upon stacks of paper covered Leander's desk. They were sketches, mostly still-life, of things he could see from his window or objects from the room. The only drawing he had taped to the wall was a perfect rendition of a Lily of the valley done in pen.

Even more impressive than the sketches were the words — thousands of them, in Leander's perfect penmanship. In my absence he'd flown through the notebook I gave him and moved on to fill up two others. Like everything else about his outward appearance, his handwriting was a reflection of his controlled perfectionism. It was perfectly neat and perfectly straight, despite the extraordinary amount of writing he'd done. Then I remembered a tiny, six-year-old Leander accidentally scratching the table and getting beaten.

I thumbed through the pages, trying to absorb the gist of everything he'd written. The latest notebook was almost filled. Each page was covered in ink, front and back, with no discernible breaks between entries. Just a stream of consciousness. Writing was one of the most basic tools of therapy but I never imagined Leander had this much locked away in him.

He wrote about everything from literature to history, nightmares he had, and his experiences with the people here. Martha, in particular, seemed to fascinate him. He correctly diagnosed her as a paranoid schizophrenic and though he didn't have the term for tardive dyskinesia, he suspected her lifelong use of antipsychotics were partially to blame for her stiff, jerky movements. The fact she drove a screwdriver into her skull didn't help.

Curiously, there was no mention of me in any of the pages I thumbed past. An emotion I didn't quite know how to describe stabbed through me. Disappointment? Why should I be disappointed? It was ridiculous. Maybe it was a case of out of sight, out of mind. Or maybe I was just imagining the slow, steady bond I thought we'd developed.

Shaking my head to dispel the ludicrous thoughts, I set the notebook on the desk where I found it. It didn't matter what or who he was writing about as long as he had a positive coping mechanism, a way to process everything that was happening. If he wasn't open to talk therapy, journaling was the next best thing.

Turning to leave, I slammed into a wall of black. I jumped and stifled a shriek, skipping back a couple steps. It took me a few, embarrassing seconds to realize it was Leander, dressed again in a black suit.

"Leander! I'm so sorry!"

He remained rigidly still, his hands glued to his sides. "Not that I am not elated to see you've returned, Doctor, but what are you doing in here?"

Exhaling a steadying breath, I hoped it would calm my racing heart. "I, um, I heard you've been busy. So I came to see what Dr. Atwell was talking about."

Leander looked around the small room pointedly before settling his gaze on me. "Was there something else I could help you with?"

"Move your ass, Welles, we ain't got all day!" Russ barked from the hallway.

"If you'll excuse me, Doctor, I have to change. I wouldn't want Russell there to think I've hung myself with my tie."

"You really shouldn't joke about that." The image of

Todd's spotty skin and purple neck swam in front of me, unbidden.

"Who said I was joking?" If it weren't for his sly smile, I might have been worried of a repeat hanging.

"I'm just saying… if someone who didn't know you heard you say that, your privileges would be revoked."

"Are you fucking deaf?" Russ shouted, stepping into the doorway. "Oh, sorry, Doc. I didn't know you were in here."

"I was just leaving," I replied. "See you tomorrow Leander." I stepped around him and crossed the short distance to the door in swift strides. My eyes narrowed as I stopped in front of Russ, blocking his entry to Leander's room. "Was that necessary?"

"What?" The guard looked confused.

"Do you speak to all of the patients this way?"

"Look, Doc—"

"No, you look, Mr. Brewer. I understand you're used to working with convicted felons but this isn't DOC. This is a private facility and in case you forgot how the legal system works, Mr. Welles is pre-trial which means legally he's no more a criminal than you or I."

Russ finally had the decency to look chagrined. "Sorry, Doc."

I nodded curtly and walked away. Perhaps it wasn't the wisest move to chastise another employee in front of a patient, but the horse was out of the barn now. Besides, if the administration wasn't going to bother disciplining employees for serious violations, what did I have to worry about for putting someone in their place?

CHAPTER 16

*L*eander shifted in his chair, the top of a pen skimming across his lower lip. He caught it between his teeth for the briefest second before he leaned forward to write something. When he was done, he laid the pen in the center of the paper and pushed them toward me.

"Thank you." I tucked the pen into my coat pocket, out of his reach, and glanced over his answers.

"Are you going to evaluate it now?"

"No. I just want to talk."

"What is troubling you, Dr. Clayton?"

I couldn't help the smile that always came when he tried to play therapist. He was just as persistent as I was. "No, I meant you do the talking."

He smiled as well, a small quirk of a motion. But I also noticed he was picking at the edge of his sleeve. Was he nervous? "I thought perhaps you wanted to unburden yourself. This is a safe space, after all, or so they keep telling me."

"It is a safe space. We can discuss whatever you'd like."

"What did you find in Easton?" He studied me as he spoke, his eyes mossy green in the dim lighting.

Shifting under the intensity of his gaze, I tucked a lock of hair behind my ear. I still wasn't used to being looked at so openly by him — or anyone. I was used to doing all of the scrutinizing, looking for signs of truth and deception, flashes of micro-expressions to confirm or betray a person's words. "What do you think I found?"

"Ghosts." He said the word so softly and so seriously it took me by surprise. Folding his arms over his chest, he pressed his back against the chair, like he needed support all of a sudden.

"Your friends Elijah and Cole seem nice," I ventured, hoping he'd relax.

"They are. Until they're not." The conversation with the old clerk rang in my ears. He'd said something similar about Leander's parents. Maybe it was a turn of phrase from down there, or maybe Leander spent more time with the old man than he'd let on.

"What does that mean?" I asked, hoping for clarification.

"Don't pretend you're not aware of their criminal backgrounds."

"Elijah may have mentioned something to that effect. He also gave me a message for you. 'Mind over matter'?"

Instead of a smile, I was rewarded with a scowl before Leander looked away, his jaw clenching. Damn it, Elijah. Instead of comforting him, all it seemed to do was throw fuel on his already irritated state.

I cleared my throat quietly, hoping to redirect the conversation. "Your other friend, Jake, wasn't around for me to talk to. Do you know where he is?"

"How would I? I've been shut off from the outside world for weeks." I was surprised he was so surly. I thought he might have been happy I'd returned, but apparently I was mistaken. Maybe he ultimately preferred Dennis' company to mine.

"You got another letter." I withdrew the envelope from my pocket and slid it across the table to him. "Not as creepy as the first one."

He didn't appear amused. Unfolding the slip of paper, he scanned it quickly before flinging it back to the table without comment.

I refrained from sighing and picked it up, re-reading the typewritten text.

And the lilies sighed one unto the other in the solemnity of their desolation.

"Is it more Poe?" I asked, hoping a conversation about his favorite writer might put him in a better mood. While I'd read the passages he marked for me, by no means did I have any of it memorized.

"*Silence.*"

"Excuse me?"

"*Silence,*" he said, on the verge of growling. "It's from *Silence — A Fable.* One of Poe's earlier works."

"It sounds pretty."

The look he shot me made me wish I could retract my words. "It's about a demon torturing a man."

"Ok then…" Since he was already in a bad mood, I figured I might as well continue with a more relevant topic. "I have to talk to you about some things I heard. I'm hoping you can clarify them for me."

His arms tightened around himself. "Such as?"

"The police think you killed more than four people."

He didn't blink or stir or twitch a single muscle. It looked like he was waiting for the punchline.

"The chief doesn't have any proof," I continued, choosing my words carefully. "But he thinks you poisoned some people. Do you know why he would think that?"

His thumb tapped idly on his bicep and he shrugged.

"Leander..." I wondered if what Olivia said about him abhorring liars was true. If he wasn't a liar, maybe he needed a push.

"I might have, at one time, told the chief he would regret his decision to cross me. And then I told him to enjoy his coffee... Obviously he has held a grudge ever since." He fought a dark, little smile, amused at the memory. "It's not my fault he didn't realize he was pouring salt into his cup."

Outwardly I was expressionless; inwardly I snickered. "How old were you?"

He squinted slightly. "Fifteen? Sixteen?"

I shook my head. A grown man shouldn't be that upset by a teenage prank, if you could even call it that. But given everything else the chief said, I had a feeling Leander was right — the man was holding a ridiculous grudge. "Ok. Next question, have you ever poisoned or vaguely threatened to poison anyone else?"

"Do the rats in the basement count?"

"No. But while we're on the topic, have you ever harmed any other animals?"

He swallowed hard. What little color there was drained from his face, all mirth disappearing in the blink of an eye. "You know about the rabbit."

I feigned an innocent expression, picking at the cuticle on my thumb. "Rabbit? What are you talking about?"

Rage flashed behind his eyes and the muscle along his jaw clenched. Several, tense seconds passed before he all but growled his next words. "It wasn't a question, Doctor. You know about the rabbit."

"Can you tell me about it?" My voice lowered again, treading even more carefully than before.

The rhythm of his breathing changed, his chest rising and falling faster. He turned his face away, staring daggers at the far corner of the room. I'd already pushed on the poison thing. I wanted him to tell the rabbit story on his own time.

"I can still hear it screaming," he said after a while, his voice barely above a whisper. A shudder rippled down his spine and he closed his eyes, hugging himself so tightly I worried about his ability to breathe. "She put the shovel in my hands and told me to... I tried, but I missed. It screamed and screamed and she was screaming and I kept swinging until all of the screaming stopped."

"What happened next?" I scarcely recognized my own voice when I spoke.

His eyes opened slowly, revealing the same emerald shade as before, but no tears fell this time. He inhaled sharply before exhaling the same breath, locking away any visible emotion on his face. Thanks to this story, I could rule him out as a sociopath. Besides his impeccable organization and no history of impulsive or reckless behavior, this level of control over his emotions was remarkable. Of all of the topics we'd covered, none had this kind of an effect on him, which meant if he was going to take my head off over anything, it would have been the bunny.

"She wouldn't let me bury it," Leander continued. "So I took it to the edge of the bluff and threw it in the river. She told me to stop crying over a stupid rabbit, or else I should throw myself in after it. Then she took a belt to my back because I got blood on my clothes."

I clamped my mouth shut, swallowing back a string of hateful words for a woman who'd been dead for over a decade. How anyone could side with her was a mystery to me. Anyone who stood by as she abused a child deserved to rot for their complicity.

"I started cutting after that." His gaze went hazy, drifting downward. "I was numb for so long I needed to feel something. The pain was all I had to sustain me, to remind me I was alive. And when I couldn't take it anymore, when I couldn't take her anymore, I hoped it would be my salvation. Sadly, it wasn't."

"I couldn't find any medical records treating you for cuts, or your past suicide attempts. Did she take you to the doctor?" Apparently Irene and Reggie operated on a cash-only system, which made their finances difficult to account for.

His eyes flitted back to mine, cold and distant. "Of course not. Could you imagine her embarrassment? The disgrace? Dr. Van Deveer came to the house when it was necessary."

"What about the time you were in the hospital? You said you thought your grandmother tried to poison you?"

His eyes narrowed sharply. "I believe my associates and I need to have a little chat on the meaning of discretion. As charming as I'm sure you were, Doctor, it seems they've been lax in my absence."

I laid a hand on the ever-present and ever-growing file. "It's in your chart. Along with a note from the attending doctor. He suspected abuse and notified the authorities. What I couldn't find were any follow-up reports from either the police or social services. Do you remember if anyone ever came to the house?"

Sneering, he shook his head. "Every time a new face appeared, asking questions, I thought maybe this would be it. And every time they left, convinced by her grace and her money, a part of me died until all that remained is the soulless shell of the man before you, the ghost of what I could have been."

I wanted to hold his hand. I wanted to hold *him*. I wanted him to know not everyone was evil and he wasn't alone. Instead, all I could offer were weak words. "I'm so sorry you went through all of that. No one should, let alone a child."

"May I go now? I feel the beginning of a migraine." He rubbed his temple with two fingers. The crease between his eyebrows was back, along with a pained expression.

"Of course. I'll see you tomorrow."

I let him out of the interview room and into Calvin's custody.

"Make sure he gets something for his migraine, please," I said to Calvin.

"Sure thing, Doc."

The beginning stages of my own headache thumped inside of my skull as I tried to come to terms with Leander's story. My heart broke for him, for the abused boy he'd been and the tormented man he'd become. I wished I could go back to the first day I'd met him, when I said he didn't look desperate, and slap myself. Hard. He was right — what did I know of desperation?

⋯

That night over dinner, as I stared at the steak knife in my hand, I understood how a person could overcome their sense of self-preservation in order to kill themselves. I put the blade to my pork chop instead of my wrist and did a few rounds of box-breathing, trying to dispel as much cortisol as I could.

"Well?" Mom prodded, bringing me back to reality.

"Was there a question?"

"Are you ever going to answer Darren? He said he's texted you a dozen times."

"I'm too busy to deal with him right now. There's too

much going on at work."

She swirled her wine in the bottom of the glass and took a slow sip. "There's never a perfect time. You'll keep finding reasons to put it off. Believe me. Why do you think you're an only child?"

Metal clanked against china as I stabbed my fork through the pork chop. "I am not going to have this conversation again."

"Do not take that tone with me, Lorelei."

"Respect my boundaries, Mother."

She sniffed. "Fine. What do you want to talk about, then?"

"I don't know." I wiped my mouth with the edge of my napkin. "I mean, I had a dream about Dad the other night..."

"Andrew!" Mom hailed the waiter and tapped the rim of her wine glass.

"You can't pretend he doesn't exist," I hissed at her as Andrew topped her off.

"He doesn't," she snapped back, her eyes flashing a warning from across the table. "You berate me for bringing up Darren and yet here you go dredging up things best left alone."

"Best for you, you mean."

"What has gotten into you? These past few weeks you've been so catty. I didn't even know you were out of town until after you were back. What if something happened while you were gone?"

"That's what cell phones are for. And the last time I checked I didn't have to clear my schedule with you."

"It's called common courtesy."

I chomped on a piece of meat instead of answering. It was safer for everyone if I didn't. What elegant turn of phrase would Leander use in this situation? Which Romantic would he quote? Because frankly, all I could think of was "Shut the fuck up."

CHAPTER 17

*P*ushing the file away, I leaned back in my chair, mimicking Leander's posture. I was losing him.

He'd been sullen the entire session, with a clenched jaw and disinterested stare. Scratch that — he'd been sullen since I returned from Easton. The shadows under his eyes were much darker than usual, exacerbating his paleness. Maybe this was the crash from his mania, the pendulum swinging back to the depressed state. I didn't want to stick him with bipolar yet, but it looked like I wasn't going to have much of a choice.

"Let's just talk today," I said, trying to sound cheerful. "No trick questions. No evaluation. No collateral data. Just talk."

"Fine. I want to talk about you."

"Let me clarify — we can talk about anything your heart desires as long as it pertains to you."

"Yes, but as we've previously discussed, I already know me. My heart desires *you*. I want to know why you're here. I want to know why you... why you care so much."

It was another harmless question in the long run, I supposed, but it didn't stop my cheeks from getting warm or my heart skipping a beat. Besides, throwing out nuggets of information always seemed to be rewarded with another stretch of honesty until he threw up a wall or dodged a serious question with some sort of dark joke.

"Well," I sighed and laid my hands flat on the table. "My father was a federal prosecutor. My mother is a judge. She, of course, wanted me to go to law school like them. But I saw the impact these kinds of cases have. I saw the kind of people the system chews up and spits out. I knew I couldn't do anything to help as a lawyer. So I went to med school."

"A broken mind, lost in a broken system," he echoed my words from weeks earlier. "Do you fix them? The broken ones?"

"I try." I smiled sadly.

"What happens when you don't?"

The smile slipped. I pulled my hands back and put them in my lap, under the table. It didn't take long to find a cuticle to pick at.

"Tell me," Leander continued, sounding as casual as ever. "Which theory do you subscribe to — Baumeister? Joiner? Who do you believe got it right in terms of assessing one's risk of suicide?"

The fact he could rattle off suicidologists shouldn't have been the least bit surprising. At this point in the game, I shouldn't have been surprised by anything that came out of Leander's mouth.

"Leenaars — the multidimensional approach. To me, it offers a more complete view of a person. Let me guess. You favor Shneidman's view, that suicide isn't about death, per se, its just a means of ending one's psychological pain?"

"Or maybe I'm just mad." His words hung in the air between us, dark and heavy. I knew he wasn't talking about anger — he was talking about insanity.

"Let me tell you a little secret they teach us in school." I leaned forward, speaking in a mock whisper. "Crazy people don't know they're crazy."

He mirrored my posture and my tone. "Broken people know they're broken and deep down they know it can't be fixed." While we spoke, his thumb disappeared inside his sleeve, mindlessly stroking the scars on his left wrist. His gaze was unfocused, his thoughts clearly elsewhere, as they had been with greater and greater frequency.

Taking a risk, my hand resurfaced from under the table and rested on top of his.

Blinking himself back into the present, Leander looked down at our hands with a blank expression. I half-expected him to pull away. He didn't, not even when I rolled his left arm over and pushed the edge of his sleeve back slowly. His most recent injury was dark pink now as the skin tried to repair itself for the umpteenth time. Tracing the tip of my finger over the jagged line, I wondered what he saw when he looked at it.

"This doesn't mean you're broken," I said quietly.

"But I am. Why can't you see that? If you believe what people say, I kill everyone around me and yet I never die despite my attempt. If that is not the epitome of failure, then what is?" His voice was strained, his eyes turning a shade darker and glassier with each word.

"Failure is giving up. Failure is giving in. You didn't give up, Leander. You're here, now."

He pulled his wrist free from my hand and stood swiftly, retreating to the window. After our breakthrough in the dayroom, I'd decided to let him attend sessions without the shackles. So far I hadn't regretted it. Except for times like this, when he physically distanced himself and began shutting down by staring out the window.

"Your definition of failure sounds like the definition of surrender," Leander said from across the room. It was raining hard, blurring the view of the outside world like watercolors. Trailing a finger down the glass, he followed a raindrop as it raced along.

"I suppose… If you want to look at it that way."

"Aren't some things worth surrendering for?"

"Death isn't one of those things."

"As a doctor you have to say that, of course. But as a woman…" He turned to face me again. The way he looked at me sent a shiver down my spine, like every inch of me was exposed. "I imagine there are times it is far easier to submit than to keep fighting the inevitable."

Clearing my throat, I tried my best to remain aloof. I had a clear visual of submitting to him and it had nothing to do with self-harm. "I don't know what you're referring to, Mr. Welles, but I was speaking strictly of suicide."

He blinked slowly and turned back to the window. "So was I."

My face was on fire. Before I could make a bigger fool of myself, I turned my attention to his most recent written evaluation. Every time I thought I had a read on him, he up and changed lanes. It was dizzying.

Based on Leander's answers and the observations I was able to make through our interactions, along with what Dennis observed, bipolar looked like the strongest diagnosis, along with Generalized Anxiety and Attachment Disorder, but the verdict was still out on any others.

The past history of self-harm complicated things, along with his reservations about food. He was thin on his first day but the hollows under his eyes had become more pronounced as of late. I debated calling Elijah to see if he had any helpful recommendations in convincing Leander to eat. Even with the improvements to the menu, the staff noted Leander continued to skip meals altogether or subsist on nothing but a few bites here and there, which made me question bipolar in favor of Major Depression.

"How are you sleeping?" I asked. Sleep was one thing I could at least help with immediately. I didn't like that he was broaching the topic of suicide again. It set off alarm bells, especially considering the downturn in his overall mood.

"Fitfully." He chased another raindrop with his finger, his lids heavy. "'A dream has power to poison sleep.'"

"Poetic. Poe again?" I didn't remember it from any of the passages he underlined.

He sighed. I didn't know if it was at me or sheer exhaustion. "Shelley."

"Percy or Mary?" I may not have been able to quote Gothic authors off the top of my head, but I wasn't a complete moron. I remembered enough from English Lit to hold a fairly intelligent conversation with the average person — except Leander wasn't the average person.

"Mary." Noted.

I flipped through the pages of his chart to make sure there were no conflicts with the medications he was already on. "Would you like me to give you something to help you sleep?"

"Medicine is for the weak."

"If you were a Type I diabetic would you chastise yourself for taking insulin? No. You'd take the insulin because it's what your body needs. Besides, you're already taking escitalopram and alprazolam."

He didn't move. In fact, his finger stalled on the glass, even though the raindrop had already pooled on the bottom of the window.

My stomach knotted and I pushed away from the table so quickly the chair scraped the floor. Just because he was prescribed medicine didn't mean he was taking it. Given his lack of interest in anything as of late, I had more than a sneaking suspicion he wasn't taking anything at all.

"Where are you going?" He spun away from the window, watching me with wide eyes.

"Wait here," I said, more out of habit than anything. It's not like he could go anywhere without a key card or an escort.

I let myself out of the interview room and stormed down the hallway.

Calvin intercepted me outside of Leander's room. "What's going on, Doc?"

"I think Mr. Welles has been stashing his meds." Pulling on a pair of gloves, I marched inside and went straight for the corner with the sink and toilet. I groped along the gleaming metal, feeling every crevice while Calvin opened each of Leander's books and shook them out before checking the underside of the table and chair.

Finding nothing, we both turned to the bed. I grabbed the pillow while Calvin felt along the mattress. As he searched, something small clicked on the tiled floor. Laying a hand on Calvin's shoulder, I knelt next to the bed and reached underneath it.

A white, oblong pill sat in the middle of my gloved palm. I glared at it. I didn't want to be right. I wanted to be wrong, just like the phone incident. I didn't want to believe this was Leander's plan.

"Flip it," I said.

Calvin grabbed the mattress by the far edge. As soon as it was on its opposite side, a small tear in the mattress became visible. I pulled the fabric apart while Calvin cupped his hands, catching the waterfall of tiny ovals and circles.

"Why wouldn't he just flush them?" Calvin asked.

"Because he was going to overdose." Grabbing a handful

of pills, I stuffed them into my pocket and stomped out of the room.

I heard the commotion before I even swiped through the security door. From the opposite end of the hall, I saw the door to the interview room was open, guards and nurses streaming inside. The staff issued commands to Leander as well as each other. Above it all, Leander screamed.

Sprinting down the hallway, I caught the heavy door before it slammed shut. I heaved it open again in time to see Leander shove a syringe-wielding Nora backward into a guard. Russ tackled him to the floor and the two writhed on the linoleum.

"What the hell is going on?" I shouted.

The other guard launched himself onto the pile. Together the men pinned each of Leander's arms to the ground. He continued to fight, yanking at the human restraints and trying to kick them off.

The younger nurse backed into one corner, away from the swinging limbs.

"He went fucking nuts," Nora said before diving at Leander with the needle again.

"Leander, stop! They're trying to help." I doubted it would work, but it was worth a shot, at any rate.

Predictably, either Leander couldn't hear me over his own yelling or he didn't care. It was hard to convince anyone with three people restraining you they were there to help.

Nora jabbed the needle into Leander's arm.

His eyelids fluttered and he stopped fighting. "No," he breathed, blinking hard, still resisting even as he lay motionless. "Lorelei…"

Before I, or anyone, could speak, Leander's eyes rolled up. His head fell to the ground with a heavy crack as his body went limp, the anguish receding from his face.

Closing my eyes and rubbing my temples, I tried to stem

the building pressure. "Someone tell me what happened. 'Fucking nuts' is not acceptable."

"Look at the fucking room," the other guard said. Paul, I realized, now that things calmed down.

I surveyed the damage. The table was shoved across the room. One chair was thrown into a corner. The other had a metal leg stuck in the window, a spiderweb of shattered glass radiating from the opening. A few larger pieces had fallen out. There was blood splattered on the floor along with streaks of it along the wall and windowsill, bright red against the white surfaces.

"Is he bleeding?" I pushed Paul away from Leander and grabbed his wrists one by one, pushing up each bloody sleeve. It wasn't his wrists, but both hands had lacerations all over the palms and fingers.

"Yeah, I'm good, too. Thanks." Russ glared at me. He was holding his left eye, as if that would stop the swelling.

I suppressed the urge to roll my eyes at him, the poor baby. "Paul, why don't you two go get checked out? Make sure Russ here isn't going to lose his eye."

I turned to Nora next, raising my eyebrows at her expectantly. "Could you go get a kit?" The young nurse had already slipped out, probably to go submit her resignation letter. The timid didn't last long around Parkview.

Nora heaved a sigh and disappeared with the guards. The three of them grumbled their way out the door. I didn't care to listen. It was more of the same. Their desire to help had long-since died, replaced by dedication to the good pay and benefits. I supposed I didn't blame them. They didn't get to know the patients like I did. They didn't try to understand how a person ended up here.

Kneeling over Leander, I felt the back of his head, probing gingerly through his disheveled hair. As I thought, there was a lump forming, but my fingers came away without blood. He was going to have a headache regardless.

Laying his head on the ground as gently as I could, I smoothed his hair away from his sweaty face. Disappointment surged through me — at him, but mostly at myself. I should have known better. I should have known he wasn't progressing the way he should have been. I should have seen the signs.

Nora returned and flung the kit from the doorway, leaving again without a word. So much for caring for one's patients. I made a mental note to discuss her transfer again with Kim since the last one ended up going nowhere.

I opened the plastic box and rifled through the supplies. Once I'd wiped the blood away from Leander's right palm, I found a large shard of glass lodged in his skin. Frowning, I picked it out with a pair of tweezers and glanced between it and the broken window. He wasn't trying to kill himself. He was trying to escape. He used the chair to break the treated glass and pulled it free, piece by piece, since the design meant it wouldn't shatter like regular glass.

"Where were you going?" I asked aloud, wrapping his hand in gauze.

Of course, I didn't get any sort of answer. Leander twitched now and again as I sat there, watching him sleep. His eyebrows furrowed and his fingers curled, as if he was still fighting. Even in a medicated sleep, his mind tormented him. Was it the upcoming trial? Whatever happened in his past? I had no way of knowing and that frustrated me more than it should have.

The door buzzed behind me. I angled myself toward it, relieved to see it was Calvin and one of the new orderlies with a gurney. What was his name? Mike? Mark? It was hard to keep track of the new people sometimes.

"Hey Doc. Heard you might need some help in here."

I scooted away from Leander, out of their way. "Yes, thank you."

Calvin and the other orderly scooped up Leander and settled him on the cot as if he was nothing more than a rag doll. They clicked the straps into place along his body and wheeled him out of the interview room again.

"Mark, hold up." Calvin paused in the hallway. "I'll have the custodian come clean this up, Doc. Why don't you go grab lunch or something before your next appointment?"

"Thank you." I patted Calvin's bicep before disappearing into my office. I wasn't the least bit hungry, but it was the sentiment that mattered.

Sinking into my chair, I stared at the computer, trying to figure out what the hell happened in the last thirty minutes. Thank God for the cameras. They would explain what Nora's definition of "fucking nuts" was.

Leander watched me leave, took one step toward the door. He raked his hands through his hair and lashed out at the nearest chair, sending it sailing. Even through a camera lens, I could see him start to hyperventilate. He paced in a tight circle, shoving the table out of the way to give him a wider area to prowl. That's when the second chair went through the window. He pawed at the glass frantically, tearing off pieces of it.

Russ entered the room first and grabbed ahold of Leander's waist, earning him an elbow to the eye. Leander was still trying to tear the glass out of the window when Paul grabbed him in a headlock and yanked him back. Leander was able to duck out of the hold in time to see Nora approaching with the sedative, which is when I walked in.

Closing out of the camera system, I slumped in my chair. He wasn't trying to escape. He was having a panic attack — a bad one, clearly — and was probably desperate for fresh air. And it was my fault. I'd made a point of telling him when I was leaving town, but I left him in the lurch when I abruptly left our session. After what happened with his parents, it made sense abandonment would be one of his triggers. I smacked my palm against my forehead, once, then a few more times for good measure.

"Stupid, stupid, stupid!"

CHAPTER 18

*L*eander slept for the next two days.

On the third morning he woke long enough to refuse his meds. According to his chart, he continued to be aggressive with staff which resulted in all of his privileges being revoked. That was bound to make his situation worse, but I couldn't argue with policy or show preferential treatment no matter how much I disagreed.

At lunch, I decided to see if he was awake yet and what the nurses meant. Just like "fucking nuts," I was sure "aggressive" was open to interpretation.

I was nearly to his room when a tray of food went flying across the hall. It clattered at Nora's feet, followed by a string of curses from her mouth. She stopped in front of me with a glare, chunks of orange jello dripping down the front of her uniform.

"Pretty boy is awake," she snapped.

"Did he say anything?"

She snorted and stormed off, her soggy shoes squeaking on the floor.

Stepping over the scattered remnants of his lunch, I continued to Leander's room. Leaning against the doorframe, I watched him through the glass, waiting for the right moment to announce my presence.

He prowled back and forth like a caged animal, snarling at himself and muttering things I couldn't hear. Both hands were buried in his hair, pushing against his skull from either side. I couldn't imagine the headache he had and refusing meds meant he wouldn't even get a simple pain reliever.

When he noticed me, Leander jerked to a halt, his hands falling to his sides. He approached the door slowly, watching me with wary eyes. Instantly, I knew the thread of trust between us was frayed. What I didn't know what how much longer I had until it snapped completely.

"How are you feeling?" I asked.

He didn't look happy to see me. He looked irate. "If you're here to inject me with something, you can forget it."

"I'm not. I'm sorry about the other day. I shouldn't have left like that."

Scoffing, he looked away, his jaw clenched.

I bristled at the rejection. Doctors who apologized to anyone were a rare breed — it was even rarer for them to get over their God complex and actually apologize to a patient. "Well, if you would have taken your medication, this wouldn't have happened at all."

"Medicine is for the weak." It sounded like a refrain his grandmother probably beat into him. God, I could strangle that woman if she wasn't already dead.

"So you've said." I crossed my arms over my chest, trying my hardest not to glare at him. "And yet you have no qualms about suicide."

"Suicide's not weakness."

"No, it's cowardice."

Seething, he slammed his bandaged fist against the glass, anger flashing in his eyes.

I jumped, cursing myself silently. I struck a nerve but at least I knew how he really felt about taking his own life — he viewed suicide as honorable. Given his literary preferences, I should have known. His regret wasn't his attempt, it was that he'd failed to complete it. He said as much, but at the time I wanted to believe it was his depression talking and not a genuine sentiment.

Leander put a hand on either side of the window and leaned in, pressing his forehead against the glass. He looked up at me from under his dark lashes, his eyes almost yellow in the light from the hallway. Inexplicably, the hue signaled danger in my brain. When he spoke, his voice was low and quiet, and eerily calm. "And what would you know about it, Doctor? What do you know about any of this other than what you've read in books?"

There was no way I was going to back off. Not now. Personal or not. A gauntlet had been thrown and I was going to meet the challenge. "My father died by suicide when I was eleven. He took the easy way out and he didn't care who he hurt in the process."

If the news was shocking to Leander, it didn't register. At all. His face remained frozen, a breath from hostile. "How?"

"He shot himself." I couldn't believe I was having this conversation. I hadn't had this conversation in years and certainly never with a patient. What was I thinking? How was this helpful in the slightest? And yet, I couldn't help but feel the need to defend myself and my experience.

"I admire his resolve."

My lip curled before I could stop it. "I'm sure he'd be flattered."

Leander angled his face upward, staring at the ceiling as if he were in the midst of a dreamy thought. "What you call cowardice, Doctor, is a moment of power. A reclamation of power, if you will. Perhaps instead of denigrating your father and his choice, you pick up a razor and put it to your wrist. See if you have the strength to pull it back."

My mouth hung open, dumbly. Nothing but a squeak came out in reply.

"Of course you could always use a gun... I can't imagine the mess." Leander rolled away from the window without looking at me and drifted to the bed like a waif. Sitting in one fluid motion, his head dropped into his hands.

Giving him one last speechless glare, I forced myself to walk away before I said something truly damaging to my career and his psyche.

*

Our less-than-productive conversation replayed itself in my head for the rest of the day, through all of my other sessions, and all the way home. I tried to ignore him while I showered, while I paid bills, and while I pulled out all of the requisite items for a salad. It didn't matter. Leander was with me every step of the way, his anger and condemnation as sharp as the knife in my hand.

He wasn't really telling me to kill myself, was he? No. He couldn't have been. He was angry. I should have never engaged in that conversation with him. Maybe it was the unmanaged bipolar. Maybe his mania was irritation and anger, along with bouts of frenetic creativity. Or maybe it was his depression at work, driving a wedge between us and our progress. Or the attachment disorder, decades of abuse and neglect festering in his mind... Push them away before they push you away. It made sense.

Shaking my head, I sliced down across a carrot. Wrong. The blade cut through the side of my finger instead.

Hissing out a curse, I dropped the knife and darted to the sink. I let the cold water run over it for a moment before wrapping it in a kitchen towel. My finger throbbed and burned at the same time, the nerves screaming in tandem with my brain at what an idiot I was. It was an unpleasant sensation without any endorphins to take the edge off. I squeezed harder until it went numb, making my way to the bathroom.

As I wrapped a bandage around the cut, I couldn't help but notice the veins in my wrist. It wouldn't have been hard to cut into them. They were there — visible, right beneath the surface, just like Leander's. Tracing the tip of one finger down my forearm, like he did, I shuddered at the thought. I slammed the medicine cabinet shut and stalked out of the bathroom.

I needed a break.

I needed to focus and reevaluate where things stood with Leander. His case was complicated and I needed to make sure I was on top of all of the work that needed to be done before the trial.

Without a second thought, I emailed Dennis my plans to work from home for the next few days. I also made it clear I was leaving Leander solely in his charge, since they seemed to get on relatively well in my absence. The last thing I needed was another doctor coming in and setting us back even further.

Maybe I shouldn't have gone to Easton… Leander had taken a turn for the worse since I came back. It wasn't much of a stretch to think they were somehow linked.

"Stop," I scolded myself. There would be no more thinking about Leander. No more worrying. And no more taking his case personally. There would be plenty of time in the morning to go over his files, I didn't need to invest any more of myself into it until then.

With that settled, I swept my bloodied carrots into the garbage and grabbed the phone. It was safer to let someone else make my dinner from now on, at least until I got my head on straight.

CHAPTER 19

I didn't see or speak to Leander again until out of the blue I was summoned to court by Scheible. Despite my self-imposed isolation, Leander was never far from my thoughts. I spent nearly every waking moment wading through his life, piecing together one horror story after another. Try as I might to see things from the prosecution's side, all I could see was injustice — cruel, blatant injustice.

According to the latest email from Dennis, Leander had a terrible night. He had to be sedated again, forcefully, when he wouldn't stop hitting his head against the window of his room. So they claimed.

Doubt nettled me all the way to the courthouse. I made a note to look into the situation after I was done putting on a dog and pony show for the judge.

My doubt turned to certainty the minute I saw Leander in person. I nearly gasped when I laid eyes on him.

Once again, Leander was dressed in head-to-toe black. There was no sign of leg restraints, just a flash of silver handcuffs at his wrists. A bandage crossed his forehead, mostly hidden by his hair. There was another across the bridge of his nose. The most shocking part of his appearance were the dark purple bruises beneath both eyes. It wasn't the mask of extreme sleep deprivation. They broke his nose.

Leander didn't look up when Scheible called me forward to speak to the judge. He sat, staring at the table in front of him, slumped into the corner of his chair instead of his characteristically rigid posture. It didn't take long to figure out they'd drugged him again before he was transported. Knowing how he felt about medication, I was furious on his behalf. Even if it meant they were difficult to deal with, I'd rather have my patients be coherent than zombies.

"Dr. Clayton, as the person currently in charge of Mr. Welles' care, can you inform his honor as to the state of things inside Parkview Psychiatric?" Scheible asked.

"Well," I shifted my weight from one foot to the other, pivoting my attention from the attorney to the judge — Phil Linden. I hoped he would stay on point today and not reminisce about the days when I ran into his chambers with blonde braids and Mary Janes looking for peppermints. "Your honor, when Mr. Welles first came to Parkview a month ago, he appeared forlorn and apprehensive, but in complete control of his mental faculties. We were making some solid progress in his mental health evaluation."

"And now?" Phil asked, glancing behind me. He didn't look impressed with what he saw. Was he offended by Leander's posture or by his injuries? With a middle-of-the-road judge, it was hard to tell whose side he would ultimately end up on. If my mother was on the bench, I knew without a shadow of a doubt how she would rule. Leander would have never left the county jail.

I resisted the urge to follow his gaze. "I don't know, your honor. These past few days have been nothing short of a setback. Mr. Welles has had to be sedated several times after alleged bouts of self-harm."

"Alleged?" Phil raised his eyebrows at me. Sharp as ever, Phil. Thank you.

In my periphery, I saw Scheible nodding as I continued. "Your honor, this is the first chance I've had to see Mr. Welles since his latest episode but I can tell you, even at this distance, his injuries do not correspond with an attempt at self-harm."

"What exactly are you saying, Dr. Clayton?"

"I don't believe Parkview Psychiatric is the safest environment for Mr. Welles anymore."

"Objection!" Tom Martin, the State's Attorney, shouted from the other side of Scheible. "Your honor, with all respect to Dr. Clayton, she can't possibly be suggesting that her own facility — a facility specifically designed to house the mentally ill — is not adequately equipped to house the defendant!"

The judge turned his attention back to me. "Dr. Clayton, are you insinuating abuse by the staff at Parkview Psychiatric?"

I hesitated for a moment before nodding. If I was wrong, Parkview's reputation would be in ruins and I'd be out of a job. If I was right, patients were in danger. "Possibly, your honor. As I said, this is the first chance I've had to see Mr. Welles, but I intend on launching a full investigation into this incident upon my return."

Phil fiddled with his pen, his jowls working as if were literally chewing the scenario over. He kept glancing between Leander and I with the occasional glance at Tom. At last, he spoke. "The state grants Mr. Scheible's request to house the defendant, at his expense, in a private residence for the duration of this case. However, in addition to house arrest and electronic monitoring, the defendant is hereby mandated to continue his sessions with Dr. Clayton or another psychiatrist of the defense's choosing. He is also prohibited from any contact with anyone except his legal team and medical staff." He knocked the gavel on his desk as Tom tried to voice another objection.

Scheible kept his smile hidden until he turned his back on the bench. "Good job, Doc. That was perfect."

"I told the truth, Mr. Scheible."

He ignored me, hurrying back to the table where his briefcase lay. "I've got the house all lined up. As soon as he gets his bracelet, we'll be on our way. I'll text you the address."

Nodding, I continued walking down the aisle, making sure I didn't linger too long. I didn't want Tom accusing me of favoritism, since I'm sure he was already fuming Phil sided with me.

Leander didn't look at me, or Scheible. His eyes were downcast and he swayed ever so slightly in his chair, jerking upright again when Scheible thumped his briefcase on the table. Goddamn tranquilizers.

I was on my way to my mother's chambers for an obligatory check-in when Darren exited another of the courtrooms. He stopped short when he saw me, then zeroed in like a torpedo.

"Lorelei!"

Oh, God. Not today, Darren...

Spinning on the ball of my foot, I retreated as quickly as I could. His footsteps echoed behind me, long, quick strides made by expensive shoes.

"Lorelei, goddamn it! Wait!"

I didn't chance looking back, even when I felt him looming up behind me. With each step he took, I could smell his aftershave getting closer and closer. My heartbeat quickened with the click of my heels. Did I yell for security? And say what? I was avoiding my ex and the public spectacle we'd inevitably have?

The doors to Phil's courtroom opened as I rushed by. Tom stormed out, narrowly avoiding a collision with me. I mumbled an apology and darted to the side while he went the opposite way.

"Oh, Darren. We need to talk," Tom said behind me.

I stared straight ahead and kept walking. At last, Darren's aftershave disappeared, along with his footsteps.

Relief flooded through me with the breath I expelled. I didn't normally dodge my exes, but Darren was different. His ego made him unpredictable. That conversation he desperately wanted to have could have gone one of two ways: civilly, or with court security escorting us out. With everything going on at Parkview, I didn't need to be distracted by Darren or his drama.

While I waited for the text from Scheible, I called Calvin on his cell phone, hoping he snuck it on the floor today. I wouldn't normally have a conversation like this over the phone, but I had an itch that needed to be scratched.

"Can you do me a favor?" I asked as soon as he answered.

"Anything."

"Can you see who was working last night besides Dennis?"

"Yeah, give me a sec." His shoes squeaked over the floor as he navigated the hallways. Papers rustled. He said a cordial hello to someone before more squeaks from his shoes. A door creaked open and closed. "Jeanette, Nora, Russ, and the new guy, Mark."

I thanked Calvin and hung up before someone caught him.

There was a sinking feeling in my stomach. I still had to confirm it with Leander, but I was pretty sure I knew what happened — Russ got his revenge for the swollen eye. How many other patients had he mistreated behind my back? The possibility was enough to make the bile rise in the back of my throat.

The text from Scheible flashed across my screen, putting a momentary hold on my raging thoughts. I couldn't worry about other patients at the moment. Right now Leander was my priority.

※

The ritzy subdivision Scheible picked wasn't too far away from the courthouse. Leander's temporary housing was large and fairly secluded from the rest of the neighboring McMansions. I imagine it was meant to make him feel more at home, even if the houses were built a century apart. How long had Scheible been planning this move?

I rang the doorbell and waited, glancing around at the wooded property. It would be beautiful in the fall. Was Leander still going to be here in the fall? Some cases lasted that long, especially when lawyers kept getting the trial date pushed back as Scheible seemed intent on doing.

Scheible's assistant opened the door with a beaming smile. "They're in the dining room." She must have seen my puzzled expression, since she pointed in the appropriate direction after she took my coat.

I murmured my thanks and headed that way, mindful of how loudly my heels sounded on the dark wood floors. The last thing I needed was to gouge someone else's expensive flooring.

Leander was seated at a large, ornate table with a tray of food in front of him. Sort of. He'd already pushed it away, leaning to one side, as if repulsed. His head rested in one hand, his eyelids heavy. He'd draped his suit jacket on the back of the chair. Otherwise, he looked the same as the courtroom, save for the fact his top button was undone and his tie was loosened.

"You have to eat something," Scheible said in a quiet voice. He slid a plate of fettuccini toward Leander, stopping when he saw me walk in. "Look, Dr. Clayton is here."

Leander didn't appear to care about me any more than the food. He didn't move an inch or cast any looks in my direction.

"Mr. Scheible can you give us a moment, please?" I asked with a smile to soften the request.

"Of course. I'll be across the hall if you need anything." He closed the french doors on his way out.

I laid my hand on the back of the chair next to Leander's. "May I sit?"

Swallowing thickly, Leander dropped his head from his hand and leaned back in the chair, resting his head against the carved wood instead. When was the last time he ate? He looked almost lifeless. "Do what you must."

I didn't know if I should take it as a good sign he finally spoke or be annoyed at his response. His words always had a proper, polite ring to them — old-fashioned, if you will. But this time his tone was neither soft nor charming, it was bitter. The thread of trust snapped completely.

I sat, regardless of his feelings, and stared at him. Since he wasn't moving, I took the time to study him and assess his injuries. Up close, I found more evidence to support my theory. There was a fresh bruise marring his jawline. If he was hitting his head, how did his jaw get bruised? And where did the split lip come from? What other injuries would I find if I pressed hard enough?

"What happened last night?" I made sure to keep my voice soft and neutral, even as my nails dug into the arm of the chair.

He closed his eyes with an exhausted sigh. "Didn't you hear? I had a psychotic break."

"We both know that is not what happened."

His eyes drifted open again and found mine. For a moment I thought he would say something, but he didn't. He remained frustratingly silent. I wanted to shake him.

"Leander, let me help you. You once said you wanted someone to listen. I'm listening. I'm trying to help."

He was on his feet and across the room with a quickness I didn't know he was capable of in the moment. Just like in the interview room, he folded his arms across himself and leaned against the window frame, staring out at the woods behind the house.

"If you don't tell me what happened, there is a strong probability that man will keep his job," I continued, after it was clear he wasn't going to speak. "Don't you want to stop him from hurting someone else?"

"No."

"No?"

"Did I stutter, Doctor?" He turned away from the window, an eyebrow lifted. He wasn't teasing this time. There was no coy smirk or smile behind his eyes.

"No. I thought you would want to see him held accountable." He's hangry, Lorelei. Don't take his head off... He's got to be starving, he's hurt, he's under stress. Don't take it personally.

"Holding him accountable and saving other people from his wrath are not the same thing. Do not confuse me for some sort of a benefactor. I told you once, I am no one's hero."

"You're right. Heroes don't play the martyr." I bit my tongue a second too late. I shouldn't have been petulant with him. I needed to be supportive, especially during the transition to a new, yet confined, environment. Sometimes it was easy to forget about his mental state, whatever it was, since his intelligence and demeanor masked so many of his symptoms.

A dark smile curled the corners of his mouth. "This is an interesting tactic you've been pursuing as of late. Does antagonism often work on unstable patients?"

I sprang to my feet and strode over to him. If he wanted antagonism, I'd show him antagonism. "You're as unstable as this house, Leander. Let's pretend for a moment that we see through each other's bullshit. Now that you're here, what do you plan to do? Cut your bracelet off and run? Open another vein? Stash some more pills to try and overdose? This trial is coming whether you want it to or not. And regardless of the outcome, you have a life to live. I can help make it better if you would just let me in."

His hand flashed out and caught me by the throat. My gasp was cut short as he swung me back and slammed me against the wall. He pinned me in place with his body, his leg shoved between mine as much for balance as it was to keep me from kicking him. He had more strength than I originally gave him credit for and far, far more anger.

"Do not presume for one moment you have any sort of control here." He spoke the words softly, but through his teeth, the same way he'd called me on my bluff about the bunny. "We are not in your world anymore, Doctor, and I am not one of your lab rats to play games with."

"I did—"

Shushing me, his forehead pressed against my temple while his fingers tightened on my throat, enough to stem any attempt at talking. I tried not to squirm as his hot breath caressed my ear. "Do not lie to me."

Without any way of communicating effectively, I shook my head. I watched him out of the corner of my eye, trying to predict what he would do next. Except, he was completely unpredictable. Even after showing aggression during his panic attack, I pegged him as non-violent. This moment demonstrated how wrong I'd been.

"No more lies, Lorelei..." His hand fell away from my throat before he peeled his body away from mine. "You may show yourself out," he said as he turned on his heel.

I remained rooted in place, watching him drift out of the room, his shoulders rounded and his head bowed. His footsteps ascended the curving staircase and he disappeared without saying a word to Scheible. It wasn't until the sound of a door closing echoed down the stairwell that I dared to move.

Wobbling on my heels, I pushed myself away from the wall, trying to ignore the trembling in my limbs. I expelled a shaky breath and willed the butterflies in my stomach to give it a rest already.

I was surprised by Leander's reaction, not scared, if that was his intent. I'd seen worse. Much worse. Leander didn't exactly frighten me, though this week taught me to be wary of his erratic mood swings. Being threatened with strangulation was an element I wasn't expecting out of him, and it made me start to reconsider my assessment.

CHAPTER 20

*T*he grandfather clock in the corner ticked away the seconds, the pendulum swinging back and forth hypnotically. I wished it would stop. The ticking made my head hurt.

At last, Gene looked up from the document on his desk and took his reading glasses off. As Parkview's resident attorney and head of the internal review department, he'd been my first point of contact in regard to Leander's assault. "This is not good."

"No, it isn't." I laced my fingers together in my lap.

"What does Mr. Welles have to say? I noticed his statement is missing."

"He refused to talk about it."

"That will make things more difficult." Gene shuffled through the papers again and squinted at another statement. I could tell from the back of the paper it was Jeanette's loopy handwriting. "Alright. Let's get this show over with."

I nodded and followed him to the conference room.

The board of directors were seated around the table with a stack of files. I took a seat in the corner and watched as

Gene moved to the head of the table. Kim eyed me from her position next to the chairman. She seemed less than thrilled with my recent claim against Nora but I stood firm in my decision to bypass her and go straight to Gene with the complaint.

"Thank you everyone for clearing your schedules," Gene began, laying out several pieces of paper in a particular order. "We're here today to review the complaints against Russell Brewer and Nora Kelly."

I stole a glance at the pair from across the room. They were sitting next to one another, whispering and openly glaring at me. Probably planning their revenge. Good luck to them.

The door opened and Calvin snuck in, cramming himself into the chair next to me.

Relief washed over me the second I felt his arm squish against mine on the armrest. Russ and Nora could glare all they wanted now that Calvin was there. They wouldn't actually be stupid enough to try anything in front of him.

"Ms. Kelly, would you mind?" Gene gestured to the chair at the far end of the table.

Nora stood and took the hot seat, clearing her throat.

"Can you please tell the board what happened last Thursday while you were on shift?" Gene asked, peering over the top of his glasses at the date on the paper.

"I was doing my rounds and I heard a banging sound coming from room three. I could see through the glass that the patient was having an episode, so for my safety I called for security to help extract him so he could be sedated. Ru— Mr. Brewer was the senior guard on duty and he responded, along with Jeanette and eventually Mark. We extracted the patient, sedated him, and secured him in the padded cell, per policy." She slid a glance at me. I balled my hands into fists to keep from lashing out.

"Can you explain what you mean by 'having an episode'?"

"He was punching the wall, he hit his face against the glass, and when we entered the room, he attacked us."

Lies. Leander's hands were pristine when I saw him. If he was punching walls, he would have had bruises or scrapes or something.

"Was he yelling?" Gene asked.

"Yes, he was yelling," Nora replied.

"What did he say?"

"I don't know. He was just yelling."

"Was he yelling words? Howling like an animal? You work with all sorts of patients, Ms. Kelly, surely you can describe how someone might be yelling."

"I don't remember."

"But the banging was loud enough to be heard over the yelling, is that correct?"

"Yes."

"Thank you, Ms. Kelly. Mr. Brewer?"

They exchanged seats.

Calvin nudged my elbow gently, frowning at me. I frowned back, but I got the hint. I stopped picking at my cuticles, forcing my hands to lay flat in my lap.

"Mr. Brewer, can you give us your recollection of that evening?"

Russ shot me a nasty look before directing his attention to Gene. "I was called to assist with an extraction. When I got on scene, the subject was already covered in blood and in an agitated state. He fought us until he was successfully sedated and then transferred to the padded cell."

"In what manner did you restrain the patient?"

"It all happened so fast."

Gene slipped his reading glasses off and folded them, laying them on the table "Try to remember, Mr. Brewer."

"I, um..." Russ huffed, rubbing the top of his knee. "I don't know. I think I grabbed his arm while Jeanette grabbed the other one. Nora had the needle."

"And what did Mark do?"

"He, uh, helped Jeanette get control of the other arm."

"It took three people to secure two arms?"

"The guy was going crazy. Three people was barely enough."

"Uh huh." Gene picked up a stack of papers from the far end of his arrangement. "What time did this happen?"

"I don't know. It was late."

"Around three in the morning?"

"Yeah, sounds right."

"None of the other patients recall hearing any commotion until after the staff was on scene."

"What?"

"Ms. Kelly stated Mr. Welles was having an 'episode,' and the banging and yelling drew her attention. You stated he was 'going crazy' and was 'agitated.' So why didn't the patients hear anything prior to the staff's arrival?"

"'Cuz they're fucking nuts?"

Shock rippled through the board in a series of murmurs and shaking heads.

"No, listen. You're going to take the word of some psych patient over us?" Russ stood up, driving a finger into the center of the table.

"This is just an inquest, Mr. Brewer. Please take your seat," Gene replied with a huff.

Russ was sinking himself with every word. At this point we wouldn't need to wait for the board's decision, Gene would fire him directly. If it wasn't for the pressure from Calvin's arm, I might have bounced out of my chair in excitement.

Russ wasn't finished. "This isn't an inquest — it's a sham. All because some wet-nurse over here gets her nose out of whack if we so much as look sideways at one of her precious patients. They're criminals — they don't need to be babied. They need to be taught a lesson."

"Is that what you were doing? Teaching Mr. Welles a lesson?" Gene stood as well, staring Russ down from across the table.

Russ started backpedaling. "I mean. That's not what happened. He did it to himself!"

"Did he? Did he, Mr. Brewer? Or did you take it upon yourself to dole out some extrajudicial punishment with the help of Ms. Kelly over there? Can you explain why *your* keycard swiped into Mr. Welles' cell twenty minutes before Ms. Kelly's did?"

The chairman of the board cleared his throat and raised a hand, effectively raising a flag between the two. "I think we've heard enough from Mr. Brewer. Dr. Clayton, your statement?"

Calvin bumped his arm against mine as I stood. Expelling a quick breath and pushing my shoulders back, I stepped up next to Russ, my gaze fixed forward. Looking at him would only make my blood boil.

"As the primary doctor on Mr. Welles' case, I have been exposed to varying degrees of his temperament and personality. He has never shown violence or aggression similar to what Mr. Brewer or Ms. Kelly have described." I swallowed the bitterness of the half-truth. He never was violent at Parkview. His reaction in the dining room was an entirely different matter; one they didn't need to know about. "I observed Mr. Welles the day after this alleged episode and I found his injuries were not consistent with the explanation given by Ms. Kelly and Mr. Brewer."

"In what way?" Gene asked, resuming his chair and his civil tone.

"The cut on his forehead was too high to have been self-inflicted. His hands showed no sign of severe bruising as one would expect from punching a brick wall repeatedly. His nose was broken, which, again, is inconsistent with the claims made by the staff. The same is to be said for the laceration to his lower lip. And lastly, there was a distinct bruise along the left side of his jaw, indicative of a punch delivered by a right-handed individual."

"And there's no way he could have injured himself?"

"Of course it's possible, but not this combination of injuries or their specific locations. His wounds are reminiscent of a man in a fight, not someone who is in the midst of a psychological episode intent on harming themselves."

"Thank you, Dr. Clayton. If you'll all excuse us for now." The chairman dismissed us with a cordial smile and a wave of his hand.

Nora made a beeline for the door, Russ on her heels.

"Bitch," Russ muttered as he passed, loud enough for me to hear but not so loud as to cause a scene.

"Excuse me?" I took a step toward him, my hands clenched.

Calvin was at my elbow, looming over my shoulder at Russ. "Say it again."

"You heard me. If I get shit-canned because of you, you're going to fucking regret it," Russ sneered.

"Is that a threat?" Calvin demanded, circling around to my front side and squaring off with Russ.

Russ didn't seem to care about their size difference. A career manhandling inmates probably gave him more confidence than he should have against a man Calvin's size. "I never laid a finger on that sick prick other than when I had to."

I scoffed. "Save it. If all you get is termination, consider yourself lucky. I'd like nothing more than to see you hauled into court and spend the rest of your life writing restitution checks out of your dwindling little pension."

Nora intervened at that point, laying a hand on Russ's arm and steering him away with placating whispers and gentle pats. What little professional respect I might have had for her once upon a time disappeared in an instant. If she concerned herself with patient welfare as much as she was concerned with babying a foul-tempered alcoholic, we wouldn't be in this situation.

I watched them leave, glaring a hole in the back of Russ's head.

Asshole.

I hoped Leander sued the shit out of them.

CHAPTER 21

J'd just pulled into Leander's when Gene called.

"The board made their decision," he said as I held my breath. "Russ has been let go. Nora was suspended."

Suspended? Was he kidding me? After everything else she'd done? Somehow, I managed to keep my reaction professional. "Well, I'm sorry it turned out this way."

"Me too. Talk soon."

Leander was already outside when I climbed out of the car. As usual, he was dressed in head-to-toe black. This time it was a long-sleeve shirt and trousers, despite the warm day. He appeared to be in the middle of walking the perimeter of his electronic leash.

"Good morning, Doctor." He gave me a small smile, his hands clasped behind his back. It reminded me of the day he gave me the sprig of Lily of the valley. Back to being a gentleman as opposed to the surprisingly powerful, intimidating man from the other night. I'm sure the stress of the day had something to do with his forceful disposition, or maybe it was a reaction to the medication. Maybe that's the real reason he refused to take anything.

"Good morning. You look well." The bruising on his face was starting to fade and he didn't look as gaunt. Maybe it was the sunlight, but he looked better than he had at Parkview. Certainly better than the last time we saw each other.

"I am, thank you. And you look equally well-rested."

I wasn't. I'd been on pins and needles for a week, waiting for Gene to call with the verdict, but I was happy my concealer was doing its job. I wanted to look unflappable and completely at ease around him. I didn't want Leander thinking he got to me. "Shall we head inside?"

"I'd prefer to walk, if that's alright."

Nodding, I set my bag on the hood of my car before joining him in the yard. Keeping a safe distance, I made sure to match his pace and stay out of arm's reach. He may have been calm now, but I was all too aware of how suddenly a tempest could blow in.

"I would like to apologize for my behavior the other night," Leander said, as if he could read my mind. His gaze remained straight ahead, his brows drawn together. "I shouldn't have lost my temper."

"Thank you for the apology. I'm fine. Trust me." I offered him a friendly smile, but he wasn't looking at me.

"That is the problem I'm afraid — I don't trust anyone. Not... really."

"Given your history, it's not hard to see why. Try to remember not everyone is out to hurt you. You have people who care about you. I think you have enough control over your thought processes to recognize when emotion is over-ruling rationality."

"That is a subject on which we will have to disagree, if history has taught us anything." He gave me a faint smile. Was he seriously joking about his outburst? He must have been feeling better, or he was still trying to downplay it.

"Well, I'm not out to hurt you."

The smile vanished entirely, replaced by a wince. "Your very presence pains me."

"How so?" I furrowed my brows at him. I'd lost my filter a time or two, yes, but I never intentionally set out to hurt him. I could never hurt anyone. Except maybe Russ. Or Nora.

He stopped walking and turned slightly to face me, his hands still clasped behind his back. "You see through the masks we wear, Lorelei. You try to save people from the darkness in their mind, in their very soul. What you fail to understand is that it is the light that hurts the most. For those mired in melancholy, it is a reminder of what can never truly be."

He sounded hopeless again. It made my heart stammer. "Why do you say that?"

"I told you. I destroy everything — everyone — in my life. Perhaps there was some part of me hoping to scare you off the other night, to spare you from the inevitable. I don't think I could bear it if I were the reason you lost your way. There are too few good people left in this world."

I wanted to reach out for him, to pull him against me and hug him until he stopped hurting. It was one of the kindest things someone ever told me, born from one of the saddest reasons. "There is nothing you can say or do to scare me away. I promise."

He squeezed his eyes shut, as if the words physically hurt him. "Please, don't."

"I'm telling the truth, Leander. I am here for you. Whatever you need. We'll get through this."

"Your confidence is inspiring. And yet..." He opened his eyes and began walking again. "I have my doubts."

We walked on in silence. At one point my arm brushed his elbow. I drifted to the side again and picked a point in the distance to focus on, hoping it kept me in a straight line. When it happened again a few yards later, I knew it was his doing. What I didn't know was if it was intentional or not.

I stole a glance up at him. His hair formed a wall of dark curls, obscuring his eyes. I couldn't even tell if they were opened or closed. He chewed on his lower lip, turning it redder by the minute.

All of a sudden, he whispered, "She's back."

"What? Who?"

Shushing me, he unclasped his hands as he stooped down, walking in a crouch toward the base of a tree. Stopping short of the woods, he dropped into a squat, holding his hand out and making a soft clicking noise with his tongue.

A few seconds later a thin, orange cat darted out of the trees. Ducking and bobbing around his hand, the cat sniffed it tentatively. When it rubbed against his leg, it left a trail of orange fur on the black fabric.

Leander scooped up the cat and cradled it against his chest, nuzzling its head. For a moment, I remembered the bunny story and I held my breath, waiting to see what he would do.

"Perhaps there is something you can do for me, Doctor."

"The cat?" Both eyebrows went up incredulously. It was clearly a stray, so I wasn't sure what, exactly, he needed help with.

"Animals are said to be effective therapeutic tools but I wouldn't want to be in violation of the court order."

I scratched the cat's chin and chuckled, dismissing any irrational fear for the cat's wellbeing. "Ok. I'll add it to your treatment plan."

"Did you hear that, Annabel? You get to stay." He smiled brightly, the first genuinely happy smile I'd seen since I'd known him. My heart seized at the sight. If he was stunning in his melancholy, he was downright breathtaking in his jubilation. I longed to see that smile again, but Leander was already gone, heading back toward the house with the cat in his arms.

We were barely inside the front door when Scheible's assistant greeted us. Was she living here now? I didn't see another car in the driveway, unless she parked in the garage to avoid the scrutiny of the SA's investigators who were no-doubt surveilling the house. I'm sure Tom was itching to throw Leander back in jail any way he could.

"Greta, do you mind running to the store to fetch things for Annabel?" Leander asked.

When the woman looked at me, I pointed at the cat. "That's Annabel. Your new houseguest."

He didn't wait for her to acknowledge her errand, since he was already halfway up the stairs, the cat's orange tail swishing behind him.

Lingering at the bottom for a moment, I was unsure if I should follow or not. Ultimately, I decided to use the time to catch up on some work in the dining room. I put in an order for a therapy cat and submitted it to the judge and the lawyers, then set to work typing up my notes on Leander's marked improvement since leaving Parkview.

I was thankful he was doing well, both for his sake as well as for the sake of my career. Disciplinary action against two staff members, while a sore point for the facility itself, at least had the added benefit of boosting my professional reputation and legitimizing my concerns for patient safety. The SA's office couldn't come back and claim bias after my concern turned out to be valid.

Leander found me in the dining room a short time later. He still had Annabel, wet and wrapped in a towel. Taking a seat in the chair across from me, he rubbed the dry edge of the towel on the cat's head gently while looking at the mess of paperwork. "Are there more tests today?"

"No. No more tests. I just need a bit more background for one of the assessments your lawyer asked for."

He nodded, looking down at the cat and drying methodically under her chin. "What sort of information? I feel there's nothing left to cover."

"I've read the police reports. I've read the witness statements. Everyone has had something to say about you and your family, but I haven't heard much from you directly. I think it's time we talked about your grandmo—"

Annabel leapt out of the towel and shook herself on the floor before trotting off, her tail held high.

Leander frowned and plucked at the damp spot on his shirt. "I need to change."

"Lean—"

He was gone.

Gritting my teeth, I pushed away from the table. Following him to the foyer, I stopped when he darted upstairs. I wasn't in the mood to play tag.

My nails tapped the newel post as I tried to guess how the rest of this session was going to go. It was as if he were afraid to be open for too long. A moment of vulnerability was followed by more evasiveness and deflection. I didn't know if he was afraid to let himself feel for any length of time, or if he was afraid of my reaction, despite my promise not to shun him.

Leander appeared at the top of the stairs a moment later in new clothes — still black. Wearing blue at Parkview must have been tortuous. I could only imagine what Camden County orange had been like.

He took his time descending the stairs, buttoning the shirt as he went. I cleared my throat and looked away.

"I'll be in the living room," I said as he hit the landing.

I took a seat in one of the wingback chairs, leaving him the couch or the other wingback. Smoothing my skirt over my knees, I waited for him to make his choice, curious to see which one he'd pick, how close he wanted to be to me.

He opted for the other chair — the closer of the two options. "Where shall we begin, Doctor?"

"From my understanding of the charges against you, the prosecution's case stems from your grandmother's murder ten years ago. So how do these three men factor in?"

He licked his lips and shrugged, his hands splayed. "I don't know how to answer that because anything I say looks incriminating."

"Try."

"When you have a family like mine, the list of enemies grows with each generation. If I were to hazard a guess as to who murdered those people, I could finger half the town. I'm the last in a legacy built by coercion and corruption. Any one of them would be happy to see me gone."

"Why? What does the town have to gain?"

"Their freedom."

I raised a brow at him. "How so?"

"The Welles Corporation has diverse interests. If it could be bought, it was. Real estate, businesses, endeavors. By the time my grandparents took over the company, it was as if everyone had entered a feudal state. Nothing happened without Albert and Irene's blessing and nothing happened without their permission. People began to chafe under the yoke. My father tried to get away from it and look how that turned out."

"That may explain your grandmother's murder, but what about you? Why didn't her murderer kill you and be done with all of you? If that's what they really want?"

Leander folded his arms across himself, his gaze lowering. He chewed on the corner of his mouth for a minute before blurting out the answer. "I wasn't in my room that night."

"Where were you?"

"In the cellar."

"The cellar?"

Shifting in his seat, he ran his palms over his knees. "As I got older, I found I could climb out of my room. Grandmother caught me. She always did. That's when she started locking me in the cellar, until I'd earned the 'privilege' of returning to my bedroom. Sometimes it could take days. Sometimes I lost count..."

I averted my gaze for a moment. Keep it together, Lorelei... "The police said the same murder weapon was used in all four killings. Do you know anything about it?"

"The conservatory was leaking and there were workmen there to repair it. The crowbar came from one of them. The police said I found it and used it one night in a fit of rage. The prosecution, on the other hand, said it was speculative and circumstantial and anyone who came into the house had access to it. When they found out a locksmith had to be called to the scene to let me out of the cellar, they dismissed the charges altogether."

"What happened to the crowbar? I assume they took it as evidence, so how could it have been used in three more killings?"

"When the mechanic was killed, they theorized it was an irate client or even someone passing through town — a crime of opportunity with the nearest available weapon. The police weren't concerned until the retired officer was murdered. Then, they discovered evidence from Grandmother's case was missing — misplaced, mislabeled, stolen, no one knew. The crowbar included. The attention came back to me shortly thereafter and I haven't been able to escape it since."

"Aren't you afraid the murderer might come back?"

He looked up, his jaw set. "Once the monster was dead, there was nothing left to fear. Nothing and no one. Besides, why would they murder me now when I am the perfect scapegoat for their schemes?"

"It's ok to be afraid sometimes. Everyone has fears. It's not a weakness. It's human — a natural response to the threat of danger, programmed into us over a millennia."

He tilted his head, considering me. "What are you afraid of, Doctor?"

Blinking, my brows furrowed. I supposed I walked right into that one. "I don't know. The usual things I guess. Snakes."

He smirked. "That's a phobia."

Damn it. Leave it to Leander to know the difference. "You tell me, since you're so perceptive."

"Failure."

Nodding, I motioned for him to continue. I wanted to see how clever he thought he was.

He leaned forward, his exquisite gaze fixed on mine. "Surrender."

The hair on the back of my neck stood up and my breath caught in my throat. "The last time we talked about surrender, we were talking about suicide. Are you having suicidal ideations again?"

He jumped to his feet. I stood just as swiftly, blocking his path. He moved in the other direction. I sidestepped with him, putting my hands up to help keep him from escaping. He could have easily shoved me away, but something about his mood this morning told me he wouldn't.

"Let me see your arms, Leander."

He scowled yet remained where he was.

I reached for his left wrist and touched it gently, hoping he didn't explode. He let me lift his arm and take out the silver cufflink, flinching only when I began pushing the sleeve out of my way. His chest rose and fell in quicker succession the higher the fabric went. There were no new marks on his arms, just dozens of old scars.

I repeated the process on his other arm, satisfied to find fewer scars than the first. None of them were fresh. Nevertheless, I didn't feel a sense of relief. "Are you cutting somewhere else? Somewhere you think I won't look?"

"Would you like me to undress for you?" His words were so soft that if they weren't being uttered near my ear, I might not have heard him.

"That's—" I cleared my throat, staring straight ahead at the smooth whiteness of his throat. It was safer than looking up at his mouth or his eyes. "That's not necessary."

"I didn't ask if it was necessary." His fingertips grazed the side of my hand, trailing down the length of my pinky. He toyed with the very edges of my fingers, sending a spasm of yearning through me. The memory of his body against mine came back, along with the butterflies dive-bombing my stomach.

"Leander…"

The front door opened and slammed again, bags rustling and heels clicking on the floor. Greta, back from her shopping trip. "Leander, I'm back! I got you that coffee you like."

I spun away from him as she came into the living room, a paper cup in one hand and a fistful of bags in the other. "Sorry, Doctor. I didn't realize you'd still be here."

Hoping she was too daft to notice what she'd interrupted, I waved her off with a smile. "It's ok. I was on my way out."

Smiling brightly, she handed the coffee to Leander. "I'll go set this stuff up."

171

And just like that, she was gone again, disappearing deeper into the house.

I didn't wait for Leander to say anything, if there was anything to say. What was there to say? My God, Lorelei. What were you thinking?

Retreating to the dining room, I stuffed my laptop inside my bag as fast as I could. There was a lump in my throat as I slung it over my shoulder and headed straight for the front door.

Leander was in the foyer, sipping his coffee. His sleeves were down again, the cufflinks back in place. Was I the only person he let actually see his scars? Elijah knew about them. Greta was intimate enough to know his coffee order, yet he wasted no time hiding them again.

Shaking my head, I chided myself at how ridiculous I was being. Who cared who he was comfortable around? Who cared who he cared about at all? I was his doctor and he was my patient and this — whatever *this* was — wasn't going to happen. It couldn't happen. He was beautiful and intelligent and mesmerizing and — and completely off limits. Full stop.

I opened the door, pausing in the threshold to glance over my shoulder. Leander watched me, one hand in his pocket, the other holding the white cup. He didn't seem the least bit frazzled about the interruption as he blew across the top of the steaming black liquid.

"I thought you drank tea?" I narrowed my eyes at the cup.

"I drink anything with caffeine."

"But you prefer coffee?"

His eyes crinkled. "Is there some psychological significance as to what beverage I prefer?"

"No. Just curious."

"Curiouser and curiouser." He hid a small smile behind another sip of the coffee.

"Goodbye, Alice." Rolling my eyes at him, I closed the

door. That was one novel I was familiar with. Lewis Carroll quotes were nothing new when you worked with the mentally ill — they just rarely came from patients themselves. At least Leander's sense of humor was re-emerging, even if it was dark and dry. In a way, I expected nothing less from him.

CHAPTER 22

The sound of my heels clacking over the linoleum echoed down the hallway as I hurried toward the conference room. I double checked my watch to see how late I was running.

Shit. Shit. Shit.

Tom's secretary emailed last week and asked to set up an appointment in reference to Leander's upcoming case. She didn't say what it was about. I assumed he was trying to call in a favor and get inside scoop on something Scheible wasn't willing to disclose. Fat chance, Tom.

Smoothing both my hair and my skirt, I opened the door, uttering my apologies. I stopped dead in my tracks when I saw who was sitting at the table.

Darren.

My heart stopped. I grabbed the back of a chair to steady myself. "What are you doing here?"

"Nice to see you too, Lorelei." He smiled his brilliant smile, perfect white teeth against tan skin.

"Where's Tom?"

"I'm taking over as the lead prosecutor," Darren replied

without even bothering to stand. Such a gentleman. Opening his briefcase, he pulled out a stack of files and dropped them on the table. A pointless intimidation tactic given the fact I had ten times the amount of information on Leander.

Still, it felt like a trap. I tried to see what Darren's angle was, since I knew he wouldn't reveal his hand willingly. My legs refused to move. "You didn't answer my question. Where's Tom?"

"Tom had to recuse himself — a family emergency came up." Darren shut his briefcase forcefully, as if the loud, swift click would stop me from asking more questions.

"What kind of family emergency?"

"Jesus, Lorelei, what does it matter?"

"Why are you being so defensive?" My hackles were up now. This was wrong. Darren shouldn't be here. Darren shouldn't have anything to do with Leander's case. As the State's Attorney Tom handled high-profile cases, not Darren. Tom was staunch and resolute, but he was also conservative and fair-minded. Darren was ruthless. There would be no leniency if he won a guilty verdict.

Darren pulled at the knot in his tie before smoothing it down. "Why can't you ever take anything at face value? Not everyone has a hidden agenda."

Rolling my eyes, I pulled out the chair I was holding and forced myself to sit. "Fine. Whatever you say. What can I do for you, Mr. Perkins?"

He cleared his throat and flipped open a file, leafing through the pages. "I'm looking for the forensic opinion. Scheible said you had it."

I smirked. He wasn't walking out of here with what he wanted and it gave me great pleasure to know it would rankle him the rest of the day. "There must have been a miscommunication. I don't have it yet."

"Why not?" He narrowed his eyes at me, like I was an uncooperative witness on the stand.

"Because it's not ready yet." I returned his glare. Maybe if he'd taken an actual interest in my work while we were together he'd know these assessments didn't happen overnight, especially not ones of the magnitude Scheible asked for. "The trial isn't supposed to happen for another two weeks anyway."

"I'd like time to review it."

"You mean you're having someone else review it. Who?"

"Why? Does that change the outcome?"

I tried not to glare at him again. "As I said, it's not ready yet. So who is your expert?"

"Lisa Goldblum."

I snorted. Of course he would use a hired gun like Lisa. She was an expert alright — at padding her bank account. She had no more sympathy for the mentally ill than she did for bugs she crushed under her shoe. It didn't change my opinion of Leander's mental state in the slightest, but I was already reformulating my approach to explaining it. It needed to be Lisa-proof now so she couldn't rip it apart on the stand.

"What?" Darren asked, eyeing me suspiciously.

I gave him a bland smile. "Nothing. It's just an interesting choice, is all."

"How long until that opinion is ready?"

"I'll do my best to get it to you by the end of the week. Is that all?"

He opened his briefcase and slipped the files back in. "That's all when it comes to this. Did you get the flowers?"

I got to my feet. "See you in court." I was a step away when his hand locked on my wrist, hauling me backward.

"Can we talk?" He almost looked remorseful. Almost.

"About what, Darren? It's over. Let's not drag it out."

"I don't get it, Lor. You didn't even try."

"I have work to do." I tried to pull out of his grip. He held on tighter.

"Is there someone else?" Of course. That could be the only explanation he'd come up with. He couldn't possibly imagine a scenario where he was not a prized catch — his ego wouldn't allow it. There had to be some external force keeping me from running back to him.

Still, I figured I'd throw him a bone. "If I didn't have time for you, what makes you think I had time for a lover on the side?"

"You make time for what's important."

Deep. Did he get that from a fortune cookie? "Goodbye Darren."

I didn't wait for a response. The moment I felt his grip slacken, I ripped my arm free and hurried out the door. It wasn't a lie — I did have work to do and since it was Tuesday I couldn't stay late. Unfortunately.

⁂

Halfway through editing my opinion for Leander's case, I was interrupted by a knock at the door.

Amanda came in with a stack of mail, giving me a cringey smile. "Sorry to bother you," she said, holding out a handful of envelopes.

"Thanks." In truth, I was somewhat grateful for the interruption. It gave me a valid excuse to take a break.

One envelope in particular caught my eye — plain white with no return address, simply addressed to Lorelei Clayton.

I sliced it open.

I know what you're doing. You won't get away with it.

Without a second thought, I tossed the letter into the trash.

Back to work I went, until my cell phone buzzed violently, reminding me of my standing dinner reservation.

◦◦◦

The restaurant was busier than usual for the middle of the week. I came armed with a list of topics to keep the conversation going in a safe, steady direction. Somehow Darren snaked his way into my thoughts and before I knew it, he was the star of our conversation as well.

"You'll never guess who the prosecutor is on the case I'm testifying in," I said, skewering a piece of asparagus.

"Darren," Mom replied blithely.

I set my fork down a little harder than I intended. "Of course you already know."

"It was the talk of the courthouse. Not Darren, Tom." Mom waved off my irritated look and took a sip of her wine.

"What's going on? Why did he recuse himself from such a high-profile case?"

Mom shrugged. "No idea. He met with Phil this morning and said he needed to take a leave of absence. I heard later in the day his secretary called Marcie and told her to pack up the kids and he'd pick them up. So, of course, Sheila had to drive over to their house to stick her nose in and she said they're gone. Even the dog."

"That is so strange. Maybe their parents are sick?"

"Tom's are dead and Marcie's are already in assisted-living. Besides, even if they were sick, Marcie's parents aren't that far away. There's no need to pack up everything, including your dog." She shook her head, cutting her chicken into smaller pieces. "I hope whatever it is, it's worth it. His career will never recover from a stunt like this." Leave it to Mom to be more worried about his career than his actual well-being.

"Unless, of course, the defendant wins." I pushed a piece of my own chicken around the plate, making patterns in the sauce. "Then the blemish is on Darren's record and not Tom's."

Mom gave a lofty snort. "Tom would have never taken the case if he didn't think he could win."

I shrugged, chewing the chicken glumly. Everyone was convinced of Leander's guilt and he wasn't even on trial yet. What happened to innocent until proven guilty? Had the rules been changed and someone forgot to send me a law update? I glanced at my mother, instantly regretting it. She'd put her utensils down and was staring at me intently. "What? What are you looking at?"

"Don't 'what' me, Lorelei. What are you not telling me?"

"Nothing." I sipped my water, trying to appear as nonchalant as possible.

"You're not a very convincing liar, dear. Maybe to those lunatics you coddle but not to me."

"Patients, Mom, they're called patients."

She made a face and waved me off again. "Yes, of course. Patients. Now are you going to sit here and try to tell me you're not getting a bit too attached to this murderer?"

"What?" I gaped at her, hoping none of the nearby tables were eavesdropping. People tended to zero in on the word "murderer" and I didn't want anyone listening to whatever lecture was on its way. Not to mention the blatant HIPPA violation. I never told her Leander was my patient. I didn't have to — the gossip mongers at the courthouse did it for me.

"You think he has a chance of winning. You've declined other cases — paying cases — to focus solely on this one. You even went to his house, for God's sake. If that's not attached, then I don't know what is."

"I have to do an opinion! How else am I supposed to form an opinion without getting a full understanding of his background?" I couldn't believe I had to explain this to her again. She knew what my job consisted of, more than Darren did, and yet she seemed continually baffled by the investigative aspect of a forensic opinion.

"He's a murderer, Lorelei." She stabbed the table cloth with the tip of a perfectly polished finger, as if that settled it.

My blood boiled. As a judge, you'd think she would know better. "Alleged, Mother. Charges don't automatically mean a conviction."

She let out a sharp breath, shaking her head. "Even if he isn't, there is your career to think about."

"What about my career?"

"If anyone even so much as whispers that you have been inappropriate with a patient, you'll lose your license like that." She snapped her fingers right under my nose. "Then what? All that schooling down the drain. All those years wasted. For nothing."

I rubbed my temples, willing away the sudden ache. "I am not dignifying this conversation any longer. We're done talking about Leander."

She plowed on anyway. "You see? That's what I'm talking about. I'm not blind, dear. I've seen the newspapers. He's exceptionally handsome and he must be charming to make you so foolish that you would lose focus like this. But don't you forget for one second how you met. Forget the murder charges. He tried to kill himself." She practically choked out the last few words.

Squeezing my eyes shut, I cringed, beseeching her silently to stop talking. I didn't want to hear it. I knew where it was going and it wasn't anywhere good.

She leaned in, lowering her voice. "Is that what you want? To throw away everything for a man only to come home one day and find his blood all over the house? To find out, after everything he's said and done, that he'd rather die than be with you a minute longer? That it was all a lie? That you meant absolutely nothing?"

Jumping to my feet, I threw my napkin on the plate. "Enough!"

Now everyone was definitely listening to our conversation. Wrong move, Lorelei…

I grabbed my purse and hurried for the door, hoping I made it outside before the tears broke free.

Leander wasn't Dad. He wouldn't do that.

Wouldn't do that? What was I saying? Leander was my patient. Nothing more. Why couldn't she see that? I wanted what was best for my patients. I wanted what was best for *all* of my patients.

If she wanted to vilify me for humanizing my patients, for caring about them when no one else did, then fine. But I would not let her heap blame onto Leander for something he didn't do. And I wouldn't let her shame me for something I didn't do.

CHAPTER 23

*L*eander was reading in the backyard when I arrived. Greta pointed him out from the kitchen window, lounging beneath a tree. As I got closer, I saw his cat was with him, curled up on the end of the blanket, basking in a patch of sunlight.

He looked up as I approached, shading his eyes with his free hand. "Doctor." He patted the blanket next to him, in the shade.

I debated for a moment. Standing was more professional, but far more likely to put him on edge. On the other hand, sitting would be more comfortable. But after my regretful conversation with my mother, I didn't want to prove anyone right. I looked around the property, making sure there weren't any investigators hidden in the trees with cameras.

Finally, I sat, as far away from him as I could while still being on the blanket. "What are you reading?"

"*Le Comte de Monte-Cristo*." Dog-earring the page, he handed it to me, as if I didn't believe him.

Taking the book, I flipped it over, trying to read the blurb on the back. It was in French, which meant my Spanish did practically nothing to assist me. Dredging up a memory from AP English, I vaguely recalled it was about revenge. I handed it back to him with a small smile. "Impressive."

Setting the book to the side, he drew up one knee, resting his arm across it. In that position, he was angled toward me, his eyebrows lifted slightly. "Is everything alright? I didn't expect you until this afternoon."

The feeling of his hand around my throat jumped to the forefront of my memory and I dismissed any thought of lying. "No, Leander, everything is not alright. Have you talked to Mr. Scheible?"

"About?"

"About the prosecutor?"

He shook his head.

I paced my words as evenly as I could, trying to remain calm and detached from the situation. "Tom Martin, the State's Attorney, recused himself the day before yesterday."

"And why should that concern me?"

"His replacement — Darren Perkins — is going to make your life hell."

The corner of Leander's mouth lifted into a smile. "I'm afraid he's a bit late for that."

"This isn't a joke." I found a hard bit of skin on my thumb and scraped at it with another nail, trying to figure out how I was going to get him to see the reason for my concern. He didn't know Darren like I did. He didn't know how badly things could go. "I'm worried about you. I'm worried *for* you."

"Your concern is touching, but wholly unnecessary."

I stared at him, trying to make sense of his composure. "I don't get it. When I first met you, you were... scared. You were desperate for someone to listen. You said this was all a mistake. And now you're just… completely fine? So were you lying then or are you lying now?"

He smirked, his eyes narrowing. It was hard to tell if it was at me directly, or against the sunlight. "Unfortunately, dear Doctor, I am not at liberty to discuss my legal strategy. But Richard assures me all is in hand."

"So where was this strategy when you were first arrested? When you were arraigned? When you were bleeding out in a cell in jail?"

He frowned at me. "You're quite agitated today. Perhaps we should talk tomorrow when you're not so upset."

I could have screamed. I could have throttled him. I could have done a dozen things to show him how agitated I was. Instead, I sat there, glowering and digging my nail into the side of my thumb until a spark of pain shot down my finger.

Picking up his book again, he flipped it open to where he'd left off. Licking the tip of his index finger, he turned the page, the absolute picture of ease on a beautiful spring day.

Irritation swelled inside of me. Without thinking, I snatched the book out of his hand. "No, we're talking today. I have let it go in the past, Leander, because I didn't want to push. But not today."

He swiveled to the side and shot forward on his hands and knees, reaching for the book.

I held it backward, as far away from him as I could — a completely professional and adult move. I had questions that needed answers, damn it. He wasn't going to weasel his way out of yet another serious conversation. And he certainly wasn't going to use *my* bad mood as his excuse.

"Lorelei…" He canted his head to the side, giving me a stern look.

I arched a brow at him and tipped my chin up.

He made another swipe for the book. I jerked back a second before he crashed into me. We fell backward, an unattractive "oomph" escaping me along with the air in my lungs. The book flew into the grass, well beyond either of our reach.

Leander braced his weight on his forearms, his face hovering over mine. His green eyes were practically glowing. I'd never seen anything more beautiful. I completely forgot why I was angry with him. I forgot everything except the way he was looking at me, the way he felt on top of me.

Patient! My mother's voice screamed inside my head. Squeezing my eyes shut, I turned my face away, trying to get a grip on myself. He was a patient and this crossed the line, the line I swore never to cross. The line I *couldn't* cross.

Before I could work up the nerve to shove him away, something skimmed across my lower lip. A tingling sensation rippled through me, unbidden but not entirely unwelcome.

I opened my eyes and my mouth so the tip of his finger slipped in. He inhaled a sharp breath, his hips pressing against mine as my tongue swirled around his finger.

His other hand tangled in my hair, knotting at the nape of my neck. When I closed my lips around his finger and pulled it in deeper with my tongue, he twisted my hair until I gasped. Once his finger free again, trailing its way down my throat and across my collarbone, he let go of my hair.

"What I wouldn't give," he whispered, "for one night…"

"It won't always be like this." What was I saying? Doctor. Patient. Line! Had I completely lost my mind?

The more my head screamed in horror, the more my body buzzed with anticipation. I couldn't control it anymore than I could control lightning.

"I'm sorry, Lorelei." Before I could comprehend what he was doing, Leander was on his feet, retrieving the book.

He held a hand out and helped me to my feet, ever the gentleman. My head was relieved, meanwhile my treacherous nervous system kept firing on all cylinders, aching to feel him again. It was a small comfort when he didn't let go, even after I was vertical.

"Help me understand," I said, holding his hand with both of mine. I tried to get him to meet my gaze, but he refused. I couldn't have been that far off base, could I? He touched me first. He wanted this, just as much as I did.

"I can't." He tried to pull his hand away. I held on tightly. He couldn't walk away. Not this time, not like this, not after that.

"Try. Quote something. Anything. What was that poem about Psyche and the star?" Leander's marginalia flashed in my mind. I tried to recall exactly what he wrote — something about the power sexuality had over reason? Or was it how love was the ultimate human delusion? Ok, maybe that wasn't the best example...

Leander succeeded in yanking free of my grasp. Whipping the book at the blanket, he raked his hands through his hair, stalking a few feet away before turning again. The same desperate look as the first time I met him was etched onto the perfect angles of his face. "I don't want to hurt you!"

"You won't!" I took a tentative step toward him.

"You don't know that!" He moved backward, folding his arms across his chest.

"Yes, I do."

"You have to believe people are good at the core. It's your nature. Believe me when I tell you there is nothing good inside of me. There may have been at one time, but it died a long time ago. Anything you think you see is only a fabrication of your mind, a hope that should never see the light of day."

"Don't push me away, Leander. Let me help you."

"Stop trying to fix me!" His rage was swift and sudden. When he unfolded his arms, his hands clenched into fists.

Even from a distance, his words practically reverberated through me. Gritting his teeth, he looked away, his chest rising and falling rapidly.

He took two steps toward the house and retraced them again, shaking the hair out of his eyes. His face softened as he folded his arms over his chest once more, his voice lowering. "I'm terribly sorry if I gave you the impression I could be mended. I can't. I am too fractured to ever be made whole and it is a waste of your time to keep trying. I'm sorry Richard brought you into this mess."

"You're not a vase I'm trying to glue back together!" I closed the distance on him before he could run away. He turned, but I seized his face in both hands. It was a risk, one I hoped I calculated correctly. "Look at me! We all have a darkness inside of us. It's part of being human. It's ugly and it's scary and no one wants to see that side of themselves, let alone have anyone else see it. It's too raw and fragile. I get it, you don't want to trust anyone with that side of you. Just like your scars."

My hands dropped to his left wrist, pushing the sleeve back. Without thinking, I pressed my lips to the white ribbons criss crossing his skin. His arm tensed under my hand, but he didn't pull away.

"I see you, Leander, and I'm not scared. I'm not looking away. I'll never look away." I touched his cheek gently.

He expelled a breath and a rush of tears in the same moment. Shifting from side to side, his green eyes were wild as they darted about, looking for his next path of escape.

"You don't scare me," I whispered, leaning up until our foreheads touched. Snaking one arm around his neck, I slipped the other around his waist and pulled him closer, slowly. I was prepared to be hit. I was prepared to be shoved away. It was worth it — he needed to know he was redeemable. He needed to know he was lovable, no strings attached.

He crumpled against me, burying his face in the side of my neck. Had it not been for the tears dripping onto my bare skin, I would never have known he was crying.

Stroking his hair, the dark curls slipped through my fingers like silk. I could have stayed like that forever, pressed against him, feeling his hair. The voice in my head was completely drowned out by the thrumming in my blood, relishing the seconds until reality set in.

When it did, it was hard and swift, like a kick to the abdomen. It came in the form of someone clearing their throat behind us — a male someone.

We pulled apart, both turning toward the sound.

It was Darren, clutching his briefcase, with Scheible in tow.

"Are we, uh, interrupting?" Darren asked, though his mouth barely moved.

"Of course not." Pulling my spine straighter, I lifted my chin. "What are you doing here?"

"I could ask you the same thing but I think it's obvious," Darren sneered.

"You mean counseling a patient? Yeah. Pretty obvious." I mirrored his expression and his tone.

"Why don't we move this inside, hmm?" Scheible asked, glancing between Darren and I.

"Let's." I glared at Darren, waiting for him to leave first.

Scheible clicked his tongue and spun on his heel. Darren stalled for a moment, shaking his head before following.

"Doctor," Leander murmured, gesturing me forward.

I ran my hands down the front of my dress and pushed my shoulders back.

By the time we entered the house, Greta was setting

glasses of water on the dining room table. Darren sat on one side, Scheible on the other.

"Are we ready to begin?" Scheible asked.

Darren took a sip of the water, steadfastly ignoring me, and I him.

"Mr. Scheible, I'd like to talk to you whenever you're done. I'll be in the kitchen," I said. Better to get in front of this disaster than wait for whatever punishment Darren would trot out during the trial. Knowing him, he'd sink his entire case if it meant publicly humiliating me for rejecting him.

Scheible nodded, unzipping his padfolio and retrieving a pen.

Leander slumped into a chair next to Scheible, holding his forehead. Was he getting another migraine?

Closing the french doors behind me, I met Greta in the kitchen. She was in the middle of preparing a charcuterie board, artfully arranging a variety of colors and textures.

"Are you serving wine too?" I asked, only half kidding. I could use a bottle right about now. Or two.

She shook her head. "No. Leander isn't allowed to have any alcohol." Duh. I was the one who wrote his treatment plan.

"Are you staying here? With him?"

She shook her head again, but the blush in her cheeks was obvious. "No. Of course not. Mr. Scheible just asked me to check in on him, run errands, that sort of thing. Helps to have a friendly face from home."

I stole a grape and popped it into my mouth, using it as an excuse not to comment. Once I swallowed it, I gestured to the board, thankful for a segue to something other than Greta's sleeping arrangement or the fact she journeyed all the way from St. Louis to assist with this case. "Have you seen him eat recently?"

"Oh yeah. We had pizza last night."

"That's good." Pizza was so... mundane. So, normal. I couldn't picture him cozied up with Greta on the couch eating pizza, even if the "we" part of her reply replayed in my head over and over.

We stood in silence for another few moments, Greta arranging and rearranging the bits of food and me watching her fuss. I wondered what Olivia would have to say about another woman moving in on her boss, providing these little comforts for him. Not that I could picture Olivia making prosciutto rosettes.

When footsteps approached, we both looked up. My stomach knotted and not in a pleasant way.

It was Darren.

"Do you need something Mr. Perkins?" Greta asked cordially.

"Can you make a couple copies of this?" He held out a piece of paper to her, but his gaze was on me.

"Of course." She took it and disappeared, trotting up the stairs.

Once she was gone, Darren advanced on me. "What the hell was that? Huh? Is he the reason you broke up with me?"

"Oh my God. You are clueless, you know that?" I pushed past him. His hand seized my bicep, yanking me back in front of him.

"Are you fucking him?"

"Get your hands off of me!"

"Answer the question, Lorelei."

"You're hurting me."

He let go and raised both hands, palms open, as if he realized the seriousness of the line he was crossing. "You just make me so crazy, Lor," Darren said, as if that constituted an apology. Should I be flattered?

"That's a 'you' problem. Might want to work on that with someone."

"If you won't tell me on a personal level, then answer me professionally. Are you or are you not sleeping with him?"

I glared at him, personally and professionally. "Stop being ridiculous. Of course I'm not sleeping with him. He's my patient. And for your information, we were broken up before he became my patient, not that it's any of your goddamn business. Our lack of a sex life wasn't because I was stepping out on you, Darren, it was because every time you opened your mouth it made my skin crawl."

Grabbing my arm again, rage flashed in his blue eyes. He jerked me up against his chest, like he intended to prove me wrong right then and there. "I could report you for what I saw. Get your testimony excluded. File a complaint with the board. Even look at a malpractice suit. I could end you, Lorelei."

Narrowing my eyes at him, I drew myself up as much as I could. I was neither intimidated nor impressed by him. I never was. "Do it. I dare you. I'll turn around and have my new friend Mr. Scheible hit you with a slander suit so fast it'll make your head spin. That's if I decide not to pursue domestic battery charges against you. I think I'm in fear for my life right now. Maybe an order of protection is also warranted. What do you say, Assistant State's Attorney?"

Darren smirked and unwrapped his fingers, one by one. I doubted any female had ever talked to him like that in his life. "You fucking bitch."

I wanted to wipe that haughty look off his face. I wanted to deck him or at least knee him in the balls, but I knew better, especially with Greta prancing back into the room with the stack of copies.

Ripping them out of her hand without a word, Darren stalked back to the dining room.

"What'd I miss?" she whispered, making a face at Darren's back.

I was about to answer with a dismissive "Nothing" when Leander appeared in the doorway. Instead, I cleared my throat and shook my head at her, hoping she wasn't stupid enough to bring it up again in front of him.

"I hope you're hungry!" Greta chirped, grabbing her charcuterie masterpiece and holding it up for Leander as he approached, like a puppy waiting for a pat on the head.

"Leave," Leander said without ever taking his gaze off of me. If it wasn't for the way he angled his head toward Greta, I might have thought he was talking to me.

Frowning, she set the board down and shook her hair over her shoulder. A part of me felt bad for her as she slunk out of the room. A small part. The rest of me felt a warm smugness. Or maybe it was residual anger at Darren.

Leander's jaw clenched again, his lips pressed into a disapproving line. I was acquainted enough with his facial expressions to know an outburst was imminent. The question was, why? I'm guessing his conversation with the lawyers didn't go the way he wanted.

He stopped in front of me, his gaze drifting downward. I didn't know what he was looking at until his fingers grazed my bicep, the same spot Darren left reddened.

"Think carefully before you answer me," Leander said, his voice a level above a whisper as he dragged his eyes up to meet mine. "Did he do that?"

A shiver raced down my spine at the icy calmness of his tone. Dumbstruck, I nodded. There was something dangerous behind his eyes. They were practically glowing again, reigniting the lightning in my blood.

"Good girl." Leander folded one arm over his abdomen and propped the other on top of it, covering his mouth in a pensive posture. He took one step backward and turned, disappearing back into the dining room.

Afraid my legs might give way, I gripped the countertop to keep myself upright. I couldn't shake the feeling something terrible was going to happen to Darren as a result of my answer. Another shiver rippled through me, not out of fear for him, but a deviant sense of exhilaration.

CHAPTER 24

$\mathcal{T}$uesday night, same dinner time, same dinner table. It was so routine at this point, I could go through the entire meal on autopilot. I virtually was when Mom dropped a bombshell on me.

"Did you hear what happened to Darren?" she asked, twirling a strand of pasta around her fork methodically.

"No and I don't care." I thought I'd made it clear by now we were through, but apparently she was holding out hope for some sort of reconciliation. Maybe I should tell her I was seeing someone so she'd lay off for a while.

She wasn't listening since she continued talking, all in one breath. "Someone attacked him the other day. They broke his hand, Lorelei. He just got released from the hospital. I can't believe you didn't hear. It was on the front page of the newspaper this morning."

My fork clattered against the plate, my eyes wide. Leander's question from the previous week returned to the forefront of my mind, making my heart skip a beat. "What?"

"He had to have surgery on it. Apparently he needed all sorts of pins and things to reconstruct it. It's his dominant hand too. The poor man. Can you imagine? He's out of work for weeks now. The junior attorneys are going crazy. First Tom, now Darren. They're all getting quite paranoid about the whole situation. They're considering bringing in a special prosecutor to help with the caseload until this whole thing sorts itself out."

"Oh my God... What happened? Exactly?"

She appeared delighted I had finally taken an interest in her gossip. "I know! It's shocking. They smashed his hand right in his own car door. If it wasn't for the fact someone heard him screaming, there's no telling how long he would have been stuck like that. Well, the police are investigating but who knows. When you work for the State's Attorney's office you deal with so many criminals I guess it's hard to predict who is going to snap. Or when. Remember when we got all of those threats when you were little? You didn't leave the house for a month."

I wiped my mouth with my napkin. "I have to go." I had to see Leander. I had to know for certain.

Mom frowned at me. "What? You haven't even finished."

"I'll see you next week." I pecked her cheek and threw my bag over my shoulder, hurrying for the door.

⁂

The drive from the restaurant to Leander's was relatively short, but the seconds dragged by until the massive brick facade came into view.

I was breathless by the time I ran up the front steps and rang the doorbell. The possibility of my complicity in Darren's attack wasn't lost on me. My insides knotted together, a tangle of emotions I didn't want to sort through at the moment. What I wanted was to see Leander.

When the door didn't open immediately, I pushed the

doorbell again. Where was he? I would even take Greta at that point.

At last, the handle turned. Leander himself opened the door. He was dressed, but his button-up shirt was undone at the top, exposing his smooth chest. His hair was disheveled, his curls even wilder than usual. He rubbed the sleep from one eye while squinting at me with the other.

"What's wrong?" he asked, leaning against the door. "What time is it?"

Stepping past him into the foyer, I tried to shake the tingling out of my hands while also trying to figure out how to phrase my jumbled thoughts in a way that didn't make me sound absolutely crazy, or self-centered, or anything other than concerned. I kept coming up blank.

"Where were you yesterday?" I asked, turning to face him.

A yawn delayed his answer. His next move was to look at his watch, furrowing his brows. "Is it eight am or pm?"

I crossed my arms over my chest, one hip jutting to the side while I waited for his brain to start firing all of its synapses. I wasn't used to slow responses from him. Coy, yes. Cryptic, yes. Even silence. But not this stunned, sleepy version of him.

He raked a hand through his hair and cleared his throat. "Yesterday? Yesterday I was in a meeting most of the day. Why do you ask?"

"Here?"

"What?"

"The meeting. Was the meeting here?"

"No. Richard's office. Why? What is going on?"

"Someone attacked Darren."

"Who?"

I refrained from growling. He must have been dead asleep to be so damn fuzzy. "Darren Perkins. The ASA who took over your case."

Leander rubbed his hands over his face vigorously and looked at me again, his eyes a bit clearer. "I don't follow."

"This is the second prosecutor to be taken off of your case, Leander. If you had anything to do with it you're expediting your way to prison. Especially if they bring in a special prosecutor to oversee your trial. They're not going to let some junior lawyer, fresh out of law school, try your case. They'll bring in a professional, even if it eats up the rest of their budget."

Furrowing his brows, he nodded every once in a while, apparently trying to process what I was saying. "To be clear, you think I absconded from a meeting with my lawyer to attack another lawyer in view of the courthouse and the numerous security cameras they have in place? All while having my every move tracked by an ankle bracelet with GPS monitoring?"

"I don't know. That's what I'm asking."

"What, exactly, are you asking?"

"Did you break Darren's hand?"

"Of course not."

"Then how did you know he was attacked at the courthouse?" I made sure to keep my voice and my expression as neutral as possible. I didn't want him to think I wasn't on his side. I was. I just needed the truth. I needed to know if it was him, and if it was, why.

The sleepy haze was gone from his eyes, replaced by confusion. Or was it sadness? It was hard to tell when they were so dark, even with a glittering chandelier hanging overhead. "Do you still have feelings for him?"

I almost laughed, except I could sense how serious he was. "No, of course not."

"Then why do you care what happens to him?"

"I don't care about him." My true meaning hung in the air. Hopefully he'd pick up on it, especially after last week.

Leander closed the distance between us, fixing me with a predatory look. He tipped my chin up with one finger, bedroom eyes aglow once again. "Do you believe in karma?"

"No. I suppose you do?"

A slow, dark smile curved his lips. "I believe in retribution."

My stomach fluttered. It was the closest thing to a confession I knew I would ever get. He might not have done it personally, for all the reasons he said, but he sure as hell had something to do with it. I decided to press the point and see what it would yield.

"Was that why those people in Easton had to die?"

That chilling smile never faltered. He didn't even blink. "We'll all die one day. That's what we're born to do." His fingers encircled my throat. Without applying any extra pressure, he walked me backward until I was pressed against the wall, reminiscent of the first time he did it. "You could die, right here, right now, if I wanted you to. And who's to say it's not fate?"

My pulse quickened beneath his hand and my breath came in short bursts. He was bluffing, trying to throw me off the path I was on without outright lying about it — the one thing that seemed to be at the center of his moral compass.

"You won't kill me," I said with complete confidence.

His fingers tightened, eliciting a gasp from me. Still, my faith in him didn't waver.

"How can you be so sure?" His gaze fell to my mouth.

It was time to call his bluff. Pressing my hand against the front of his pants, I bit my lower lip. He sucked in a surprised breath through his teeth, lust blazing in his eyes. A sense of power rippled through me; I wanted to pull more sounds out of him — gasps and groans and my name. The line of professionalism was completely gone, obliterated into nothingness. More shocking than my boldness was the fact I didn't care.

My chin dipped demurely before I looked up at him through the fringe of my lashes. "I just know."

His hand shot up, abandoning my throat to capture my jaw. Forcing my head back, he held my gaze with an intensity unlike anything I'd seen before. "You're playing a very dangerous game, Doctor."

"Are you worried you'll lose?"

"I never lose."

"Then kiss me."

His mouth crashed into mine, hungry and demanding. My fingers dug into his hips, pulling him as close as I could while his hands tangled in my hair. I wanted to feel every inch of him, to strip away everything that stood between us.

"Fuck." He groaned against my throat, dragging his teeth over my skin. "I need you. Now."

All of a sudden he pushed away, leaving my head spinning and a rush of cold air in his absence. His hand locked on my wrist, pulling me up the stairs as quickly as my heels could carry me.

Once we were on level ground again, he grabbed my face between his hands and kissed me, harder than before. Twisting and stumbling, we slid over walls and each other until we found the master bedroom. We broke free, panting for air and tearing at each other's clothing.

"I'm not gentle," he said as I kissed his jawline feverishly.

"Good." I grabbed handfuls of his shirt and ripped it open, sending a spray of black buttons to the floor.

A feral smile crossed his face as he lunged for me, toppling both of us onto the center of the bed.

CHAPTER 25

*O*f course he hadn't been lying. He was not gentle. Time seemed to stop, replaced by a series of pants and gasps and sordid exclamations. By the time the morning light crept into the bedroom, every inch of me was sore and my legs were like jelly, but I felt rejuvenated. The same dark sense of exhilaration I felt when Leander decided Darren's comeuppance flooded every cell.

Rolling onto my side, I propped myself on an elbow, watching Leander sleep. In the pale yellow light, he looked like an angel. It was a complete contrast to the insatiable devil he was the night before.

As if sensing he was being scrutinized, Leander inhaled and stretched languidly before opening his beautiful chartreuse eyes. He reached for me and pulled me closer by my hips until we were tangled together again.

"Good morning," I murmured, tracing idle patterns on his chest.

He groaned in response, nuzzling my hair.

The doorbell rang, shattering our blissful moment.

I bolted upright, the shamelessness of the night before evaporating with the sharp slap of reality. "Who is that?"

Leander sighed and rolled out of bed, retrieving his pants from somewhere on the floor. "Stay here." He swiped his shirt off the lamp and padded out, closing the bedroom door behind him.

Scrambling out of bed, I started the scavenger hunt for my own clothing. The top button on my skirt was missing and I vaguely remembered hearing my silk blouse rip when he yanked it over my head.

Swearing under my breath, I shimmied into my skirt and hurried over to the dresser. Unsurprisingly, each drawer revealed piles of black fabric. I found a lightweight sweater that looked promising and pulled it on, leaving it untucked to hide the top of my skirt. Please, God, let the zipper be strong enough to keep everything in place for the walk of shame out to my car.

As decent as I was going to get, I crept toward the bedroom door and cracked it open. Voices from the foyer echoed up the high stairwell.

It was Scheible. Shit. No doubt Greta wasn't far behind, probably with a stack of Belgian waffles and homemade jam for Leander. I suppressed a groan. The last thing I wanted was to deal with her chipperness first thing in the morning, or explain what I was doing there so early.

"I'll get it taken care of," Scheible said down below. "I'm going to the courthouse as soon as I leave here."

"How much longer?" Leander asked.

"Tomorrow at the earliest, I'm hoping."

"You're hoping? What was it Shelley said about hope? 'Worse than despair, worse than the bitterness of death.'"

"I know. Ok? It could be longer. It all depen—"

Something loud echoed up the stairs. I heard Leander's voice, but it was too quiet to make out what he was saying.

Scheible cleared his throat. "Greta will be here soon. I'll let you know when it's done."

"Good."

Heavy footsteps crossed the foyer and the door opened.

"Oh, and get rid of the doctor, hmm? She's turned into a liability," Scheible said before the door slammed shut.

Covering my mouth with my hand, I backed away from the door, a sudden dread replacing the euphoria that had been there only a moment ago. My confidence from last night was also gone, especially since Leander didn't challenge his lawyer's final instruction.

I was a liability? And how, exactly, was Leander supposed to get rid of me? I didn't know, nor did I want to find out.

I looked around for another exit. There wasn't one. The windows were too far off the ground. There weren't any phones in the house to speak of and my cell phone was still in my purse. In the car. Outside. Twenty feet below the window I couldn't climb out.

Leander appeared in the doorway before I could figure out my next move. There was murder in his eyes, the same dark gleam I saw when he asked about Darren grabbing me. But then he blinked and it was gone, his brows drawing together. "What are you doing?"

"What?" I backed away from the window as nonchalantly as I could.

He came closer, biting his lip before speaking. "Lorelei..."

I danced out of his reach, scooping up one of my heels and clutching it to my chest. "I have to go."

"What? Why?"

He reached for me, but I ducked beneath his arm under the pretense of searching for the other shoe. I found it in the corner by the bathroom, which put me further from the bedroom door and my only route of escape.

"Lorelei." He closed the distance until I was backed into

the wall again, all without ever touching me. Now I knew what Olivia meant when she said he commanded a room just with his presence. It was his eyes — they had the power to bend people to his will.

"I don't know what you and Scheible were talking about, but I'm gone. Ok? I'm leaving." Last night, I wasn't lying when I asserted he wouldn't kill me. But in the morning light, with his lawyer calling me a liability, I wasn't so sure. And I certainly couldn't trust my own judgement after everything I'd done.

"I don't want you to go." He looked wounded, his eyes soft and imploring once again.

"I can't stay." I edged around him slowly, watching for any sign he was about to snap.

He stayed where he was, folding his arms over his chest. Swallowing thickly, his gaze followed my every move, further and further away from him.

Once I was well out of arm's reach, I bolted for the stairs, in case this was all part of a game of cat and mouse. I yanked open the front door and crashed into something warm and solid.

We both screamed.

It took me a moment to realize it was Greta, coffee dripping down the front of her shirt.

We blurted our apologies to each other as I squeezed past her in the doorway, ignoring her question about why I was there with more apologies about her outfit.

Climbing into my car, I sped away as fast as possible before Leander could pull me back into his web.

CHAPTER 26

The days crept by in the wake of my tryst with Leander. I kept myself busy at Parkview, focusing on the work I'd been neglecting by spending so much time on his case. It was never ending, a sad testament to the state of mental health in America.

Case in point: another letter from my most recent "admirer" arrived, same as before. Except this time it was far angrier.

You WHORE!
You're going to regret this! You're going to regret everything!
I know everything you FUCKING SLUT!

Darren was the first person who sprang to mind. While I didn't picture him as the anonymous-note type, he was the only one I had pissed off recently. Other than Ray. But the last I heard, he was on his way to DOC in the southern part of the state for a twenty-five-year sentence. Oh, and Russ. And Nora… I guess I had been on a roll lately.

Dennis stopped in my doorway and knocked, a stack of files tucked under his arm.

I slid a pad of paper over the top of the note, shielding the giant, irate letters from him. "Shouldn't you be at St. Mary's?" I asked, stealing a glance at my watch.

"Headed there now. You got a sec?"

"For you, Sensei, always." I eyed the folders, instantly regretting not telling him "No." There was only one reason to cart around patient files outside of your office.

"Can you take a look at these?" He set the pile on the only free space he could find in the corner of my desk. "Just want to get a second opinion."

"Of course. Is there a deadline?"

"Not really. So, whenever you have time."

"I have to finish my article for the *AJP* first, but I'll get to them as soon as I can."

He smiled and pointed finger-guns at me. "You're the best."

"Uh huh." I waited until he left before slumping in my chair. At this rate, I was going to have to work through the weekend too. I didn't mind being busy, but the pounding in my skull was not an ideal work companion.

My cell phone buzzed on the desk. It wasn't a number from my contacts, but that didn't mean anything. I got random calls all the time, usually seeking an assessment or a second opinion. Unfortunately for them, Dennis just siphoned off what little generosity I had left. I answered anyway, shuffling the stack of files around on my desk, trying to create some semblance of order while also looking for that notepad I just had.

"Hello Doctor."

Leander's voice hit me like a slap in the face. Two little

words were all it took to resurrect the buzzing in my veins.

Shooting out of the chair, I slammed the door to my office and locked it just in case. I was grateful he was calling my cell and not my desk phone, but I didn't trust anyone not to eavesdrop. Especially Nora, freshly back from her suspension.

"What are you doing?" I asked, pressing the phone closer to my ear.

"I had to talk to you."

"You're not supposed to have a phone. You're violating the court order."

"I don't care." He swallowed hard enough I could hear it on the other end of the line.

Sighing, I closed my eyes. I didn't want to admit to myself, let alone to him, how much I missed his voice — how much I missed *him*. These self-imposed exiles I tried implementing did more to stoke the fire than to extinguish it, even if I'd had the most ridiculous thoughts the last time I saw him.

"Lorelei..." His breathing was ragged.

The skin prickled on the back of my neck and I strained to listen to the background for any clues as to what he was up to. There was a rushing noise. The room sounded cavernous, but I didn't hear any other voices. Was he in a bathroom? Somewhere in the courthouse? "Leander, where are you?"

He sniffed and exhaled sharply, like he was working up the courage to say — or do — something. "It doesn't matter. I'll be gone soon enough and you'll be free of me."

"What are you talking about?" I hoped he wasn't saying what I thought he was. I didn't want my mother to be right. I didn't want my worst fear to come true.

Silence.

Grabbing my keys and hurrying out the door, I tried to

keep myself from panicking. Tried and failed. Even I could hear my voice turn shrill despite my attempt to sound casual, as if we were having any other conversation. "Leander? Where are you going?"

"Why did you leave, Lorelei?"

"What?"

"On Wednesday. Why did you leave?"

"I don't think we should be having this conversation right now. Not like this. Just tell me where you are. I'll come to you. We can talk in person."

"Wednesday. Goddamn Wednesday..." It didn't even sound like he was talking to me anymore. He laughed, a short bark of a laugh, and sniffed again.

"What about Wednesday? Tell me about Wednesday. Leander?" My heart raced faster than the seconds ticking by. I needed him to keep talking. If he was talking then hopefully that meant he wasn't doing anything we'd both regret.

"But you left..." He sucked in a breath and groaned, murmuring something I couldn't understand.

A wave of nausea roiled in my stomach. I knew. I knew right then and there what he was doing. "Leander, stop! I'm sorry. I'm sorry I left. I heard you and Scheible talking. I got scared. It was stupid. I was being stupid. Just please, stop. You don't have to do this."

"Fuck!" There was another groan and a whoosh of liquid. A lot of liquid.

Numbness seized every cell in my body, like ice water coursed through me instead of blood. He was making it worse. Ten times worse. I knew it. He was doing everything he could to make sure this time wasn't a failure.

"You're not powerless, ok?" I cast about for anything to say, anything to make him stop. "You have control. Right now, at this moment. You can choose to stop. Choose to stop, Leander! I'll help you. I'll help you find another way to deal with this. Ok? You're not alone anymore. I'm here. I'll always be here for you. Just please stop hurting yourself. Please!"

"Thank you... for listening. For everything." He drew in another ragged breath.

"No! Leander! Do not hang up this phone! Talk to me. Ok? I want you to keep talking. Let's talk about me. You always want to talk about me. What do you want to know? I'll tell you anything. Anything you want. Just ask." I stomped on the accelerator.

"I'm sorry, Lorelei. I really didn't want to hurt you. I tried. You don't know how hard I tried..."

"Lean—"

The line went dead.

I screamed and pounded on the steering wheel. He couldn't be doing this! It couldn't be happening again. Not when I worked so goddamn hard. Not when I gave so much of myself to him. He couldn't do this to me!

My hands shook as I dialed 911. I all but screamed at the dispatcher to send an ambulance to Leander's temporary address. He had to be there. There's no way he would do something so stupid in a public place where the risk of intervention was too high.

My next phone call was to Scheible's office.

"I'm sorry, Mr. Scheible is on a conference call right now," the receptionist said with an unhurried cheerfulness.

I wanted to scream at the top of my lungs. Instead, I opted for "Put him on the goddamn phone!"

A moment later, he was on the line. "This is Richard Sch—"

"Where is Greta?"

"Dr. Clayton?"

"Leander just made another attempt. Where is she?"

"She, she's at the house. She just dropped off some stuff for him."

"Call her!" Was he kidding me? Standing around like a gaping moron while his client bled to death and his assistant puttered around downstairs?

"Ok. Ok. Hold on." The phone clicked. Gentle music streamed through the speaker.

I drove faster, praying the ambulance would get there soon. I didn't want to be the first one in. Not again.

Scheible came back on the line. "She's not answering."

"Goddamn it!" Throwing the phone against the dash, I blew through a red light, narrowly avoiding the front end of a pickup truck.

Don't die. Don't die. Don't die. Don't you fucking die! Over and over, I chanted it in my head. I whipped my car into the driveway, seething that mine was the only vehicle there. Where was the goddamn ambulance?

Sprinting into the house, I ignored a startled shout from Greta and took the stairs two at a time. The rushing sound was louder the closer I got to the second floor. My stomach twisted viciously, knowing exactly what I would find when I burst through the bathroom door.

"Leander!" I steeled myself for the inevitable.

Steaming water spilled out of the tub. A sizable pool had already formed on the marble floor. Leander was mostly submerged. A cloud of red surrounded him, turning a yellowish-brown the further it drifted away.

Plunging my arms into the scorching water, I hauled the top half of him out. His pale skin had a bluish tint. He wasn't breathing. I tried to calculate how many minutes had passed since he hung up on me.

As I struggled to pull him over the edge, Greta appeared. She shrieked and babbled at me, flapping her hands.

"Get his legs!" God, she gave blondes a bad name. If seconds didn't matter, I would have slapped her — hard.

She stuck her hands in the water and shrieked again,

yanking them out. "It's too hot!"

"Greta!" Worthless. Utterly worthless.

She tried again. With a chorus of "Ow, ow, ow" she finally got his legs out of the tub and helped lower him to the floor.

I tilted Leander's chin back and gave him rescue breaths.

"He's bleeding," Greta said.

"No shit! Get that towel and put pressure on it!" I started chest compressions while she fumbled with the towel, trying to contain the bright red spurting from his left arm.

Suddenly, he heaved and wretched. I pushed him onto his side in time to avoid a wave of vomit. It was mostly water, since he'd apparently gone back to not eating over the past few days. Gasping and coughing, he slumped onto his back, his eyes closed.

I glared at Greta and her sniveling. "Keep his arm elevated!"

Nodding, she lifted his arm again, pressing on the towel with a horrified look on her face.

I unbuckled Leander's belt and ripped the leather strap free. Slipping it around his bicep, I yanked on it as hard as I could, buckling it into place.

"Do not take that off," I snarled at Greta as blood began to seep through the compress. Like a moron, I could just see her taking the towel off to look.

Thankfully, the medics rushed into the bathroom, shooing Greta out of the way.

"There's an arterial bleed," I said as they assessed his vitals. "And a near-drowning. I don't know how long he was under the water."

They nodded and got to work, calling out things to one another like a well-rehearsed dance. Even though Leander was technically breathing, they bagged him and started the rhythmic ventilation for him.

I staggered backward, soaked and bloody, as another

medic took over Leander's arm. They left my tourniquet in place and added more compresses to the wound. The third sliced open Leander's pant leg before unwrapping a giant syringe and jamming it into the inside of Leander's leg, just below the knee. A bone gun. Good. They weren't wasting any time poking around his hand for a suitable vein.

The first medic hoisted a bag of saline into the air while the other two slid Leander onto a backboard. Once he was wrapped in an insulated blanket, the trio hauled him out without so much as a backward glance at the carnage left behind — blood, water, wrappers and two shaken females.

Alone with Greta, I stared at the stupid cow. Anger curled inside of me like a serpent ready to strike. "Where the hell were you?"

"Downstairs. He said he was getting ready."

I shook my head at her naïveté and went to the tub.

A straight razor sat at the bottom of the white porcelain. With a shaking hand, I pulled it out and turned to Greta, bloody water dripping from the blade.

My words were slow and drawn out so the dumb bitch wouldn't misunderstand me. "What is this?"

"Umm…" She shifted, rubbing her arms vigorously.

"What the fuck is this?" I screamed, inches from her face. "You gave him a fucking straight razor? How stupid can you be? Nothing in the house, Greta! That was part of the treatment plan! No knives. No razors. Not even a pair of fucking safety scissors! And you literally gave him a goddamn straight razor?"

Cowering away from me, tears brimmed in her eyes. "He said he needed to shave. He said he had a meeting. It was in the kit Mr. Scheible got for him. I, I—"

"If he dies it's your fault." I whipped the razor into the sink and shoved past her, slamming her into the door. She was lucky I didn't throw it at her fucking face.

CHAPTER 27

*M*y fingers trembled as I undid the buttons on my shirt. Leander's blood streaked across the fabric in red splotches. Soaked and shivering, I yanked it off. Wadding it into a ball, I threw it on my bathroom floor, as far away from me as I could get it. It was ruined. Even if the blood could be cleaned, I would never touch it again except to shove it into a garbage bag. My entire outfit was going in the garbage. I didn't want any reminders.

I made it to the shower before I broke down crying. Sliding down the cold tile wall, I hugged my knees to my chest, sobbing into my arms. My thoughts were a mess of swirling anger and fear. They refused to be soothed by the spray of warm water beating down on me.

Why would he do that? I understood before — I understood why, when he was younger and why, when he was in the jail. I didn't — couldn't — understand this time. I didn't know what happened on Wednesday, other than me leaving in the morning. But how could he do it? How could he call me and do it, like it was nothing? Knowing what he knew...

The rest of the shower provided little clarity. When the

water turned cold and goosebumps dotted my skin, I climbed out, giving up any hope of understanding. I was numb anyway, chilled from the inside out with a despair I'd spent decades trying to suppress.

Staring at the clothes in my closet was like staring into a void. The rows of sheath dresses and blazers didn't register in my brain. Nothing did until I spied the black sweater I'd stolen from Leander. I pulled it on before yanking on a pair of jeans and headed out the door.

꒰꒱

Scheible was at the hospital by the time I got there, along with a correctional officer from the jail.

"What's he doing here?" I asked.

Scheible made a face, assessing the guard down the hall. "Technically Leander is still in custody, so they have to watch him."

"I'm here. He can be in my custody. Besides, they still have GPS monitoring on him, right?"

Shaking his head, Scheible led me to the row of empty chairs in the waiting room. "They cut off the bracelet before they took him into surgery. At least they had the sense to tell me, so I could call the sheriff's office and let them know. The last thing we need is the cavalry charging in."

I slumped into a chair and held my head in my hands, staring at the flecked linoleum floor. "What the fuck happened, Richard?"

He sat next to me, his briefcase clicking on the floor at his feet. "You're the shrink. You tell me. Did he give any sort of indication this was coming?"

"He kept talking about Wednesday on the phone. What happened Wednesday?"

"He called you?"

Ignoring him, I continued to stare blankly, my jaw set. He didn't need to know I was a large part of whatever the Wednesday scenario was in Leander's brain. Something else had to have happened. He wouldn't be so distraught over me leaving. He couldn't be. It was nothing. We were nothing and certainly nothing worth killing himself over.

Scheible sighed in defeat. "There's been another murder in Easton. Same M.O. as before. A woman named Florence Strand."

"That's great!" I winced, realizing a little too late how it came out. Talk about karma. "I mean, not great great. Great for the case. Right? So why don't you look happy?"

"I petitioned the court to dismiss the case. Leander's been under house arrest so he obviously had a solid alibi for this new murder." Scheible rubbed his forehead, chuckling in an unamused sort of way. "The judge doesn't agree. He said there's not enough evidence to convince him it's the same killer."

"What is he looking for? A signed confession?" My God, Phil. This was not the time to be a stickler for technicalities. How many people were running around Easton wielding crowbars? The odds were highly unlikely.

"They're waiting on lab results. The wound pattern matches, but they want to see if there are any fragments or DNA that either links or excludes Leander."

My heart sank. At least it was starting to make sense now. After being locked up for months for crimes he didn't commit, it must have been agonizing to hear this new murder wasn't enough to set him free. "That could take weeks." And that was being generous...

Scheible huffed, gesturing at the pastel surroundings. "I guess that's why we're here. I knew Leander was getting restless, but I never imagined..."

We sat in silence after that, listening to the nurses chattering and the mechanical beeping all around us. I wondered if Scheible called Olivia. Or Elijah. Someone from Leander's circle. Or, if it was just the two of us — three, including the guard — waiting on word of Leander's surgery.

The silence, along with the gnawing curiosity, needled me until I couldn't take it anymore. "There is something that has been bothering me," I said, looking at Scheible.

"Oh?"

"How am I a liability?"

He chuckled, which was not the reaction I was expecting. "I might be old, but I'm not blind. I see what's happening."

"There's noth—"

He held up a hand. "I'm not going to report you. Frankly, I'm thrilled for him. But he needs to focus — you both do. If this goes to trial, I can't have you up there blushing like a schoolgirl and making eyes at him from across the courtroom."

It was almost a relief someone knew — and approved. I also understood his point. Mostly I was grateful he didn't launch into a lecture like my mother would have. "So what did you mean by getting rid of me?"

He looked at me incredulously. "Your car was in the driveway, for Christ's sake. If you're going to sneak around, at least be discreet. I'm not the only one keeping tabs on who comes and goes from that house. If the SA's office caught wind of it, you bet your ass they'd find a way to throw Leander back in county and get your testimony stricken from the record. Then we're back at square one."

I felt like an even bigger idiot now. I'd let my imagination run wild instead of thinking logically, which was the exact opposite of everything I'd spent my life learning. I couldn't believe I was so stupid. I knew Leander wouldn't hurt me. Not really. His anger was surprising, yes, but as with most people, anger belied a deeper emotion. It was a defense mechanism, nothing more. Why didn't I remember that when it mattered?

After another hour of waiting, a thought occurred to me. "Excuse me a moment, Richard."

Hurrying around the corner, I pulled out my cell phone and dialed my mother's number before I lost my nerve.

"Lorelei, what a pleasant surprise. Is everything alright? Please tell me you're not already canceling dinner for next week, are you?"

"Yes. No. I'm fine. Mom, I need a favor."

"What is it?"

"I need you to talk to Phil." I bit my lip, waiting for her to respond.

There was nothing but silence.

"Mom?"

"I can't do that, Lorelei."

"You don't even know what it's about."

"Yes, I do. It's that boy."

I gritted my teeth. I knew it wasn't going to be easy, but I didn't expect a blanket refusal from the get-go. "He's a patient."

"Whatever. I'm not going to argue with you over semantics. I won't do it. I don't know what your infatuation with him is, but I won't do it. You're too involved."

"Mom! Listen to me. Someone else was murdered while he was in custody. How can you still think he's guilty?"

"That isn't as compelling of an argument as you might think, Lorelei. He probably paid someone to do it. He has the resources. You know it. I know it. And Phil knows it."

"Oh my God." Slumping against the wall, I tried not to crush the phone in my hand. We might as well have been speaking different languages for all the good it did.

Mom plodded on anyway. "Is this some sort of late teenage rebellion? Hmm? You didn't do it as an actual teenager, so now you have to do it as an adult? Can't you dye your hair or go pierce something? Go backpacking through Europe?"

"I have never asked you for anything and I have certainly never asked you for help when it comes to work but I'm asking now. Mom, please help an innocent man. He's already been robbed of his freedom for this long — how much longer does he have to suffer?"

She sighed, a deep, dramatic sigh that didn't bode well for our conversation or our relationship, for that matter. "Dear girl, when are you going to learn? No one is ever entirely innocent. Especially not men who land themselves in the middle of a murder trial, no matter how pretty the face or how sad the story."

A tear rolled down my cheek. I squeezed my eyes shut, trying to hold the rest of them back. Frustration welled inside my chest, seconds away from unleashing as a scream so loud she'd be able to hear it across town — without the phone.

Hanging up without another word, I slid down the wall, hugging my knees to my chest. Leander may have dubbed me an optimist but right now I felt like the exact opposite. I knew the world wasn't a fair place. I'd known that since I was eleven, but logic was cold comfort at the moment.

Scheible found me in the hall, curled up into myself and wishing for the impossible. He jerked a thumb over his shoulder. "He's out of surgery."

I scrambled to my feet and followed him to a room in the ICU. There were flowers everywhere, a touch I was not expecting. Only one bouquet sat on the table next to the bed — a small vase of Lily of the valley, scenting the air. I wondered who sent it, Elijah or Olivia? At least now I knew Scheible called them.

Leander was awake — barely. A splint stabilized his left

wrist and he was still on oxygen. An IV dripped next to him, along with a stack of beeping machines and monitors.

"How are you?" Scheible asked.

Leander closed his eyes and sighed. "Go away."

Scheible nodded and patted the end of the bed, apparently unperturbed with the dismissal. "I just wanted to check on you. I'll be back later. I'll send Greta with your things."

"Don't," I snapped before I could help it. "I'll get him whatever he needs."

"Don't be silly. She's at the house already. Save yourself a trip." Scheible smiled, not to be argued with, and walked out.

Glaring at his back, I hoped he could feel my anger down the hallway. I never wanted to see that girl again. If she was in charge of packing for Leander, then I sure as hell would be the one unpacking for him and making sure she didn't give him something else to hurt himself with.

Setting my violent thoughts to the side, I turned to Leander and approached his bedside slowly, my arms crossed.

He turned away from me, his gaze fixed on the window. "Don't."

"Don't what?" I tried to keep some sense of calmness by regulating my breathing. Don't scream at him? Don't lecture him? Don't tell him how mad I was? How scared I was?

The muscles in his jaw twitched, but not before I saw his lower lip quiver. His face remained resolutely turned away.

I didn't know what to do. I couldn't make him talk any more than I could make him put down that fucking razor. If he didn't listen to me then, why would he listen to me now? Point of fact, when did he ever listen to me? Our conversations were almost always on his terms. Pressing resulted in him lashing out or shutting down, neither of which I wanted to occur while he was in such a delicate state.

Uncrossing my arms with a sigh, I sat on the edge of the

bed with my back to him. Even if he wouldn't listen, I still had to say it. "You scared me. I thought I lost you. And I hated you. I hated that you could do that to me, knowing what you know. I hated that I was the one who had to find you."

He exhaled, but didn't say anything.

"I get it," I said with a small shake of my head. "Logically, I get it. Scheible told me what happened. I understand you must feel alone, and trapped, and scared, and a thousand other things you'll never admit to. Things I could never know unless I was in your position. But how could you? How could you do that, knowing what it would do to me?"

I summoned the strength to look at him, to face his dark gaze, full of torment and betrayal at my confession.

He hadn't moved while I spoke. His eyes were closed again, his chest moving in a steady rhythm. Leaning over him, I brushed the dark strands from his face.

He was asleep.

The story of my life. I finally work up the nerve to say what I am really feeling and it literally falls on deaf ears.

With nothing else to do, I assumed a watchful position in the chair in the corner of the room. The nurses came and went and still, Leander slept.

Eventually, Greta crept in. Eyes wide, she clutched a leather bag to her chest and glanced around.

Flying out of the chair, I ripped it out of her hands, shoving her back out the door.

"I'm so sorry. Is he ok?" she asked.

"No thanks to you."

She looked like she was on the verge of crying again. It didn't make me feel any better. If she fell groveling at my feet, I still wouldn't feel better. Even if it was completely irrational, I would blame her for the rest of my life for endangering Leander.

"I didn't know he was going to do that!" She looked at Leander, as if he would suddenly wake up and save her from my wrath. "He seemed fine."

"Oh, did he now? Well, there's a reason you'll be fetching coffee and making copies the rest of your life."

Her eyes flashed. "Yeah? Well, he's your patient and he still wants to off himself. So what does that say about you?"

If I wasn't clutching the bag, I would have slapped her right in her insolent mouth. "Stay away from him. You've done enough damage." I spun on my foot and stalked back into the room, sliding the door shut.

Dumping the contents of the bag onto the counter, I rifled through them, leaving nothing to chance. I groped the pockets and ran my hand over the seams and the lining, looking for anything that twit could have overlooked, like a giant fucking razor.

Satisfied she wasn't giving him yet another opportunity to hurt himself, I put everything back in the bag and resumed my place in the chair.

I couldn't help but think about my dad. Washing Leander's blood off of my hands summoned memories from the other worst day of my life. Right now, the two events were neck-and-neck in a competition I wished didn't exist.

School had let out like any other day. I was blissfully unaware of what awaited me at home. There was nothing remarkable about the way the house smelled, or the way it sounded. It was simply our house. I didn't have any expectation of Dad being there until I got off the bus and saw his car in the driveway.

Maybe he didn't know I was coming home at the regular time that day. Maybe he forgot when I said soccer practice was canceled because Mrs. Klassen broke her foot. Or maybe he just didn't care. He was too far gone at that point.

Offloading my backpack at the front door, I sprinted

inside the house. He was always so busy lately — working late, avoiding my mother — I was thrilled to have him all to myself, if only for a few hours.

I called out for him.

There was no answer.

There was only one place he could be — only one place he ever was when he was home. His office.

I skipped through the door. My smile turned to horror. I screamed at what lay beyond.

The neighbors called the police with all my screaming. They thought I was hurt. I *was* hurt, just not in the sense they thought.

I didn't remember the police arriving on scene. I didn't remember the paramedics showing up.

I did remember the coroner coming. I remembered seeing my father wheeled out of the house in a big, black bag. The officer tried to get me to look away, tried to shield me with a fierce hug, but I saw — I saw under his arm when they shoved the husk of my father into the back of that black van.

When they closed the doors, my mother was there. She didn't even cry.

Decades later, I still felt dazed — frozen — at the memory. Where I should have felt warmth in her arms, I felt nothing. It took years to look her in the eye again, to not blame her for what he did. Then, my hatred flipped to him and his selfishness. His cowardice. How could he do that to me? How could he leave me like that, leave me with her? With no explanation. No apology. Nothing. Just the emptiness in my life where my father should have been.

As I watched Leander sleep, I worked hard to keep that hatred from rearing its head again. Consciously, I knew I didn't hate Leander any more than I hated my father, but it didn't stop my heart from cursing his name and regretting the day he walked into my interview room.

CHAPTER 28

"*L*orelei."

Stirring, I woke to find Dennis standing over me. I jerked upright, instinctively looking at the bed.

Leander was still sleeping. The sky was pitch black. The room was calm and mostly quiet, aside from the monotonous beeping next to his bed.

"Go home and get some sleep," Dennis whispered. "I'm here all night. I'll keep an eye on him."

"No, I'm ok." I rubbed my eye, trying to get my contact to un-glue itself from the top of my eyeball, hoping it didn't pop out in the process.

"No, seriously. You know how it looks."

Of course I knew how it looked. I still didn't care. I'd rather get the side-eye from fellow doctors for caring too much about a patient than letting anything else happen to Leander. They could talk all they wanted.

Dennis sighed and patted my shoulder. "If you don't want to go home, then at least go to the on-call room."

That was reasonable. Close, but not career-ending close. "Ok. Come get me if you need me."

I trudged to the on-call room and crashed onto the couch.

◄◊►

The next morning, I woke to the sound of someone paging out a code on the hospital speakers. An army of nurses and the closest doctor barreled down the hall with a crash cart.

I burst out of the on-call room and sprinted after them, far faster without my usual heels. Relief overcame me when the herd thundered past Leander's room and disappeared into another at the far end of the hall.

I caught myself against his doorframe, my chest heaving.

"Are you alright?" Leander asked.

Rushing to his bedside, I had to stop myself from throwing my arms around him. "I thought… never mind. How are you feeling?"

He was sitting up, which was a good sign. The oxygen and the IV were gone, though the splint remained, as it would for weeks to come.

"I've been better." He looked downward as he tried to flex the fingers on his left hand. Wincing, he turned away, glaring at who knew what. His hand? His stupidity? Me?

"Leander?"

He looked up again, his features softening.

I tucked a curl behind his ear, trailing my fingers along the side of his jaw. Now the panic of yesterday was gone, I could afford to be the calm, supportive person he needed instead of a raving lunatic operating near hysteria. "I'm here for you. Tell me what you need."

"Would it be too much trouble to check in on Annabel for me?"

"Yeah, of course." Disappointment elbowed relief out of the way. His request was centered on a cat, of all things, but I took it as an indication he wasn't feeling hopeless anymore. I was worried he would wake up angrier than before, furious at himself for what he perceived as yet another failure. Surprisingly, he seemed at peace with his surroundings.

"She doesn't seem to like Greta," he said with a hint of a smile.

Instead of saying anything, I tried to smile back. I couldn't blame the cat — I didn't like Greta either. Not after everything that happened. No, that wasn't true. I didn't particularly care for her *before* everything happened. I wondered if Leander felt the same way, if he felt anything toward the girl he duped into handing him a razor.

A nurse came in and yanked the curtain around his bed closed. I stepped away as she went to the other side, checking his splint and the gauze along the surgical wound.

"I'll be back soon," I said, ducking out.

⚜

The house was strange without Leander in it. It felt hollow, devoid of the energy he radiated. Trying not to think about it, I clicked my tongue for Annabel and called out her name. Like a typical cat, she did not appear. I refilled the bowls in the kitchen before venturing upstairs in search of her.

Hesitating in the doorway of the master bedroom, I wrapped my arms around myself. Two very opposing memories clashed in my mind. I didn't know which one hurt more. Leander's sweater, while cashmere, did little to warm the chill in my bones.

Taking a deep breath, I stepped into the room. Part of the bathroom was visible from where I stood. It was clean. Did Greta do it or did Scheible hire someone? It didn't matter.

Steeling my spine, I walked into the gleaming white

room. Thankfully, the straight razor was gone. I double checked all of the cabinets and drawers but there was no trace of it.

A sigh of relief seeped out as I returned to the bedroom, nearly tripping over something.

"Annabel!"

The cat stopped weaving around my legs and meowed at me, twitching her tail. I scooped her up and scratched behind her ear.

"He's worried about you. Are you worried about him too?"

The cat purred and head-butted my hand when I stopped scratching.

"Well, he'll be home soon. I hope. As long as he doesn't develop any sort of infection in his lungs. Oh my God. I'm talking to a cat." I set her on the bed and patted her head one last time. "See you later."

·❧·

The curtain was still drawn around Leander's bed when I returned, but the door was open. My footsteps slowed when I heard him talking. Stalling outside the room, I didn't want to interrupt his conversation with whoever it was.

"Yes, I heard. I wish she would have said something sooner. But as long as it's being handled, I can live with the rest." Leander sighed. "It's fine. A few months of therapy and it'll be like it never happened. Mmhmm. You too."

Brows furrowed, I peered around the corner again. There were no feet on the floor near his bed, nor any other audible voice to account for the conversation. No one was in the room except Leander.

Walking in the rest of the way, I pulled back the curtain.

Leander was sitting in bed, his hands folded in his lap. There was no one there. Even the TV was off.

"Who were you talking to?" I asked.

He frowned at me. "I beg your pardon?"

"Were you on the phone?" I glanced between the bed and the hospital phone. It was on his left side. His injured side. I doubted he could have reached it from where he was sitting. Even if he could, he didn't have the capability to pick it up in his current state.

He followed my gaze to the phone. "That's a violation of the court order, as you pointed out yesterday."

Maybe I was hearing things. Or maybe I was overhearing things from another room and assumed it was him. I pushed at the space between my eyebrows. I really needed sleep. Good sleep. "Annabel is fine," I said, wanting to gloss over my error and get back on friendlier footing.

He gave me a small smile. "Good. Thank you."

Silence fell between us. It was suffocating.

"You scared me," I said. It was like ripping off a bandaid. I needed to tell him when he was conscious. I needed him to hear me — actually hear me.

He blinked slowly but didn't look away. His voice was barely audible. "I know."

"You hurt me."

"I know that too."

"You asked what I'm afraid of — this. Losing a patient. Having someone else take their life on my watch and being powerless to do anything about it."

He tried to keep his face passive, but I saw a ripple of agony, like I'd slapped him. "That's all I am to you? A patient?"

"Leander…" What could I say? I didn't know what he was to me any more than I knew what I was to him. On the surface I was his doctor and he was my patient, but over the weeks he'd become so much more. He infiltrated my every thought, slipping between the crevices of my mind until he consumed me. But how do you tell someone that? How do you voice those feelings when they're not supposed to be there in the first place?

He laughed, a short mirthless laugh. "'And all I have loved, I loved alone.'"

"I can't talk about this right now," I said quietly, hoping he would sense the urgency in my voice. Besides the fact you never knew who was listening, I didn't have the words to tell him what I truly felt without sounding like a lunatic. It was easy for him to rattle off a quote and consider his innermost thoughts explained. I, on the other hand, was trained to listen, not be the one pouring out my heart.

"No, of course not. There's no need to speak of it again." His jaw shifted while the vein in his neck jumped with each betrayed heartbeat.

"That's not what I meant."

Anger flared in his eyes, the same hostile yellow-green as before. I searched beyond it for another emotion, the deeper one. There was none. The intensity of his chartreuse eyes faded, like a light going out. "Goodbye, Doctor."

I reached for his hand, hoping to reassure him with a physical gesture as opposed to a verbal one.

He pulled away. He may as well have hit me. It would have been more bearable than the crushing pain in my chest.

Defeated, I turned and left.

CHAPTER 29

The days dragged by.

Refusing to go to the hospital or even ask how Leander was doing, I busied myself with work. I didn't want to complicate the situation any more than it already was. Dennis didn't offer any updates and Scheible was too busy with the opening day of the trial.

I was surprised the new prosecutor was prepared so quickly, but ultimately it wasn't my concern. Maybe Phil didn't want to grant any more extensions. I knew I wouldn't be summoned until much later, after the state had gone through all of their evidence and the jury had been presented with the worst possible examples of Leander's character. Then, it was the defense's turn to try and do damage control.

I was in a staff meeting at St. Mary's when the call came in.

"Dr. Clayton? This is Rebecca from Mr. Scheible's office. I'm calling to inform you your services are no longer required. Final payment will be mailed out at the end of the week."

I almost dropped the phone. "What are you talking about? Did he retain another psychiatrist?"

"No, ma'am." She giggled. "The case has been dismissed!"

"What?" My legs felt like they were going to give out. I steadied myself against the wall before I toppled over. Dismissed? How could it have been dismissed? They only just started.

"Yes, dismissed with prejudice, according to the paperwork. The State's key witness was a no-show." Vera Van Deveer, a no-show? I didn't believe it. Did she have a change of heart after all this time?

"Thank you for the call," was all I managed to spit out before hanging up. I pulled up the *Easton Sentinel's* webpage on my phone and started scrolling. Our local newspapers may not have cared much about the trial, but Easton certainly did.

I clicked on the link embedded in Leander's picture and waited while the latest update loaded.

Vera's picture was positioned next to Leander's, a smiling version of her that looked like it was from a wedding or some other social event. Leander's, on the other hand, featured him sitting behind the defense table, looking rigid and severe, downright evil to anyone who didn't know him. A not-so-subtle visual remark as to the editor's true feelings.

More than the jarring juxtaposition, however, was the headline beneath the photo — KEY WITNESS DECEASED: CASE DISMISSED.

My jaw dropped. I skimmed through the text, trying to comprehend what I was reading.

According to the article, Vera was admitted to the hospital before the trial even started. The family assured everyone she'd be well enough to testify and encouraged them to proceed. So they did. The jury was sworn in. The prosecutor presented his opening statement and began with his first piece of evidence — the forensics on the missing murder weapon.

When court broke for lunch, there was a flurry of activity at Phil's bench. He and both lawyers disappeared behind closed doors for quite a while, only to reemerge with the shocking news. Vera passed away earlier that morning and the family had just notified the State's Attorney's office. As a result, the state had no witness to Dr. Van Deveer's kidnapping, thus no witness to link Leander to the subsequent murder. All of the other evidence was circumstantial. Phil had no choice but to dismiss the case with prejudice and release Leander.

According to the paper, Leander was a free man as of yesterday afternoon.

So, why didn't he tell me himself?

A hollow feeling expanded in the pit of my stomach. Grabbing my bag, I jumped in the car without a second thought and drove straight to the McMansion in the woods.

I held my breath as I rang the doorbell. It boomed inside the large house, once, twice, and a third time. There was no movement beyond the windows, no cars in the driveway. Nothing.

He was gone.

Just like that.

He left without saying a word.

There was no thought in my mind other than Leander. I wasn't even cognizant of the fact my car turned southbound until I was halfway to Easton. Each sign I passed pulled me closer and closer, like a magnet.

The sun disappeared from the sky in the time it took to pass the Easton town limits. It didn't matter. I made my way to the mansion on the hill with ease, following the lighted tower glowing above the treetops.

The gaslight fixtures flickered next to the front door as I rang the bell.

Again. And again.

The house remained dark. No one came to the door.

I shook my head at the absurdity of it all. What was I thinking? He was probably out celebrating with his friends. He'd been in custody for months. If it were me, I wouldn't be home either. I'd driven all this way and for what? What was I really expecting if he opened the door?

The breeze shifted off the river, blowing tendrils of woodsmoke around the corner of the house. On a hunch, I followed the scent to the backyard, mindful of my footing with all of the ornate landscaping.

Behind the conservatory, a roaring bonfire blazed against the black sky. Leander stood on the opposite side of the flames, his face twisted in the dancing light.

As I took a step closer, something landed in the center of the fire. Embers sparked and flew up into the darkness. He caught sight of me and froze, a stack of paper clutched in his hand.

"What are you doing here?" he asked flatly. He didn't look happy to see me, nor did he look particularly angry. I didn't know which was worse.

"You left." It actually hurt to say it out loud. It hurt even more he didn't seem bothered by it.

"You should recognize the gesture." He threw the paper into the flames. I spied the boxes at his feet — it was all of his work from Parkview. His sketches, his journaling. Every scrap of paper he'd accumulated.

"What are you doing?" It was distracting, to say the least. It also added to my irritation with him, with the whole situation. Did he want to rid himself of every memory of his incarceration, or just his time with me?

"What does it look like?" He threw another handful into

the fire. One sheet managed to escape the flames and flew away on the breeze, the edges curling as they burned. He caught it deftly and crumpled it, casting it in the heart of the bonfire.

"Why did you leave without saying goodbye? Without saying anything?" I circled around the edge of the burn pit, taking note of the direction the smoke was blowing. The last thing I needed was a stray cinder sending me up in flames. At that moment, I wasn't so sure Leander would do anything to save me.

"Why do you care?" So he was angry. There was no mistaking the sneer in his voice, even if his face remained impassive. He fished another item out of the box. One of the notebooks.

I lifted my hand as if I was going to stop him, but retracted it just as quickly. He was bordering on an outburst, I could feel it, the way the anger pulsated through the air around him. "Can you stop for a second?"

He looked at me plainly and tossed the notebook into the fire. Point taken. The tables were officially turned. He didn't have to listen to me anymore, or pretend to, at any rate. He didn't have to do anything I asked. He was the one in control, just as he was the night he grabbed my throat and slammed me against a wall.

I closed the distance between us hesitantly. It was strange, seeing him like this. Unrestricted in any way. At his home, on his turf. I couldn't explain how he was different, but I sensed it with each of his movements. He was like a wild animal set free, sleek and powerful and unstoppable.

"This isn't easy for me," I said, shifting on my heels in an attempt to keep from sinking in the grass.

"Then allow me to spare you." He kicked a box out of his way and strode toward the house without so much as a backward glance.

"Leander, wait!" Trailing after him, I picked my way over the uneven terrain. I caught up to him along a flagstone path in the middle of a maze-like garden. I snagged the back of his shirt and pulled, hoping he'd stop easily and not send me sprawling.

Thankfully he did, but he spun with a suddenness I wasn't expecting. He took a step toward me, forcing me backward to avoid a collision. "What do you want from me, Lorelei? What are you even doing here?"

They were questions I'd debated for three hours and I still had no definitive answer. Why couldn't he be the one to say what I was thinking, to articulate what was going on in my brain? He was the wordsmith, not me.

"Nothing. Everything. I don't know," I sputtered.

Furrowing his brows at me, he stared intently as if he could make sense of my answer if he thought about it long enough. I wished him luck, since I couldn't make sense of it myself. I never thought clearly when it came to him — it'd been the case since Day One.

"Being with you will cost me my career," I said at last. "Not just at Parkview or St. Mary's. I could lose my license altogether. It's not just something that's taboo, Leander, it's forbidden. Legally, ethically, morally. I will lose everything."

The firelight cast sinister shadows over his features, obscuring any chance I had of getting a sense of what he was thinking. I wanted him to say something. Say anything! His silence was deafening. Torturous, just like in Poe's fable.

"But not being with you…" I drew in a sharp breath, searching for the right words. What could I say to make him understand? I was floundering and he wasn't saving me. He just stood there and watched me squirm, silent and unmoving. "Say something. Please."

"What is it, exactly, you want me to say?"

"Something. Anything. Tell me what you're thinking."

Silence.

After a few more painful heartbeats, he spoke. "I think you should leave."

"What?" Did I hear him correctly? I drove three hours to see him. I told him I wanted to be with him. And his response was to tell me to leave? This was not going at all how I thought it would... I honestly didn't know what his reaction was going to be, but I didn't expect to be sent away, dismissed, like I was nothing.

The back door of the house slammed.

A figure rushed through the darkness, crashing into Leander and wrapping him in a fierce hug. Olivia. "There you are! I've been waiting! What are you doing out here?"

I could have sworn someone sucker punched me in the gut. I couldn't breathe. I couldn't think.

Olivia detached herself from Leander only slightly, following his gaze to where I stood, flabbergasted. She kept one arm wrapped around his waist, arching a perfect eyebrow at me. "Dr. Clayton. I wasn't expecting to see you again. Ever."

"She was just leaving," Leander said, his voice hollow and his gaze downcast. He wouldn't even look at me with her there. I didn't know whether to be heartbroken or furious.

Olivia smiled, turning her full attention to Leander. "Elijah's here. Cole is on his way."

"Jake?" he asked, lifting his eyes to meet hers.

She shot a glance at me out of the corner of her eye, her glossy lips twitching. I got the hint. I was no longer welcome by Olivia or her boss and I was certainly not privy to wherever Jake was or their plans.

Shaking my head, I stifled an incredulous laugh. I couldn't believe how ridiculous I was, that I drove here for nothing. I almost threw away everything I'd worked so hard for, and for what? A man who couldn't even look at me?

Without another word, I shook my head and wound my way out of the maze of boxwoods. I resisted the urge to look back as I followed the path around the house. I didn't care what Leander was doing, or with whom. Not anymore. He'd taken enough from me over these last few weeks. I wasn't going to give him the satisfaction of knowing how much he'd gotten inside my head.

Cole pulled in the driveway as I reached my car. I intended to slip away, but he jogged over and knocked on the window before I could put it in drive.

"Hey Doc! You staying for dinner?"

Dinner at this time of night? "No, I don't think so."

"Are you sure? We've got more than enough."

"No. Thank you. I need to get home."

He glanced at his cell phone and made a face. "It's kind of late. You might want to think about staying the night. You don't look like you're up for that long of a drive by yourself."

The sooner I got out of Easton, the happier I'd be. Coming here was a mistake and I wanted nothing more than to forget it. Forget everything. Especially Leander.

"I'll be fine. Take care." I rolled up the window and drove away before he could say anything else.

﹡✿﹡

Fireflies dotted the night sky as I sped northbound. The old buildings gave way to fields until the Easton town limits were well behind me. There was nothing in front of me except darkness, nothing behind me except misery.

How could I be so foolish? So utterly naive? No. Stupid. How could I have completely misread the entire situation? Olivia said Leander wasn't a liar. Clearly she was. She had to be. There was no other explanation for his cold shoulder or the look of triumph in her eyes.

Unless none of it was a lie. Leander said there was nothing good in him. He told me quite clearly anything I thought I saw was my imagination. Maybe I should have believed him. Maybe I felt the things I did because he wanted me to, because it suited his agenda. Now that he was free, there was no reason to carry on the charade. He got what he wanted while I was left picking up the pieces.

My headlights sliced across a blur in the roadway. I slammed on the brakes and swerved to avoid whatever it was.

The front end of my car dove into the ditch and smashed into the embankment. The seatbelt caught me across the chest, saving my face from smacking the steering wheel.

Coughing, I unbuckled the belt, rubbing at my sternum gingerly. At least the airbags didn't go off. I didn't need a broken nose on top of a bruised chest.

What the hell was that, anyway? A deer? A coyote?

I looked behind me.

The roadway was empty. It was just me and the twinkling fireflies.

"Shit." There was no way I was driving anywhere. It was going to take a tow truck to yank me out of the ditch. I prayed I didn't have any actual damage to the undercarriage. Easton was the closest Godforsaken town and I did not want to stay any longer than absolutely necessary.

Slipping my cell phone out of my bag, I slumped over the steering wheel. "You've got to be kidding me." Zero bars.

I shoved it in my work bag and popped the trunk. Climbing out of the car, I grabbed my overnight bag for the hospital, praising myself for being over prepared. It was one in a million chances like this that made me thankful I was Type A.

With nowhere left to go, I slung my bags over my shoulder and headed southbound. My shoes were going to be trashed by the time I reached civilization. Maybe that would activate some sort of emergency beacon in my mother's brain and she'd instinctively know where I was to send help.

Except she had no idea where I was. I didn't tell anyone I was leaving. I could literally die in the middle of nowhere and no one would know what happened to me. Served me right, I supposed.

⁘

A pair of headlights lit up the road while I perched on a guard rail, cringing over a blister. Squinting, I shielded my eyes with my hand as a pickup truck rolled to a stop in front of me.

"You ok there?" a man asked.

I hobbled up to the passenger window and blinked through the boxes of white lights dancing in front of my eyes. "Mark?" What was an orderly from Parkview doing way down here?

"My name's Jacob. You ok?"

"Yeah. Sorry." I blinked hard, trying to clear my eyes. "I thought you were someone I knew."

"I take it that's your car back there?"

"Yeah. Any chance I can borrow your phone? Mine's not working."

He shook his head. "Not going to in this stretch of road. You gotta wait til you get back to town. Hop in. I'll give you a ride."

I debated for a minute, weighing my options. Get in the truck with a strange man in the middle of nowhere or suffer needlessly on blistered feet and who knew how many more miles? I opened the door and tossed my bags in, giving him a small smile. "Thanks."

"Where to?" He seemed nice enough — clean cut, clean

237

clothes, clean truck. Besides, given my occupation, I was fairly confident I was a decent judge of character, even if Leander left me shaken in my abilities.

"Um, I don't know. Is there a hotel or something?" The last time I was in town I stayed at a bed and breakfast, which I doubted would be open for customers this time of night.

"Yeah, downtown." He pulled back onto the roadway and drove onward. "Must not be from around here, huh?"

"No, no I'm not."

"Figured. Tourists mostly come in the fall. Besides, you don't look like you're hiking in that outfit."

"Thank God you came along when you did."

"At least you picked a busy road to crash on."

I glanced over my shoulder. I hadn't seen another car since I left Easton. "You're joking, right?"

He laughed.

The rest of the ride was quiet, except for the radio playing in the background. I perked up when the truck rumbled across the river and parked in front of an old, corner building several stories tall. In case there was any question as to what building it was, WALKER HOUSE was carved in stone over the doorway.

"Here we are," Jacob said. I reached for my wallet, but he held up a hand. "No need, Doctor. Just happy to help."

"Thank you." Grabbing my bags, I opened the door, pausing for a moment. "How did you know I was a doctor?"

Chuckling, he gestured to my hospital bag. "The luggage tag."

"Oh. Right. Sorry. Thanks again." I smiled and closed the door, feeling like an idiot for what felt like the hundredth time lately. There must have been some magnetic field over Easton wreaking havoc on my brain. Or I was losing it. Maybe my mother was right. Spending too much time with the criminally insane was not good for my own mental health.

Stepping into the hotel, I glanced around the spacious interior. Like everything else in Easton, it was old but had a certain elegance to it. A lone clerk greeted me sleepily. He handed over a key card, along with directions to the room and a reminder of what time breakfast was.

As soon as I was in my room, I collapsed on the bed, wishing I never heard of Easton or Leander Welles.

CHAPTER 30

*G*roaning, I hung up the phone and sank onto the edge of the bed.

Good news: the mechanic was able to pull my car out of the ditch easily enough.

Bad news: I jacked up something with the tire arm and it wouldn't drive. He said it would only take a day or two to fix, but that meant at least another twenty-four hours in Easton.

Grabbing my laptop, I buried myself under the covers. At least I had plenty of work to keep me occupied. It would be nice to plow through it without distractions.

A knock on the door dashed that plan. I wasn't too irritated, though, since it meant my clothes were back from the laundry. If I had to venture outside of my hotel room, at least I wouldn't have to do it in leggings and a t-shirt.

The air was promptly sucked out of my lungs the second I opened the door.

Leander stood there, impeccably dressed as always. There were familiar shadows under his eyes and a marked pallor to his skin. If I had to guess, he wasn't sleeping again. Maybe that's why he was so irritable last night. Or, he was genuinely unhappy to see me.

It didn't matter.

Shaking my head, I closed the door. I could not deal with him anymore and I didn't want to be a part of whatever he was here for. My professional relationship was fulfilled, the contract with his lawyer satisfied. It was time my personal relationship was likewise terminated. Any concern for Leander and his wellbeing vanished last night.

He knocked again, three slow knocks.

"What do you want?" I asked through the door. It was better there was a physical barrier between us. Hopefully it meant I'd keep my wits about me instead of falling under his spell.

"I don't want to talk through a door."

"I didn't ask what you didn't want." I was on to his verbal trickery, the way he played with words to steer the conversation. It wasn't going to work this time. "What are you doing here? How did you even know I was here?"

He sighed. "Your car is at the garage. It's not that hard to deduce where you might have gone. Please open the door."

Crossing my arms over my chest, I glared at the dark wood paneling. "I don't have anything to say."

"I find that hard to believe."

I glared even harder. Now he wanted to talk? After weeks of prompting and pleading and pulling teeth? No. I wasn't going to make it easy for him, like he didn't make it easy for me. "Well, believe it."

"Lorelei. Please..."

Something in his tone stirred my empathy. Or maybe it was my curiosity. Relenting with a huff, I yanked the door open. Before he got any ideas, I blocked the way in, arching an eyebrow at him. "What?"

"Now that I'm standing here, I've forgotten everything I

want to say." He shoved his hands in his pockets and bit his lip.

"Then allow me to spare you." I hoped his words stung him as much as they stung me the night before. Swatting the door closed, I spun away, fully intent on going back to my laptop and not spending another second thinking about him or what could have been.

Two steps toward the bed and I realized the door didn't click shut. Glancing over my shoulder, I stifled a gasp.

Leander was in the room.

He closed the door firmly behind him and turned the deadbolt.

The same apprehension I felt the day after our tryst bubbled up again when I realized I was trapped. Maybe I shouldn't have been so churlish with him. Maybe this was my punishment for letting my guard down like an idiot.

"You were not part of the plan," he said softly, wagging a finger at me before covering his mouth in thought. I backed away from him until my leg hit the edge of the bed. "You... Lorelei. You were unexpected."

Swallowing the lump in my throat, I stole glances at my surroundings. I didn't know where he was going with this. He wouldn't hurt me. Would he? He never had before, not really. But he'd never been a free man before, with no one watching his every move.

"I don't get surprised very often," he continued, almost like he was talking to himself more than me. He moved forward as he spoke, a slow, unhurried saunter, until he stopped in front of me. "This whole thing has been years in the making. Everything, except you. You were the unknown." His fingers caressed my cheek before he took hold of my jaw, forcing my gaze up to his. He didn't look angry in the morning light, he looked like he was in agony.

The warmth of his skin on mine quelled any irrational

thought. My body moved closer to him, drawn in by the pull of his gaze alone and a rush of desire to be near him. "What do you want from me, Leander?"

"Stay with me," he whispered, his nose brushing against mine. His lips were so, so close. "Don't go back. I want you to stay here. Tell me what you want, it's yours. You want a clinic? I'll build you a clinic. You want a charity? I'll fund your charity. Anything. I'll give you anything, everything, you want. Just tell me you'll stay."

Squeezing my eyes shut, I tried to unravel the twists and turns of the last twenty-four hours. It was easier to do if I wasn't looking at him. One minute he told me to leave and the next he promised me the world. It made my head swim.

"I don't understand…"

"I never want to watch you leave again, Lorelei. I don't think I could bear it."

My lashes drifted open. Despite the fact his green eyes were aglow, they were touched with a profound sadness that couldn't be faked, even by the best of actors. There was no anger or ill-intent buried beneath the turmoil. He wasn't lying. I knew it in my gut.

"Last night, you said—"

"I was angry. I'm sorry." His hands circled my waist, pulling me against him.

"What about Olivia?"

"What about her?" One hand was in my hair, twisting around the strands and angling my face toward his.

It was hard to think when he was touching me. I clung to the front of his shirt for balance, hoping my legs didn't betray me. "Aren't you two…?"

"No," he breathed against my ear a moment before his teeth grazed it. "There's only you."

A shiver raced down my spine. Memories of our time in bed came back full force, along with the thrumming in my

243

blood. Another surge of dark, delicious exhilaration shot through me. Somehow he'd breached all of my defenses, all sense of reason. In spite of everything, I wanted him.

"Can I kiss you?" he whispered.

"Please."

He pressed his lips to mine gently, almost hesitantly. I twined my arms around his neck and melted against him. It was easy to forget everything when we were like this. Gone was the anger, the hurt, the confusion. In his arms, everything in the world was made right again. This was the only thing that made sense.

Unlike the time before, this time was slower, less frenzied. Our clothes survived the encounter, landing in puddles on the floor instead of being flung to the far sides of the room in tatters. The need was the same, but the urgency was gone, calmed by an implicit understanding.

Afterward, Leander wrapped his uninjured arm around me, pulling me in as close as he could. I snuggled into his chest with a contented sigh.

The surgical scar on his wrist caught my attention. It was the grisliest one yet — dark red and longer than the others. White dots, leftover from the stitches, lined either side of the incision. More than the surgeon's emergency patch-job, it was a reminder of how close he came to death. Again.

"Does it hurt?" I asked, my gaze fixated on the delicate system of veins and tendons underneath the scar.

He flexed his fingers and winced. "Does it make you feel better, knowing it does?"

"No." I skimmed my fingertips along the mark. "You could have done serious damage. You know that, right? Lost all motor skills in this hand, lost sensory function. You don't know how vulnerable hands are in the grand scheme of things."

"I do know." He kissed my temple. "It's in the past."

"Past actions predict future behavior." I shifted onto my elbow so I could see his face, see what he was really thinking. Did he regret it? If he did, was it the act itself, or the fact I was so hurt by it?

He stared at the ceiling for a minute before turning to acknowledge me. His face was soft, but his eyes were guarded, as if he was the one anticipating an outburst this time. "You're worried I'll do it again."

The unspoken fear formed a lump in my throat. Unable to say it aloud, I nodded. It was the second worst day of my life. I needed him to know it, even if I couldn't say it. I couldn't tell him how much he meant to me. It was still too fragile, like a bubble.

"Would you believe me if I said I didn't want to die that day?" The fingers of his good hand caressed the small of my back.

I chewed on the edge of my nail, working up the courage to vocalize actual words. "It's not what it looked like. Except for the part where you called me." Was I his safeguard? The one part of the plan that could undo all of the damage?

"I know what it looked like. I'm sorry you were the one to find me. I'll spend the rest of my life apologizing, if that's what it takes."

"Just tell me why." Pushing away from him, I sat up, brows furrowed. Why would he go through all of that pain for nothing? If he wanted the release from cutting, he could have cut anywhere else. Cutting that deep, the way he did... I couldn't fathom a reason except the obvious, which he now insisted was not the case.

He sat up as well, staring at his wrist while flexing each finger with a grimace. "I needed to get out of that house."

I shook my head. That wasn't it. He wasn't lying, but there was more he wasn't saying. After all of our time together, I was attuned to him in a way I'd never been with anyone else. "You could have left at any point. You know Scheible would have taken you wherever you wanted to go."

He glanced at me out of the corner of his eye, but didn't say anything.

"You wanted to be at the hospital," I said, following the breadcrumbs of his logic. "You wanted to be admitted, not just looked at and released. This was a guaranteed way to do it. Routine self-harm would have gotten you into the psych ward. You wanted to be in the ICU."

He fixed me with a stare, watching me unravel his plan. His eyes were glowing again with the predacious glint I'd seen before, the one that gave me goosebumps. I was treading into dangerous waters, but the truth was too tempting to ignore.

I wracked my brain, sorting through the events. Phil didn't want to release Leander until the DNA came back from the murder of Florence Strand. The opening day of testimony proceeded as usual until news of Vera Van Deveer's death derailed the entire case.

My mouth dropped open. I blinked, the final piece of the puzzle sliding into place. The memory of Leander's hospital room rushed in, including the vase of Lily of the valley. It was there the first day, filling the entire room with its fragrance. It was gone the next. I didn't register its absence at the time, but I remembered it now.

"You were there because of Vera," I whispered.

"Mrs. Van Deveer had a heart condition. Everyone knew that," he replied, his voice like silk.

I carried on, trying to put myself in Leander's complicated maze of a brain. "Dismissed with prejudice is almost as good as double jeopardy. And you know there's no way anyone would appeal to a higher court without a witness or a murder weapon."

His tongue toyed with the tip of an incisor as he averted

his gaze, like he was deep in thought. I knew he heard me. I knew I was close.

"What aren't you telling me, Leander?" I had a feeling I already knew the answer, but I wanted him to say it out loud, to confirm my suspicion.

"You're safe with me, if that's what you're wondering." Taking my hand, he kissed my palm before pressing it against his cheek. My heart skipped a beat with the gentleness of the gesture, at odds with the lethal look in his eyes. "I will never let anyone or anything hurt you ever again. Including me."

"You can't promise that."

"I can and I am."

It may have been the steeliness underneath his velvet voice or the burning certainty in the pit of my stomach, but I believed him.

CHAPTER 31

"*Y*ou're what!" Mom's voice shrieked in my ear.

Grimacing, I pulled the phone away. "I'm in Easton."

"Lorelei, so help me God..."

"Mom, this isn't a conversation or a debate. I'm letting you know where I am out of common courtesy." Regurgitating her phrase made me roll my eyes. "And I'm taking a leave of absence for—"

"You're what!"

"I just need some time to figure—"

"Have you lost your mind? I know what you're doing, Lorelei. You're sabotaging everything for him and you're going to regret it. You're going to wake up one day and—"

Sighing, I let the phone fall away from my ear. There was no point trying to explain anything. She never wanted to hear it.

"I'll talk to you later, Mom," I said over the top of her admonishments. As soon as I hung up, I switched my phone to silent and tossed it to the side.

The screen lit up a second later with her name. When it

didn't stop vibrating, I growled and powered the stupid thing off. Another sigh escaped me, this time from relief instead of exasperation. Flopping backward onto the bed, I closed my eyes, trying to calm my racing brain.

It's not like I came to this decision lightly. After I'd spoken with Kim and addressed my concerns about a potential for burnout, I knew it was the right thing to do. She agreed. Apparently Dennis expressed a similar concern to her a few weeks ago about the pace I was keeping.

It wasn't just Leander's case that left me out of sorts — it was the entirety of my life. I fought day and night for people who couldn't advocate for themselves and where did it get me? What was I actually accomplishing? There was always a waiting list to get into Parkview, unless you came in in handcuffs. Was I actually helping anyone or just slapping a bandaid on a hemorrhage?

Dennis told me I shouldn't kill myself trying to save them all, but that's exactly what I was doing. Splintering myself into tiny fragments in the hope that if I gave enough of myself, if I worked hard enough, somehow it would make the world right again.

It didn't. All it did was leave me drained and disheartened.

For once my future wasn't mapped out. I had no idea what tomorrow would bring. Although I was terrified, I was also ebullient. Instead of running like a hamster in a wheel, I finally had a sense of control over my own fate, even if it meant stepping away from everyone and everything I knew.

The bed dipped down next to me. A drop of cold water splashed on my forehead a second before warm lips pressed against mine. I opened my eyes and smiled, brushing Leander's wet hair behind his ear. He smelled like my shampoo.

"I take it that didn't go well," he murmured, propping himself on his good arm. He was dressed again, sadly, but I was happy to see he procured a wrist splint from somewhere and it was securely in place. At least he wasn't too proud to follow the surgeon's orders.

I picked at my thumbnail. "Am I that transparent?"

Laying his hand over the top of mine, he quirked an eyebrow but remained mute. I knew I was. Everyone told me I was a terrible liar. My perfectly polished doctor's smile was the only thing that ever masked my true feelings and the only person to ever see through it was lying next to me, dark curls dripping on the collar of his shirt.

"Tell me I'm not making a huge mistake." Since I couldn't pick, I fidgeted.

"You know I can't do that." He played with my fingers, either to stop my fidgeting or because he needed to fidget himself. "I can't tell you what to do with your life."

"Lie to me."

He smirked, his eyes crinkling. "You know I won't."

"It was worth a shot." I sat up, raking a hand through my hair. "I'm going to go shower and then we can go. Ok?"

He nodded, kissing me while I slipped off the bed.

The hot water didn't erase my concerns, but it melted the majority of them away. Nothing was set in stone. I was still employed. While I called it a leave of absence, in reality I was finally getting around to using my stockpile of vacation time. My license was still intact, unless Leander decided to file a malpractice suit against me. This was just a break, a much needed break for my mental health. A time for reflection, to see if my career was still on its best course.

Stepping out of the shower, I felt far more confident than twenty minutes prior.

Leander stood by the window, his phone pressed to his ear. Irritation marred his face.

My stomach flipped at the sight of him. Was it Scheible? Did something else happen?

"Do I have to come out there?" Leander asked. He drew the curtain closed with a snap. "Well it sounds to me like you're saying you can't handle it. If that's the case, you can disregard and I'll address it myself."

I slipped into my dress and dragged a comb through my hair, cringing for whoever was on the other end. The business-side of Leander was far different than what I'd experienced. He was cold and sharp. No wonder he liked Olivia. The pair of them must have been terrifying to work for. Maybe a little bit of his grandmother rubbed off on him after all.

"Good. Don't call me again until it's resolved." When he turned to face me, it was with a brilliant smile. The animosity from a moment ago was nowhere to be found. "Ready?"

Stuffing the rest of my belongings in my bag, I nodded. "Is everything ok?"

"It's just business." Taking the bag from me, he leaned down and kissed my cheek. "Let's go home."

Our trip through the lobby was interesting, to say the least. The employees stopped talking as we approached the desk, nudging one another. An older man took the plunge and stepped forward with a tight smile. "May I help you, Mr. Welles?"

Leander slid his credit card across the countertop. "Checking out. Room 303."

The man's eyes widened. He took the card nonetheless, typing away on the computer. "I hope everything was to your liking. Forgive me, I didn't realize you were staying with us."

Leander turned to me, raising his eyebrows. "Was everything to your liking?"

The clerk also looked at me, eyebrows raised, swallowing.

I offered a smile to the frazzled man. "Yes. Fine. Thank you."

He let out a nervous laugh and finished typing on the computer. "Good. Glad to hear it. Thank you for staying with us and please let us know if there's anything we can assist you with in the future, ma'am. Sir."

Picking up my bag again, Leander slung an arm over my shoulders, steering me toward the door.

"What did you do to that man?" I whispered as soon as we were out of earshot.

"Why do you think I did something? Maybe he has a nervous disposition." He held the door open, a mischievous grin on his face. I threw a disbelieving look over my shoulder.

"Thank you for paying for my hotel room. You didn't need to do that." I slipped my arm around his waist and leaned against his shoulder.

"Consider it part of my penance for last night." He guided me toward a black car, sleek and expensive, parked on the street. I expected nothing less from him.

A pair of women lingered near the doorway of the hotel, whispering and pointing. At first I assumed they were arguing over the hotel's lunch menu. One woman shook her head disapprovingly while the other hissed in her ear, not even trying to hide her beady gaze.

The word "murderer" drifted across the open space, fanning the flame of rebellion inside of me. Choosing to stay with Leander had been the spark; gossip mongering by a pair of judgmental hags was the accelerant.

Grabbing ahold of Leander's belt, I yanked him against me. My free hand tangled in his damp hair as I kissed him fiercely. The audible gasps behind us made me kiss him all the harder.

Breathless, Leander pulled away, steadying himself against the car. "What was that for?"

"Nothing." Batting my lashes, I gave him an innocent smile and slipped into the passenger seat.

He cleared his throat and closed the door. A second later, he was in the driver's seat, expelling a slow breath as he pulled his car into traffic. "You are certainly full of surprises..."

"Just wait until we get home." The last word slipped off my tongue so easily I couldn't believe I said it.

Leander gave me a devilish smirk and sped us across the bridge.

CHAPTER 32

$\mathcal{I}$n the afternoon light, Leander's house had none of its sinister shadows or impersonal feel. Golden light illuminated every room, coaxing the dark colors to reveal their rich jewel tones and the intricate patterns on the historic wallpaper. The first time I was there, I didn't think it was a place that could ever feel welcoming, let alone become my home. Now, after a week of being there, it seemed as familiar as my own apartment.

Leander was draped across the couch in the library when I found him, the tattered copy of *Frankenstein* in his hands. He looked up, smiling brightly, the way he always did when I walked into a room. After so many weeks of reservation and withholding, his cheerfulness was a strange, but welcome, experience. Every time he smiled, it took my breath away.

"How many times have you read this?" I asked, straddling his lap.

"Innumerable." He let the book drop to the floor and tugged at the bottom of my shirt. "Is this mine?"

I snuggled into his neck. "Maybe."

"Speaking of... I seem to remember a cashmere sweater

that disappeared from my stay up north. Do you know anything about that?"

"Nope."

"Mhmm. I thought you agreed not to lie anymore, Doctor?" He nuzzled the top of my head.

"I'm sorry, Mr. Welles. I have a terrible memory."

His fingers grazed back and forth over the curve of my hip. I squirmed away, nudging him with my elbow. Laughing, his hand stilled. "We can always go shopping, you know."

"You don't like this?" Shifting into a vertical position, I pushed my lower lip out in a faux pout. I unbuttoned the top button, then the second. By the time I got to the third, he sat up, pressing kisses along my throat. His hands disappeared up the back of my shirt, leaving scorch marks along my skin.

A pounding on the front door made both of us jump. His eyes narrowed as he slid out from beneath me. Clearly he wasn't expecting anyone, either. "I'll be right back." He strode out of the room without a backward glance, his spine as straight as steel.

Chewing my nail for a minute, I waited to see if he would return. When he didn't, I slipped off the couch and crept toward the door. Voices echoed across the foyer. Pressing myself against library wall, I only recognized Leander's.

"You have got to be joking," Leander said. He sounded neither pleased nor amused.

"No. We're not," a male replied brusquely. "So you can either bring her out here, or we're coming in."

"It's within our legal right," a second male said.

"Lorelei, can you come here please?" Leander called.

Making sure my shirt was buttoned appropriately and thanking God I was wearing pants, I smoothed my hair down and sauntered as casually as I could to the foyer.

Two police officers stood in the doorway, one looking bored while the other looked downright hostile. Leander was directly in front of them, his arms crossed over his chest, barring further entry into the house.

Butterflies did loop-de-loops inside my stomach. I hoped my face didn't betray me. Linking an arm around Leander's waist, I tilted my head, batting doe-eyes at our visitors. "Is there a problem, officers?"

"Are you Lorelei Clayton?" The tall one asked.

"I am."

"Can we speak with you... outside?"

"Right here is fine." I tightened my hold on Leander's waist. His arm circled my shoulders, squeezing ever so slightly before relaxing again, a silent acknowledgment of the line I drew in the sand. If he didn't know where I stood before, he knew it now.

The tall one looked especially irritated. "Fine. We're here to make sure you're alright, that you're not in any danger, not being held against your will. That sort of thing." He cleared his throat, his gaze flicking to Leander.

Obstinance took root, straightening my spine as severely as Leander's. "I'm perfectly fine, as you can see. Who called you?"

"A concerned citizen."

There it was. He thought I was another dumb blonde, that I wouldn't see through the charade. I gave him a bittersweet smile. "Well, by all means, you can call my mother back and let her know I'm alive and well."

The officers exchanged glances.

"Oh, and one more thing," I continued. "I'm sure this is going to happen again. So, if she intends on using the police to harass me, you may want to remind her that her judicial immunity does not cover criminal conduct outside the courtroom. Any further welfare checks will be seen as harassment and I will not hesitate to press charges."

The short one, a sergeant by the chevrons on his uniform,

smirked. Swatting the tall one on the arm, he tossed his head toward their squads. "She's fine. Let's go."

The tall one shook his head, looking like he wanted to offer some sort of rebuttal. Giving Leander a withering look, he trailed after his sergeant with heavy strides.

"She thinks I kidnapped you?" Leander asked, pushing the door closed.

Rolling my eyes, I crossed my arms over my chest. "Obviously. I can't believe she called the police."

"Does this mean she won't be coming to the Fourth of July festivities?"

Laughter escaped me before I could help it. Was he serious? The thought of my mother actually meeting Leander was unfathomable, especially not after this little stunt. "Uh, no. But tell me about these festivities."

"Come with me." Taking me by the hand, he led me to the kitchen and down into the basement.

"Umm..." I ducked under a cobweb and glanced around the cellar. "What are we doing?"

"Do you trust me?"

"Of course."

He smiled his brilliant, beautiful smile and tugged my hand, pulling me further into the dark, rocky labyrinth. Old doors lined either side of the stone walls. It seemed like mostly storage and utilities. The only room with any kind of remodeling was the expansive wine cellar we passed.

A door at the far end led into a small, pitch-black room. A bare bulb dangled from the ceiling, the only source of light after someone bricked up the one window at some point in the house's history. Shelves lined the walls, coated with dust and grime. There were a few mason jars left behind, along with a stack of wooden milk crates.

Leander pulled out a lantern from one of the crates and switched it on, handing it to me. Before I could ask what he was doing, he slid one of the shelves out of the way. A small trap door, nearly invisible in the stone floor, lay beneath the shelf. A narrow ladder descended straight down into darkness. "Ladies first."

"Absolutely not."

Laughing, he took the lantern back, disappearing down the opening with ease.

I followed him, landing on a hard dirt floor in the center of another small, windowless room. "What is this place?"

"The sub-basement. It was used during Prohibition, but rumor has it it's even older than that." He took my hand, leading me through a dark passage at the far end of the room. It turned out to be a tunnel, sloping downward through the limestone.

The tunnel opened up at the base of the bluff. The river was just a few feet away, flowing by in a steady stream of greenish water.

Leander waded in without hesitation while I stalled on the bank.

"What are you doing?" I asked, pulling him to a stop.

"Trust me." If he was exasperated with me yet, he didn't show it. If anything, he seemed extraordinarily patient.

One more gentle tug on my hand and I relented. The cold water rushed around my legs. The danger of being swept away was apparent, even though Leander plunged ahead. He kept hold of my hand, pulling me further from the bank. The water rose steadily, over my hips, up to my chest, until I was walking on the tips of my toes.

Before my head went under completely, we reached the little island I'd spied from his bedroom window. Up close, I could see the appeal. Flowers of all sizes and colors blanketed the island. Lily of the valley predominated, its soft scent permeating the air. A sense of familiarity washed over me until it clicked. This was the same spot his mother was photographed in.

"It's beautiful," I said.

"This is the best seat in town." He settled onto a flat, grassy spot and folded his arms behind his head.

I laid down next to him, mirroring his pose. Fireflies drifted overhead and the first of the stars twinkled in the purple-gray sky. The sound of the river surrounded us, accompanied by the growing song of cicadas and the occasional frog. It was peaceful. Magical, even.

"They launch the fireworks down there," Leander said, nodding toward the center of town. "You can see it all from right here. We spend the day grilling, swimming, and then the fireworks."

"Sounds wonderful."

"I hope you'll be here."

"Where else would I be?" Pressing myself against him, I hooked a leg around one of his.

A question that had been circulating my brain since I first met him finally worked its way to the surface. It was one piece of his puzzle I hadn't been able to figure out. "Can I ask you something?"

"Yes, Fourth of July is my favorite holiday. Should I be concerned about the deeper meaning of my love for fireworks?"

I ignored him and stayed on my charted course. "Why do you stay here? In Easton. And why do you stay in the house?"

When the silence dragged on a beat too long, I worried I overstepped. Finally, he answered. "I dreamed about leaving as a child, laying here on this very island. But Grandmother left me one final gift — she included the house in my trust with exacting instructions. If I walk away from the house, I walk away from the trust. She underestimated me, as usual.

259

She thought these insignificant townspeople would accomplish what she never could."

"What's that?"

"She thought they'd break me. But here I am."

And I thought my mother was controlling. "Does the trust prohibit you from changing the house?"

"No. The National Register and the state's Historic Preservation Division have their rules though. Why do you ask?"

"I was just wondering." It's not that the decor was out of sync with his personality, but I could also see his foreboding grandmother adding such a trifle stipulation to the trust to be a continued thorn in his side.

He seemed to accept my curiosity without question, running his fingers through my hair leisurely. His mind appeared to have drifted elsewhere again. Over the past few days, he'd been more pensive than usual, though he wouldn't say why.

We laid in silence, enjoying the last bit of the day's warmth and the tranquility of the river around us until a tiny white bell bopped my nose out of nowhere.

I smiled, taking the sprig of Lily of the valley from him. It was still strange, that something so small and beautiful could kill someone. Even if I'd never know for sure, I had a feeling this tiny flower helped expedite Mrs. Van Deveer from the world. Whether or not Leander played a role would remain a mystery.

"You never told me," he said, brushing my hair away from my face. "What is your favorite flower?"

"Trying to analyze me now, Mr. Welles?" I arched an eyebrow at him, smelling the fragrant Lily. An impish smirk curled his lips and I knew he wouldn't answer. "Sunflowers."

"Interesting."

"Is it?"

"Why, may I ask?"

I shrugged. "They're happy. They always turn toward the sun, which I thought was amazing as a child. My dad told me once they face each other when it's cloudy, but that's a fallacy."

"It's a charming thought, though…"

CHAPTER 33

As the days turned to weeks, Leander gradually resumed his duties at work, leaving me for longer stretches of time while he went to the office. With nowhere to go and nothing filling every second of my schedule, I relished the free time.

Like all good things, I knew it wouldn't last forever. As much as I wanted to ignore my life up north, I knew I'd have to face it eventually.

The phone was the first thing to deal with. Turning it back on after weeks of silence, I unleashed a flood of emails, voicemails, and text messages. Most got deleted, only a few garnered an actual reply.

Messages from my mother ranged from mild chiding to petulant outrage. The stream of warnings steadily morphed into threats before she called the police. There was one last message after they'd apparently phoned her back: **I told you not to involve yourself with him. Don't come to me for anything when he's ruined your life.**

Glaring, I flicked away the message.

Calvin's was far friendlier, wondering where I was and if

everything was alright. I smiled at his closing, **Hit me back, Doc**.

I typed a quick reply, letting him know what was going on. Other than Dennis, he was the only one who bothered checking in with me on any sort of personal level.

Dennis's latest voicemail, however, was the most concerning. "Lorelei, call me."

Checking the time, I debated whether or not he'd be awake after working nightshift. The urgency in his voice prompted me to take the risk. It rang three times before he picked up.

"Where have you been?" Dennis asked without the customary greeting.

"Didn't you get my email?"

"Tell me you are not where I think you are."

"Where do you think I am?"

"With him."

I bit my lip, trying to figure out what I could say to that. Nothing came to me. Chewing my nail didn't result in any brilliant answers, either. All it did was make the seconds drag by until Dennis huffed out a sigh and said, "Oh my God... Lorelei!"

Even though he was three hours away, I cringed. I didn't want to disappoint him, especially not after being his star protege for so many years. It's not like I planned for this to happen. How do you plan for someone like Leander Welles sweeping into your life and upending everything?

"Lorelei, listen to me," Dennis continued, his voice resigned. "You are not the first person to go through this. Ok? But think of the risks! If you go your separate ways, you could face a multitude of civil suits, not to mention losing your license. You'll never work as a doctor again. Is it worth it?"

On the one hand, it was troubling Leander held my

career, my future, in his hands. Power imbalances like that could, and have, ripped couples apart. On the other, I knew, inexplicably, I was safe with him. He'd promised as much. "He wouldn't do that."

Dennis groaned. "You don't know that. He's not the only one you have to worry about. If anyone finds out, they can report you." My mother's face came to mind. It wouldn't be beneath her to pull a stunt like that and then magnanimously claim it was all for my benefit.

"I know that..."

"What if this is part of some sick fantasy of his? You know he's manipulative, Lorelei. You can't argue with that. Look at how he played us at Parkview. All the tests and the evals? I worry about how stable he really is, about what he could do if he snaps again."

Each word made me bristle. I wanted to point out Leander played *him*, not me, but I refrained. "I can handle it. I can handle him."

"Can you? Three to four days, Lorelei. That's all it takes to brainwash someone."

I sighed. "He's not a cult leader, Dennis."

"I'm not convinced he's non-violent. You know how insidious domestic violence is. Not to mention, how many people did it take to put him down the last time he flipped?"

"Oh, you mean the night Russ beat him to a pulp while Nora tried to cover it up?"

Dennis ignored me. "How do you know this isn't limerence or good old-fashioned transference? He's a good-looking guy. I get it. I've seen the stacks of fan mail."

"I don't know, Dennis. I just know how he makes me feel. For the first time, I feel like I actually matter."

"You do matter, kid. You matter to a lot of people."

"Do I? It doesn't feel that way. It seems like I'm only valuable for the service I can provide or for what I look like, like

I'm a goddamn trophy. My mother, Darren. They don't care about what I actually want. Leander wants me for *me*, not what I can do for him. He's not my patient anymore. He's free. If he was only using me to help with his case, then what am I doing here?"

Silence stretched over the seconds, ticking away with each heartbeat. Dennis inhaled and exhaled again, which meant he was giving up the fight. "You call me if you need anything. Anything, Lorelei. I mean it. I'm always going to have your back, kiddo. Just please be careful."

"Thank you, Dennis." He might not have agreed, but at least he cared enough to support my decision. It was more than I could say for most people.

The doorbell rang right after I hung up. Thrilled my clothing order finally arrived, I hurried downstairs. No doubt Leander would be pleased to have his wardrobe back and I was elated to wear something other than black for a change.

Sadly, it was not my package.

It was Olivia.

"Leander's not here," I said, trying not to frown.

"I'm here for you." Oh, shit. That couldn't be good.

"What can I do for you?"

"Are you going to invite me in?" Not good at all...

Stepping out of her way, I gestured into the foyer. Breezing past me, her stilettos clicked on the polished floor. She turned to face me with a less-than-enthused smirk. "Since you're going to be staying here, I figured we should get on the same page."

"What are you talking about?"

"Leander."

"Ok..." I propped a hand on my hip, waiting for her to continue. Despite my training, I wasn't a mindreader. Surely she knew that.

"As you know, I'm his personal assistant. That means I assist him with every aspect of the Welles Corporation. But I'm also his friend, so I gladly assist him with any aspect of his personal life too."

"Ok..." I still wasn't following her. "What does that have to do with me?"

She held a business card out to me between two fingers. "I am not yours to command, but if it's for Leander's benefit, I'll try to help. Don't be a jealous bitch and we should get along fine."

Still trying to process whether or not this was a good interaction, I took the card. Was this her version of an olive branch? "Ok…"

"I thought you were supposed to be smart?" Ouch, Olivia. So much for an olive branch.

"I don't understand what any of this has to do with me?"

"I'm telling you like it is. Don't come at me all pissed off because you can't handle the fact that Leander relies on me. I'm here to stay. So either you deal with it, or move on. If you try to make him choose between us, you'll lose."

"Do you give this pep talk to all of Leander's girlfriends?"

She smiled, as sharp as daggers. "You're the first. Don't fuck it up."

"I don't suppose you want to stay for tea?"

She scoffed, her nose wrinkling. "No. I'll see you tomorrow."

"What's tomorrow?"

"Leander used to host dinner every Friday night. He stopped when you came around, but he's resuming the tradition. Hope you're ok with that." It wasn't a question.

"Sounds great. See you tomorrow."

She let herself out, giving me another once-over on the way.

Dinner should be interesting, to say the least. Thankfully

his other friends weren't so combative. Although I wondered when, exactly, Leander was going to let me know about his dinner plans.

I was about to close the door when I spied a package on the porch. It was smaller than I was expecting, which meant my order was coming in separate boxes. Great. So much for choosing the environmentally-friendly shipping option at checkout.

Snagging the box, I carried it into the kitchen and set it on the center island. After locating a pair of scissors in a drawer, I sliced it open, hoping it was at least something presentable for the dinner party I was just informed about.

I pulled back the brown paper wrapping and screamed.

A dead crow stared up at me from the bottom of the box. Its eyes were rotted away. Maggots crawled in and out of its broken chest cavity. The intestines, spilling out of the bird's abdomen, started to move and drag along the bottom of the box. A tiny black spider appeared, skittering up the length of entrails and disappearing into the empty eye socket.

Backing away from the box, I swiped my cell phone off the counter and called Leander.

"What's the matter?" he asked before I had a chance to say anything. It was unusual for me to call him at all during the day — I should have realized it would set off alarm bells.

"Is there any way you can come home? I need you to see something." Letters were one thing. Heavy breathing, hangups, even ding-dong-ditch were all things I'd dealt with and ignored over the course of my life when both of my parents, and then myself, were targeted by angry or deranged people.

Dead things being delivered to my doorstep? That was on an entirely different level. The symbolism wasn't lost on me.

"I'll be right there."

And he was.

In what seemed like no time at all, he burst through the back door. "What's the matter? What happened?"

I pointed at the box.

Tipping the edge downward, he peered inside. His expression was unreadable. If he was as shocked and horrified as I was, he didn't show it. "Where did you get this?"

"The front porch."

"I'll take care of it."

"I'm calling the police."

Snatching the box off of the counter, he opened the back door and tossed it outside. "I wouldn't do that."

"Why not?"

His cell phone buzzed in his jacket pocket. He answered it without looking, apparently relieved to avoid my question. "No, everything's fine." His gaze flicked to me momentarily. "I'm settling something at home. I'll be on my way back shortly."

Crossing my arms over my chest, I arched an eyebrow at him.

He turned his back on me, one hand on his hip and the phone pressed to his ear. "Yes, I'm sure. Oh, and tell Cole to file the paperwork."

Paperwork? Was he really conducting business while I was facing a not-so-subtle threat?

"Well, it's a good thing I didn't ask for your opinion." He disconnected abruptly and slipped the phone inside his jacket. "I have to go back to the office for a bit. Will you be alright?"

"I'd be better if you would tell me what is going on in that head of yours."

A faint smile crossed his face, almost pained. "'There are some secrets which do not permit themselves to be told.'"

"Stop quoting Poe at me! This is serious, Leander. I didn't tell you before because I didn't think it mattered... Someone was sending me letters at work. And now this, which means whoever it is is escalating. And somehow they know I'm here."

Crossing the kitchen, he caressed my cheek, his eyes solemn. "Would you like me to send someone over here until I return?"

"I don't need a babysitter. I need you to stop being coy and just talk to me."

"I made you a promise, Lorelei. If nothing else, trust in that. I keep my word, no matter what it takes." He kissed me gently. Before I could say anything else, he turned and strode out the back door as quickly as he'd come.

CHAPTER 34

*A*nnabel picked her head up a second before I heard the back door open and close. Squeaking, she uncurled herself from my feet and darted out of the library.

Setting my book to the side, I kicked off the blanket and trailed after her. Leander must be home from work, since it was far too late to be Yolanda, the cleaning lady.

I followed the cat into the kitchen. Leander's car keys and a pile of mail were tossed in the middle of the island, but Leander himself was nowhere to be found.

Hesitantly, I faced the mail. Ever since the dead bird, I'd been reluctant to open anything.

An advertisement for upcoming events in Easton was splashed across the front page of the town newsletter. The main focus was on the spring flower sale and the historic house walk Leander refused to participate in despite a little old lady named Gertrude begging him at least twice a week.

As soon as I picked up the newsletter, an envelope fell from the backside.

It was white and nondescript like the ones I'd received, but this one was addressed to Leander by hand instead of being typed. He'd sliced it open with something sharp, but the contents were shoved back inside so forcefully the page wrinkled. Out of the stack of mail, this was the only thing he'd opened.

Curiosity got the better of me. Unfolding the sheet of paper, I skimmed the handwritten note. My name stared back at me in harsh black strokes.

> *I'll give you one more chance.*
> *Pay, or I'll report Lorelei.*
> *You have the number.*
> *You decide.*

It wasn't signed but the writing looked familiar. Try as I might, I couldn't place it. The threat of exposure was my primary concern, followed by a sinking feeling. This is what had been preoccupying him lately. This is what he'd been hiding.

"What are you doing?" Leander asked, his voice right behind me.

I jumped and whirled around, clutching the letter to my chest. "You scared me."

His gaze fell to the letter before flicking back to me. Stepping forward, he plucked the paper out of my hand. "This isn't your concern."

"Isn't it? They're threatening my career, Leander. First the bird, now this?"

"I thought you trusted me." There was a flash of emotion on his face. Irritation? I couldn't be sure. He folded the letter again and shoved it into his pocket.

"How many of those have you received?"

He sidestepped me, head held high. "If you don't mind, I have to get dinner started."

"Answer the question."

Still ignoring me, he disappeared into the pantry.

I planted myself in the doorway, blocking his escape route. "How many letters are there?"

Hefting a bottle of oil in his hand, his face was unreadable once again. "I didn't want to trouble you."

"That's not for you to decide." I was flattered and angry all at once.

"It's being handled." He came toe-to-toe with me in the doorway, the muscle in his jaw twitching. Was he going to shove me aside? Literally and figuratively? The moment I wavered, he squeezed past me.

Irritated with him and myself, I circled around to the other side of the island, staying out of his way. Giant knife in hand, he chopped through an assortment of vegetables with a scary speed and precision. "What does that mean?"

"It means it's being handled." Anger shot across his face a second before he stabbed the knife into the cutting board. He moved around the island, heading straight for me.

Eyes wide, I darted the other way.

Frowning at me, he yanked open the refrigerator I'd been standing in front of and retrieved a stack of brown-wrapped packages.

Since he wasn't going to answer with any sort of details, I tried a different avenue. "You gave them to Scheible?" There was no way he'd go to the police, especially not when he vehemently opposed me telling them about the crow. His lawyer seemed like the next best bet.

"Why does it matter?" Unwrapping the first bundle of meat, he slapped it into the center of the cutting board. Yanking the knife out of the butcher block, he sliced through the side of a thick pork chop.

"Why can't you answer the question?"

"Why do you insist on knowing everything?"

"Why do you insist on hiding everything?"

He leaned against the island, still clutching the knife. "What would you have me do, Lorelei? Trust the police to resolve this? In case you've somehow forgotten, the police aren't exactly my biggest fan."

"I don't know, because I don't know what the extent of 'this' is. How long has this person been blackmailing you? Who is it? And why didn't you think I needed to know? You could have said something when a dead bird showed up on the doorstep!"

"The less you know, the safer you are."

"What does that mean? What are you doing?"

He laughed, a dark, exasperated laugh. "If I answer that, then you are complicit in any legal action that may result. If you want to keep your license, the last thing you need is a criminal investigation dragging your reputation through the mud. Savvy?"

He had a point… "Do you know who it is?"

"Yes."

"Are you going to kill them?" It was a bold question. Maybe even a stupid question. But it needed to be asked. In all our time together, I'd never asked him directly and he'd never addressed it other than to couch it in legal terms such as "alleged" and "accused" — or dance around the subject entirely.

Tossing the knife on the island, he snatched a towel from the drawer and wiped his hands. "Do you think I kill everyone I disagree with?"

I held my ground as he approached, stopping a breath from me. "Of course not."

"But you think I'm a murderer?"

"Tell me you're not."

He smirked, staring at me a beat too long. "I'm paying them, Lorelei. Elijah is withdrawing the money as we speak."

"And then what?" That couldn't be all there was to it. The last people Leander said blackmailed him ended up dead.

"That's up to you." He turned his back on me and resumed preparing the meat.

"You won't tell me who it is?"

"No. If it's all the same to you, I'd prefer not to have this discussion any longer."

I crossed my arms over my chest. He wasn't getting out of it that easily. "I'd prefer you not infantilize me and keep things from me, especially when they involve me."

Shoving the pan into the oven, he strode to the sink, his jaw set. "Is this to be our first fight? Truly?"

Before I could answer, his cell phone rang. He dried his hands and swiped it off the counter before I saw who it was. "Yes?" Bending his head, Leander hurried out of the room, obviously intending to keep me in the dark no matter what I had to say.

His voice, however muffled, echoed out of the conservatory. Leaning against the doorframe, I watched him, trying to piece together the conversation.

The person on the other end did a majority of the talking. Leander gave minimal answers in return. Pacing up and down the green aisles, he touched a plant here and there, picking dead leaves off and flicking them aside.

"Are you sure?" The pacing stopped.

A flutter of nerves danced in my stomach while I waited for him to say something else.

Swearing under his breath, he shook his head. "No. No... Thank you. Your assistance has been most helpful." Disconnecting, he turned to face the doorway, both eyebrows raised as if daring me to ask.

"I don't suppose you're going to tell me what that was about?" I already knew the answer.

"An unexpected merger."

"At six o'clock at night?"

He went to sidestep me. I moved with him, slipping my arms around his waist. Biting his lower lip, he stared past me, simmering with irritation.

"I don't want to fight," I said, keeping my voice soft.

"I made you a promise." His gaze dropped to meet mine, wary but no longer angry. "And I am nothing if not a man of my word."

"You can keep your promise. All I'm asking is that you don't shut me out. I made you a promise, too. Remember? I said I would never turn away."

Slipping his hand into my hair, he tilted my head back, pressing his lips to mine. He left a trail of kisses along my jaw, down my throat. His teeth grazed the side of my neck before biting down.

I gasped, a wave of desire rushing through me. Twisting my hand in his dark curls, I pulled his head back to glare at him. "Don't."

A devilish smile curled his lips. "Don't what?" He kissed me again, hot and demanding as always.

My hands drifted to his chest. I pushed him backward, never breaking contact with his mouth. As soon as I felt wicker against my knee, I wrapped my fingers around his throat and tore my mouth from his, shoving him into the chair. I remained standing, unbuttoning my shirt before he ripped it off. "Is this your idea of conflict resolution, Mr. Welles?"

"Is there a better alternative, Doctor?"

The tip of my tongue skimmed across his lips teasingly. When he tried to kiss me again, I pulled away, tsking him. Peeling my shirt off, I dropped it to the ground, turning slowly so my back was to him. Slipping my jeans over my hips, I stepped out of the denim and kicked them to the side.

He seized my hips, pulling me backward into his lap. His

hands roamed my bare skin until, one by one, I plucked them off and forced them to lay flat on the wicker arms. I rolled my hips in small, hard circles. The sighs and heavy breaths behind me gave me another rush of pleasure, and power. There was no doubt I had the upper hand and I was going to use it to my advantage.

As soon as I felt him lean forward, his breath hot on my back, I shot off his lap. Dancing out of reach, I turned with an innocent bat of my eyes. "I should get ready for dinner," I said, halfway to the door.

"What?" He stared at me, equal parts desire and confusion. His breathing was just shy of panting as he gripped the wicker chair.

"If it's all the same to you, I'd prefer not to have this conversation any longer," I quoted with a smirk. And here Dennis had been worried Leander was the only manipulative one.

"Wait. Lorelei!"

Slinking around the corner, I let my fingers trail along the wall, laughing. Cruel? Maybe. But it made a point. Despite his assertion, Leander couldn't control every situation. And he certainly couldn't control me.

By the time I reached the top of the stairs, I heard him in the kitchen, dishes and silverware clinking together perhaps a little more forcefully than necessary. I padded down the hallway to the guest room I'd claimed as my own, though in reality it did little more than house my clothes and toiletries. Even though I slept in Leander's bed, it felt intrusive to move into his room completely.

Sliding onto the stool at the vanity, I assessed my features in the antique mirror, turning my face from side to side to catch the light. There was that glow Mom was talking about. Turned out I didn't need Celine's help after all.

CHAPTER 35

"*A*nother exquisite meal," Elijah said, throwing his napkin on the plate. "Can I please have the recipe now?"

Leander smirked, pushing away the remnants of his beef wellington. "No."

"Would you stop asking him, already? He didn't give you the recipe for stuffed pork chops last week. He's not going to give you this one, either." Olivia rolled her eyes at Elijah and finished the rest of her red wine.

"It's too bad Jake isn't here," Cole said, glancing around the table expectantly. If I wasn't paying attention, I might have missed the look on Leander's face. It was there and gone again, a brief flash of ire, followed by a smile so sincere I questioned what my eyes had seen.

"Yes, it's a shame," Leander said, refilling Olivia's wine glass.

"I'll get dessert," Olivia said, standing abruptly and striding into the kitchen.

"Where is Jake?" I ventured, glancing between Leander

and Cole. In all the weeks I'd been in Easton, I'd yet to meet him or even spy him from a distance.

Standing and scooping up the dishes nearest him, Elijah disappeared into the kitchen as well.

"He's overseeing an acquisition for the company. He should be back soon," Leander's words sounded harmless enough, but the look he gave Cole made the hair on the back of my neck stand on end.

Olivia returned with a chocolate tort and set it on the table. Despite her cold demeanor, she was one hell of a baker.

"Before we get started," Elijah said, following on Olivia's heels. "Can I talk to you?" He raised his eyebrows at Leander and tossed his head to the side.

"Excuse us," Leander murmured, kissing my cheek as he stood.

They disappeared into the other room. A moment later, the side door opened and shut again.

Olivia and Cole exchanged a look. She hadn't resumed her seat and I couldn't help but notice the long, glinting knife in her hand.

"What was that all about?" I asked, directing the question at Cole, since I knew better than to try and get anything out of Olivia. Especially not when she was armed.

Cole gave me a brilliant smile, the picture of ease. "What was what?"

Olivia set the knife down. Or slammed it, more like. "Cole. Come help me with the dishes." She spun on her heel without a single plate in her hands.

Snatching the remaining dishes off the table with a fleeting smile thrown in my direction, Cole scurried after her.

As soon as I was alone, I let out a slow breath. Dinner last week had been filled with lively conversation and friendly bantering. Tonight, everyone was on edge and I was the only one without a clue as to why.

I didn't have time to wonder. Raised voices on the side porch drew my attention. It was Elijah and Leander, but I couldn't hear what they were saying. I peeked out the curtain, grumbling when I realized I couldn't see around the angle of the house.

Making my way into the front parlor, I pressed myself against the side of the tall windows despite the fact the lights were off. They were just outside the wavy glass, a black duffle bag on the floorboards between them.

"There's always another option," Elijah said, his arms spread wide.

Leander, on the other hand, was rigid, as motionless as a statue. "Pray tell, Elijah. What are my options?"

"Not all cop—"

"Are you serious? What would Cole say if he heard you now? Never mind my own experience to the contrary."

"I just think—"

Leander swooped forward, nose-to-nose with Elijah. I couldn't hear what his interruption was, but it made Elijah shake his head. Leander lingered a moment before retrieving the bag.

Before either of them turned and spied me in the window, I spun away. I slammed into something hard in the dark and stifled a gasp. Hands gripped my arms, keeping me upright. It was Cole.

"Whoa, easy, Doc."

"Oh my God! You scared me. What are you doing in here?"

"Same thing as you." He nodded toward the window. "Something is up between those two."

"Any ideas?"

He shook his head and pressed a finger to his lips,

miming silence. "Come help me pick out a dessert wine." It wasn't a request. His hand circled my bicep and he hauled me out of the room, through the kitchen, and into the basement. Once we were in the wine cellar, he closed the door behind us. "You need to be careful."

"What are you talking about?" I took a precautionary step backward. Cole never scared me before, but he did now. There was something about the look in his eyes, a spark of menace I hadn't experienced from him. His criminal history leapt front and center in my mind. A good tailor and impeccable grooming couldn't erase what I knew about him, about what he was capable of — just like Leander. Just like all of them.

Cole moved with me, keeping his voice low. "Outside of the four of us, you know the most about Leander. That makes you powerful in this town but extremely vulnerable."

"I don't understand."

"People will use you to get to him. It also means if they," his gaze shot upward to the house above, "sense any disloyalty, they won't hesitate to deal with it."

"You mean Leander will kill me?" There was no point in beating around the bush anymore. After all, I'd feared he was plotting it once before with Scheible. Did he have a hand in the letters, too? The death threats? Was that why he didn't even bat an eye at a dead bird?

"Not necessarily him... but yes."

Elijah and Olivia's faces ran through my mind. Of Leander's friends, they were the most zealous. "Like, Elijah or—"

"Jake," Cole finished.

"Jake?" Of course. The one member of the pack I hadn't met. The one always away on mysterious business, even now. The one I'd never see coming.

"I'm pretty sure Jake killed Old Lady Strand."

"Florence Strand? The cook?"

Cole nodded.

"Why do you say that?"

"Ever since Leander was locked up, Jake hasn't been around. Then one night he comes back to town as if nothing happened. He was gone again the next day, right before news of the murder broke. Elijah won't say anything about it, but I heard Olivia on the phone. She wired money to Jake and told him not to come back until Leander was home."

"Why are you telling me all of this?" It felt like a trap, or a test. It had to be, because if it wasn't, it was a warning I couldn't afford to ignore.

"Because Jake's the one who picked you up after you wrecked your car that night. He came back, met with Leander, and disappeared again, just like before. He's the one who told Leander you were still in town."

The realization hit me like a slap in the face. The driver said his name was Jacob. I was such an idiot! He threw me for a loop when he referred to me as "Doctor," but I believed him when he said he saw the luggage tag. How could I be so stupid? "If Jake killed Florence Strand, do you think he killed the others, too?"

"I think—"

Before Cole could finish, the door creaked open. He snatched a dusty bottle from the shelf behind my head a second before Leander stepped in.

Leander's gaze darted from Cole to me and back again. It was hard not to notice how close Cole had been standing before he leaned away, toying with the bottle in his hands. Like usual, I couldn't tell what Leander was thinking but it probably wasn't good. His face was drawn, his knuckles white on the door handle.

"There you are," he said at last. I didn't know if he meant me — or Cole.

Cole held up the bottle, as if Leander couldn't see it. "Lorelei was helping me pick one."

I swallowed hard, trying to hide the fact my heart was thumping hard enough to make the vein in the side of my neck jump. The tension in the air was thicker than the layer of dust on the aging bottles.

"The others have gone," Leander said dismissively.

"Right. Goodnight." Cole shoved the bottle back on the shelf and started for the door.

Leander didn't move.

They locked eyes, nearly nose-to-nose with each other. The temperature in the room felt like it dropped twenty degrees. Leander lifted his chin almost imperceptibly, his head held high, regally. Cole lowered his gaze, like a wolf submitting to an alpha, looking as guilty as I felt. Leander remained rooted in place while Cole squeezed past him in the narrow doorway, disappearing into the hall.

Once we were alone, Leander continued into the room. He stopped just short of me, reaching past my head to retrieve the bottle Cole grabbed. Blowing softly across the label, one dark eyebrow lifted as the writing beneath was revealed. "Did you pick this?"

I shook my head. My voice was caught somewhere in my throat. What was Cole about to tell me? That Jake was the serial killer running rampant through Easton? Or that it was Leander? Perhaps both of them, working as a team, a master and an apprentice.

"What did Cole want with you?" Leander's gaze pinned me to the wine rack, dark and piercing with suspicion.

"He said he needed help with the wine." I hoped my voice didn't sound as shaky as I felt.

"And you believed him?"

"I don't know what to believe, Leander." I fixed him with a narrowed glare of my own. If he insisted on keeping secrets, how was I supposed to know who was telling the truth? Thus far all of the evidence contradicted itself. The only one who could set it straight was the one person who refused to give a straight answer.

"This is for a celebration," he said loftily, sliding the bottle back onto the shelf. "Which is clearly not tonight."

"What were you and Elijah arguing about?"

The corner of his mouth lifted slightly. "I didn't take you for a voyeur."

"It was hard not to overhear."

"If you overheard then you know what we were arguing about."

My hands balled into fists at my side. He was so frustrating! Even when I thought I could get an honest answer, he evaded it. "I'm tired of playing games with you."

"Pity." He slipped his hands into his pockets and pivoted, strolling out of the room.

Gritting my teeth, I used every ounce of strength I had to stifle an infuriated scream.

CHAPTER 36

"*I*'m going home," I announced, adjusting my grip on the bag in my hand.

After a fitful night of tossing and turning in the guest room, I'd decided space was in order. I had things to sort out at work. Leander clearly needed to deal with his latest blackmailer, or whatever it was that had him and Elijah pitted against one another. Maybe then we could resume our attempt at a relationship in the real world, minus the secrets.

Leander halted in his tracks, cell phone in hand. I knew he had conference calls all morning and I hoped to slip out unnoticed. Clearly that went right out the window.

"You're what?" He looked stunned. For a moment I felt a twinge of guilt. Despite the sourness of last night's conversation — or lack thereof — he obviously didn't think I'd up and leave.

"My life is up north. There are things that need my attention."

"I'm going with you."

I grabbed my keys and my sunglasses, pausing long enough to throw him a look. "No you're not."

Surprisingly, he didn't look mad. He looked concerned, which was even more worrisome. "I don't like the idea of you going back there right now."

"Why? What aren't you telling me now?" My anger was gone, replaced by a growing sense of dread, tinged with irritation. Were there more to the letters and dead birds than he was telling me? Knowing him, the answer was YES!

He chewed on his lower lip before answering. "If you won't allow me to accompany you, then take Olivia."

"What? No. I told you, I don't need a babysitter." Or a spy, if that was his true intention.

"Lorelei."

"Leander."

"Please?" His eyes were soft and pleading, completely opposite to the emotions from last night. It was the same way he looked at Parkview when he was desperate for someone to believe him, to listen to him. Maybe he did have control over the look after all, adding the right amount of sadness to sway things the way he wanted.

Either way, I caved.

⁂

A half hour later, Olivia and I were northbound — her behind the wheel and me sulking in the passenger seat of my own car. She didn't seem concerned about how she was getting back to Easton. Not that she'd want it when she had a European import of her own, but I was not about to let her keep my car and leave me stranded.

The realization dawned on me — I wouldn't be staying. If I had to bet money, I was returning to Easton later that night whether I wanted to or not. Leander's possessiveness was an unusual development. On the one hand, it was endearing, a testament to how much he seemed to care. On the other, it was the same brutish behavior that made Darren so unappealing.

"Can you tell me why I'm not allowed to go home by myself?" I asked once Easton faded behind us.

Adjusting her sunglasses, Olivia reached for the radio, turning up the music. "No."

I turned the radio back down. "No, you don't know? Or no, Leander said not to tell me?"

"Yes."

I groaned. She was as difficult as ever, which meant this was going to be far from a pleasant trip.

She turned the radio up again. I let her. At least the music was somewhat distracting from the dizzying circles of thoughts. Why couldn't Cole have been tasked to drive me? Or Elijah? Unless Leander was afraid of what either one of them would let slip during a three-hour ride. I couldn't exactly fault him for that line of thinking, given how much they'd revealed during my forensic interviews.

∞

The first stop was my apartment.

A long, white box leaned against the doorframe. As I got closer, I recognized it from one of the local florists. Darren. Maybe this was an actual apology for everything that happened before his mysterious hand-smashing incident. Too little, too late.

I scooped up the box and unlocked the door.

Olivia wandered around the living room while I gathered more essentials. She zeroed in on the wall of shelves stuffed with law books, psych books, and a section dedicated entirely to murderers. Since the books on suicidology were crammed on the bottom, thankfully they didn't attract her attention. I didn't feel like chatting about the reasons for my interest in the topic.

She pointed at the books and raised an eyebrow. "You have a thing for serial killers?"

I tried not to read too much into what could be insinuated as an insult. "It's my job."

"Uh-huh." She turned her attention to the white box I'd left by the door. "Aren't you going to open this?"

"No." I had no interest in whatever Darren had to say. The heap of mail I'd dumped on the table was far more appealing than his nonsense. "Before we go, I need to stop by my office at Parkview."

"Fine." She took the lid off the box and promptly dropped it. "What the fuck?"

"What?" I crossed the living room to see what she was talking about.

Inside the white tissue paper lay the remnants of a dozen red roses. They were all dead. By the looks of them, they had been for some time. More disturbing, however, was the fact the top of each rose had been lopped off. A few fat, pinky-brown worms wriggled over the stems and the shriveled bodies of their friends. The whole thing reeked like rotten, musty dirt.

Olivia swiped the card from the decrepit bouquet and tore it open. "What the fuck?" She repeated each word slowly and deliberately before I snatched it out of her hand.

> *Roses are red,*
> *Violets are blue.*
> *Leave Leander alone,*
> *Or I'm coming after you.*

Throwing the card back in the box, I slammed the lid down and backed away from it.

"Where did this come from?" Disgust marked every aspect of Olivia's face. Either she was a brilliant actress, or Leander didn't tell her about the bird.

"Let's get out of here," I said, hurrying out of the apartment. I didn't want to stick around any longer than necessary, nor did I want to think about the fact someone was out there planning God knew what. Suddenly, I was grateful for Olivia's company.

⁕

The drive to Parkview was longer than I remembered. It should have felt familiar but in the weeks of my absence it lost any of the warmth it once had.

Olivia insisted on coming inside with me. Even though she and I were far from friends, I felt better having something of an ally by my side walking through the front doors. She stopped in the lobby, waving me on ahead. As the elevator doors closed, I saw her on her cell phone. No doubt calling Leander about the roses.

Any sense of discomfort disappeared the moment I saw Calvin. He grinned and wrapped me in a fierce hug. "Doc! Tell me you're back. We miss you!"

I frowned. "Not yet. I'm just here to sign off on some case files and grab a few things from my office."

"Well don't stay away too long. We're in the middle of another staffing crisis. Could sure use the help around here."

"Why? What's happened now?"

He rolled his eyes. "You know how it is. Nora quit. That orderly, Mark, quit. Another nurse put her two-weeks in. Kim is pulling her hair out of her head."

Hearing Nora quit was the most surprising and pleasant

news of all. I rejoiced silently for all of the patients who wouldn't have to suffer under her apathetic care. "We'll see. I'm still kind of dealing with some stuff."

"Yeah, I get it. But hey, I know Martha would love to see you if you have time."

"I'll check in before I go. It was good to see you." I squeezed his arm with a smile and headed to my office.

There was a stack of files on my desk and another pile of mail to go through. I sorted the files as quickly as I could, signing off on treatment plans and deferring future patients to Dennis. I shoved the other handful of mail into my bag and hauled the files to the nurse's station for Amanda to pick up later.

I was heading for the dayroom when Gene appeared, his face lined with worry.

"Got a minute?" he asked, his voice unusually low.

"Sure. What's up?"

He grimaced, pulling at the knot in his tie as he glanced around. "I wanted you to hear it from me first. I got a complaint about you."

My pulse spiked. "What?"

"It didn't come from any official channel, but... we're looking into an ethics violation."

"You're what? What was the complaint?" It could only have been one thing, one person — Leander. Heat rushed to my cheeks. I hoped it would register as anger and not an admission of guilt.

"That you've been inappropriate. With a patient." He looked uncomfortable even saying the words aloud. Hopefully that meant it was unbelievable to the rest of the board, too.

Feigning horror, I gaped at him. He wasn't wrong, but I could never admit it. I would have to use shock and indignation to cover for my inability to lie convincingly. "What are you talking about?"

"Leander Welles?"

"You've got to be kidding." I scoffed and tried to look as disgusted as possible. "Why? Because I exposed two vile employees who mistreated him? You're lucky he hasn't sued Parkview."

"I know. I know." Gene grimaced and scratched the back of his neck. "I'm not supposed to say anything, ok? The complaint came from Nora, so you know it's probably not going to go anywhere. But if she goes to the medical board... there could be another inquiry. And you know what happens if there's even a whiff of scandal."

"Clean slate," I murmured. Terminate every employee associated with the unpleasantness, appease the board and the investors, and start fresh.

Gene nodded solemnly.

The letter on Leander's counter popped into my head. Was Nora the blackmailer? It made sense. But Leander said he was going to pay it, so why would she turn around and complain about me to Parkview? Unless that was the motivating factor for Leander to finally pay her. Maybe that's why he didn't want me coming back here — he was trying to keep me in the dark about this, too.

"So what now?" I asked, crossing my arms over my chest.

"You know, we'll review the sessions, talk to the staff. We'll have to talk to Mr. Welles, obviously, and see what he has to say. I know it's a pain in the ass but we have to cross the Ts and dot the Is."

"I know. Thanks for the warning."

Gene gave me a bleak smile. "Talk soon, ok?"

As much as I wanted to drive straight back to Easton and have it out with Leander, I went and found Martha instead.

The moment she saw me, she flapped her hands and spun in a tight circle.

"Hi Martha. How are you?"

She wrung her hands together, shuffling from one foot to the other. Before I could say anything else, she shoved a crumpled piece of paper into my hands. It was a painting of a black and yellow blob. I smiled when I realized it was a rudimentary bee. In addition to Calvin, Leander must have shared his comparison of me with Martha.

"Thank you, Martha. It's lovely."

She clapped and handed me the angel painting of Leander as well.

"For me?" I furrowed my brows at her.

She shook her head.

"For Leander?"

She responded by giving me a lopsided smile and what I think was a wink.

I glanced around the dayroom. None of the other patients or staff were paying us any attention. Did she know? Did Leander say something to her? Or was she more observant than anyone gave her credit for?

Rolling the paintings carefully, I smiled. "Thank you, Martha. Take care."

She blinked hard and picked up her paintbrush again, swiping bright red streaks of paint over the surface.

$\mathcal{T}$he drive back to Easton was as quiet as the drive up had been.

Olivia dropped me off with little fanfare, speeding away in her own vehicle without so much as a backward glance. She didn't give me any time to thank her for being my chauffeur, even if it wasn't by choice.

Surprisingly, Leander wasn't home when I marched in the front door. Maybe he went to the office to handle the rest of his calls.

After putting away my things in the guest room, I settled into the couch in the library with my mountain of mail. Most of the stuff from my apartment was junk, thanks to the advent of paperless billing.

The mail from my office ranged the gamut from subpoenas to checks to personal letters from former patients or their doctors, updating me on their status. Other than the card included with the box of dead roses, my pen pal didn't seem to have sent any more letters to Parkview.

I sorted the mail into piles to tackle each task separately.

After the subpoenas were dealt with, I turned my attention to the professional services pile.

A letter from Scheible's office was at the top. I sliced it open and unfolded the pages inside. It was the standard completion of our contract; the final invoice and a note scribbled on the bottom in round, girly letters confirming payment had been rendered. The initials beneath the note read G. B. — Greta Burkhardt.

Rolling my eyes, I tossed the invoice to the side, happy to be rid of the nitwit once and for all.

Three envelopes later and an unsettled feeling crept into the pit of my stomach. Shuffling through the discarded papers, I pulled out the invoice from Greta and studied the handwriting, comparing it to my memory of the letter Leander received. It couldn't be her. Could it?

Slipping off the couch, I crossed the library to the large desk. A quick search of the drawers turned up nothing useful. Unless he took it to the office, there was only one other place I could think of that Leander would stash the letter.

Tip-toeing up the stairs, I called out for him in case he came in the back door without me hearing.

Silence.

I darted into Leander's room and headed straight to the writing table. Much to my annoyance, the center drawer was still locked. A silver letter opener winked at me in the fading sunlight, daring me to use it.

Biting my lip, I weighed the pros and cons. It was a blatant invasion of privacy. But it was also the only way I could find out what was going on since Leander seemed determined to keep things from me.

Consequences be damned.

I snatched the letter opener off the desk and wedged the tip inside the edge of the drawer. Like the rest of the furniture in the house, it was an antique, the lock couldn't be that strong.

It wasn't.

In another heartbeat, I held a stack of letters similar to the ones Leander and I already received. Some were to him — most were to me. While my current residency in Easton was unknown to the vast majority of people, somehow someone knew, as evidenced by the dead crow and a slew of hate mail. The letters grew increasingly hostile, from warning Leander about what a terrible person I was to outright blackmail. The ones directed at me were much more explicit, detailing what horrible things were about to befall me unless I left town immediately.

"Looking for something?" a voice asked behind me.

Jumping at the sound, I dropped the jumble of letters. They fluttered to the ground as I whirled to face the man in the doorway. It wasn't Leander.

"Jake," I said, backing up against the desk. Dark as it may have been, I remembered the man's face. I glared at him. "Or should I say, Jacob?"

He smiled. It reminded me Olivia's — smooth and cold, with none of the charm he had the night he picked me up on the side of the road. "So you remember."

"Why didn't you tell me who you were?"

"What does it matter?" He took a step into the room. I slid in the other direction, keeping the distance between us. "You needed a ride. I gave you one."

"Where have you been this whole time?" I tried to sound casual, but the muscles in my throat were tight. Cole's warning whispered in the back of my mind. He thought Jake was a killer. And now here he was. Alone. With me.

"You should ask Leander." Jake walked forward another step.

I bumped into the edge of the bed. "Is he here with you?"

"You seem really nervous. Is everything ok?"

"Never mind. I found them," Leander called out. "They were misfiled under the bridge project." He walked in with his head bent, his nose buried in a folder. Stopping short, Leander lowered the file and shot a questioning glance at Jake. "Lorelei. I didn't expect you back so soon."

"I figured Olivia told you." I stayed where I was, not sure what I was interrupting. It looked like business as usual, but I could never be sure with Leander. "I didn't hear you come in."

Leander closed the folder and handed it off to Jake as he crossed the room. "Take these to the office, please."

Jake nodded, disappearing without another word.

"Why didn't you tell me Jake was the one who picked me up?" I asked, one hand on my hip.

"I don't see how that is relevant."

"It's another secret, Leander. Another needless secret."

"Is that why you felt it necessary to rifle through my effects?" Kneeling, Leander gathered the letters into a neat pile. If he was angry, he didn't show it. He appeared to be his calm, controlled self.

I scoffed. "You should have told me. God knows you had plenty of opportunities."

Canting his head to the side, Leander studied me as he rose to his feet. Still, he said nothing.

Unfortunately for him, I was not about to let it go, not after the wormy, decapitated roses. "Tell me, is it Nora? I know she told Parkview about us. I'm currently under review for an ethics violation. So is she the one blackmailing you? Is it Jake, trying to scare me off? Or is it Greta?" I yanked the invoice out of my pocket and brandished it beneath his nose.

He swatted it away without even looking at it. "I told you I'm handling it. I wouldn't fret about the ethics review.

Nothing verboten occurred at Parkview, as you well remember."

"Did Olivia tell you about the roses?"

Pushing my hair over my shoulder, he lowered his mouth to the side of my neck. "I won't let anything dire happen to you," he murmured between kisses. "Ever."

I tried to push him away but he held on to my waist. "You can't control everything, Leander. It's impossible."

"Anything is possible with enough determination." He pushed me backward onto the bed before settling himself on top of me, pinning my wrists above my head.

"I want to talk to you." I tried to pull my hands free, to no avail. He responded by pressing them even further into the pillow and kissing me hard, until the room started to spin.

"Do you still want to talk?" he whispered, as breathless as I was. He relaxed his hold on my wrists, dragging his fingertips down the length of my arms.

"No." I grabbed a hold of his face and pulled him down again, picking up where he left off. It wasn't practical. It wasn't rational. It was pure emotion — desire and anger, all rolled into one. I couldn't explain it. I didn't want to analyze it. In the moment, I wanted to free myself from all of my thoughts and fears and worries. The easiest way to do that was to lose myself in Leander.

CHAPTER 38

*O*ur morning started cruelly with Leander's cell phone ringing. Untangling himself from me, he leaned over the edge of the bed and retrieved it from his discarded pants. He made a face at the screen before answering with a clipped tone. "Leander Welles."

I propped my chin on his chest, watching him and the myriad of expressions he made. His eyes did most of the talking while he listened to whomever it was on the other end. Curiosity, annoyance, a flash of anger, and stone-cold resolve. He offered few words to the caller, beyond an annoyed "I know who you are," and "eleven o'clock is fine." He disconnected without saying goodbye and let the phone fall to the floor again.

"What was that all about?" I asked.

"Gene Lowery. He's driving down to depose me."

"He's what?" I sat up, staring at him.

"We're meeting at the office."

"Is Scheible going to be there?"

"Among others."

"Why doesn't that make me feel better?" I frowned at him.

"I have never lost a battle, Lorelei. I'm not about to start."

◆

Pacing back and forth inside the foyer, I waited for Leander to return. The porch would have been my preferred spot since it offered a better vantage of the road leading up to the driveway, but I was under strict instructions to stay inside. I didn't know if Leander thought Gene would come to the house, or if it was about the person blackmailing him. Either way, I wasn't about to argue.

Annabel sat on the bottom stair, watching me, her tail twitching.

"It's going to be ok, right? Leander is going to convince him nothing happened and Gene will go on his way." I looked at the cat for confirmation.

She blinked at me.

"Nothing happened at Parkview." I glared at her.

She yawned and stretched her front paws out before plopping down in a patch of sunlight.

"And as for the threats… he said he'd take care of that too."

My cell phone barely finished its first ring when I swiped to accept.

"Lorelei," Dennis said after my frantic hello. "Are you ok?"

Clearing my throat, I tried to sound normal. "Yep. Fine. Just thought it was someone else."

"Like Gene?"

"I take it he talked to you?" That was fast. I thought Gene would have dragged his feet on this review. Unless he was getting pressure from the board.

"He talked to everyone. Why didn't you tell me you were in town yesterday?" He sounded hurt. I kicked myself for not including him in my itinerary, but I also figured there was no way Olivia would have agreed to go to Dennis' house after my surprise parcel.

"Sorry, I just had some quick errands. I wasn't there long. So, tell me about Gene…"

Dennis sighed. "I told him it's all bullshit. I told him you're a consummate professional and would never cross that line."

"He's here," I said quietly, closing my eyes. "He's talking to Leander."

"I did what I could for you, kid."

"Thanks, Dennis. I really appreciate it."

I hung up with a sigh. I didn't expect Dennis, of all people, to outright lie for me but I was grateful he did. Dennis' word carried weight, not just at Parkview but also at St. Mary's. As long as Gene couldn't find any direct evidence contrary to what we'd already said, the review should be fine. Right?

⁂

By the time Leander made it home, the sun had set and I was at the bottom of a bottle of Pinot Grigio. He strolled into the library, stepping over my laptop and the piles of papers I'd created on the floor.

Loosening the knot on his tie, he assessed me with an arched eyebrow. "Staying busy, are we?"

"It's either that or go crazy." I drained the rest of my wine, setting the glass down with a delicate clink.

An impish smirk pulled at his lips. "Interesting choice of word, Doctor."

I glared at him. "I've been waiting all day and you're going to stand there, not saying anything?"

He lowered himself to the floor next to me, leaning back against the couch. "There's nothing to say. He asked his questions, I gave him the answers they deserved. Before it was

299

over my lawyers informed him they already filed a lawsuit against Parkview."

"You what?" I blinked.

He smiled, but it was a bit too thin, bordering on bitter.

"But what, exactly, did you say to Gene? What did he say? Who else is he talking to?"

"I'm afraid he didn't spell out his plans for me. He did, however, tell Richard he would need to speak with him privately, as well as Greta."

My blood boiled at the mention of her name. If anyone could undo our carefully constructed fabrication, it was Greta. "Is she the one who sent all of those letters? You never did answer me."

His lips twitched as his gaze swept past me, staring at the void behind my head.

"No." I seized his tie and yanked his face closer to mine. "You don't get to not answer anymore." His eyes were glowing again, the same dangerous look that gave me the sense I was toying with fire.

"It's her, isn't it?" I pressed on, winding the black silk around my hand. His mouth was a whisper from mine. Each time he exhaled, it blew across my lips, short and hot, smelling of spearmint.

"Yes."

Shifting forward into his lap, I maintained my hold on his tie, pulling it taut until we were nose-to-nose again. "No more lies, Leander."

He shook his head, his eyes half-hooded.

I did what I wished he would have done that night in the dining room when he extracted the same promise. I kissed him until our lips were swollen, until our clothes were torn to shreds and we fell in an exhausted heap on the library floor.

⊰❦⊱

The moon was high in the sky when I woke, sore and shivering on the plush oriental rug. Massaging the crick in my neck, I looked around for Leander.

He was gone, as were his clothes.

Not knowing whether to be dismayed, confused, or absolutely furious, I gathered the remnants of my clothing and scurried up the stairs. I dressed quickly in the guest room before hurrying down the hall to Leander's bedroom. Flicking on the light, I glared at the interior.

"Leander!"

It was empty, save for Annabel, curled up in the middle of the bed.

Where was he?

I whirled through the house, checking every room, calling his name.

Nothing.

I didn't find a note during my hunt. There was nothing to indicate where he'd gone. His cell phone went unanswered. I found it on the kitchen island, along with his car keys.

All of the doors and windows were locked. Unless he shimmied down the drain pipe outside his bedroom window, he didn't leave the house. He just vanished.

Then I remembered — the tunnel.

Taking the basement stairs two at a time, I bypassed all of the rooms and headed straight for the windowless root cellar.

A hot sickness roiled in the pit of my stomach when I turned the corner.

The canning shelves were slid to one side. The trap door was open.

Retrieving a lantern from the milk crate, I switched it on and descended into the darkness, trying not to shriek when something brushed my face. I swiped it away frantically, scolding myself for being an idiot when I realized it was just a spiderweb.

The sub-basement was also empty. The sound of the river echoed off the limestone walls, surprisingly soothing in the small, cave-like room. Part of me wanted to make my way through the tunnel and go in search of him. But I knew better. I had no idea where he'd gone, not to mention I had no idea how to get from the river back up the bluff to civilization.

Setting the lantern on the dirt floor, I sat on an old whiskey barrel in the corner and waited.

And waited.

Time slowed to a crawl.

Once I lost feeling in my legs from the lip of the barrel, I started pacing, checking my watch again and again. Every creak and groan made me pause, straining to hear something over the river.

I lost track of the minutes, then the hours.

Where was he? And what, exactly, was he doing? As much as I wanted to know the answers, I dreaded the truth. I dreaded what it meant.

At long last, the unmistakable sound of footsteps echoed through the tunnel. With my heartbeat thumping in my ears, I counted each one until a figure appeared, praying it was Leander returning, safe and sound.

The shadows peeled away from the person the closer they got to the circle of light.

It was Leander.

There were dark flecks on his pale skin, along with distinct splatters across his face and his throat.

It was blood.

His hands were similarly covered in speckles. One still held a crowbar, dark and glistening wet in the lantern-light.

When his eyes landed on me, I held my breath. We stared at each other until I found the courage to use my voice, strained as it was. "Greta?"

Holding his head high, he met my gaze full on with the same smoldering severity that first drew me to him.

"Yes." There wasn't an ounce of regret in his voice, only merciless resolve.

Now I knew. I could never un-know. There could never be another doubt in my mind. If there was, it was delusion, pure and simple.

Leander was a murderer.

He killed with his own hands. His blood-covered hands. He assumed the ultimate power over someone's life — he took what was living and rendered it dead, for no other reason than he deemed it so.

Canting his head, he studied me like a panther watching its prey. His face held no discernible emotion. Even his eyes were hard to read clearly in the dim light. I couldn't tell if he was plotting my death or simply waiting for a reaction.

Tentatively, I moved forward, my eyes locked with his. As much as I wanted to keep an eye on the crowbar, to watch for a sudden jerk of his arm, I couldn't.

Stretching upward on my toes, I reached for his face. He didn't pull away as I held it gently between my hands. I didn't flinch. I *couldn't* flinch, the same way you couldn't make sudden movements in front of a predator.

What should have horrified me, didn't. What should have left me shaking, didn't.

I understood.

Like clouds parting after a storm, I finally understood everything he'd been saying all along, everything about who he was and how he thought. The final piece of the puzzle slid seamlessly into place.

My heart nearly burst with the realization, confirmed by

this one depraved act. Greta's death wasn't a random act of violence, some senseless atrocity by a serial killer satisfying his need for bloodlust.

Her death was a gift meant for me and me alone. Perhaps he'd been planning on killing her all along, but tonight — mere hours after he'd told me she was scheduled to be deposed by Gene — tonight sealed her fate. Leander kept his promise. He wasn't about to let Greta, or anyone else, do anything to harm me. Like a mafioso protecting his empire, Leander did what he had to do to ensure I was safe. And instead of hiring a hitman, he saw to the problem personally.

Leander swallowed, watching me, waiting for my reaction.

"I still choose you," I whispered, afraid to speak at full-volume with the darkness pressing in around us. Smiling softly, I nodded, hoping he believed me. "You are my sun, Leander. You are everything I've been waiting for. I will follow you no matter where you go, no matter what you do."

The crowbar fell to the dirt floor as his hands wrapped around my waist. His lips crashed into mine and I surrendered to him entirely.

THE RATIONALE OF LEANDER
WELLES — CHAPTER ONE

"'I am fearless, and therefore powerful.'"

The reflection staring back at me in the small, square mirror looked anything but.

Dark purple shadows hung beneath my eyes, matching the sharp contour underneath my cheekbones. In the weeks since my incarceration, they'd only grown sharper and more defined. All of my bones had become more visible. I couldn't remember the last time I ate anything of real substance. I wasn't complaining. It was a fair trade — giving away food in exchange for peace. Unlike most people, I was willing to make the sacrifices no one else wanted to. Like food, and my freedom.

I stripped off the hideous orange shirt the Camden County jail provided its inmates and threw it on the cot behind me. My cellmate, along with the rest of the gentlemen from D Block congregated around the communal table in the center of the block over a card game. Their laughter and coarse camaraderie buffeted me, echoing off the iron bars and cement walls.

"'I am fearless, and therefore powerful,'" I said again, trying to drown them out.

Before I lost my nerve, I balled my hand into a fist and punched the mirror as hard as I could. The reflective surface splintered and cracked, radiating out from the point of impact. One more quick hit and a larger piece of glass fell away from the rest. I caught it before it shattered in the sink and carried it to my cot.

My knuckles were smeared in blood and my hands had already begun to shake. I punched the wall behind me in an effort to still the trembling. I don't know if it worked or if the new shock of pain was merely a distraction. If anything, the surge of endorphins would help for the task to come.

"'I am fearless, and therefore powerful.'" Closing my eyes, I expelled one final breath. Fear and anger and nausea twisted inside of me. My animal brain screamed at the rational one to stop. I ignored them both.

Without another thought, I drove the jagged piece of glass into my wrist as far as I could. Gritting my teeth, I did my best to contain the yell in my throat to an agonized growl.

Fire shot up my arm while blood poured out the bottom, rushing over the sides of my wrist.

I felt sick. Hot and sweaty, yet frozen to my very core.

The mirror dangled from my fingers before plummeting to the concrete floor. I flopped onto the cot, letting my injured arm hang over the side. That should create a nice pool for the guards to find. Even they couldn't miss something quite so obvious.

"'I am fearless… and… powerful.'"

I expelled another slow, steady breath, trying to get the queasy feeling to subside. Closing my eyes didn't stop the room from spinning. It might have made it worse. The coldness spread throughout my limbs, exacerbating the shaking that refused to stop.

Too far, Leander. You went too far…

"Hey, Welles! Man, what are you doing?" Xavier, my cell-mate, called from the table. I excused myself over a half hour ago, so either he realized something had gone awry, or his so-called winning streak must have come to an end in my absence. Like the extra food, goods from the commissary went a long way in making friends in an eight-by-ten space. Fortunately, I had plenty of money to keep up with my many "losses."

Ignoring him, I counted each drop of blood that rolled off the edge of my palm. It was almost time for the guards' rounds. If I timed it correctly, they'd be walking by the main window of the block in three, two, one…

A jangle of keys, the creak of leather. Perfect.

"Dude, I am talking to you," Xavier said from the door-way. "Oh, shit man! Hey! We need some help!"

Xavier grabbed the discarded shirt and smashed it over my wrist.

I hissed in pain but otherwise remained unmoving.

Through the thick glass, the radio on the guard's shoulder chirped. A voice came over the intercom on the wall ordering the rest of D Block back into their cells. Once they complied, the heavy metal door buzzed open and several pairs of boots rushed in.

"Back off Sanchez," one of the guards said.

"Dude, he needs an ambulance!"

"Get your ass in that corner, now!"

"Everyone move!" It was a female yelling this time. Sergeant Christopher. Lovely. She wouldn't let me die. Not like this. Not without a fight.

There was a change in pressure on my arm and the distinct scent of a floral shampoo. "Stay with us, Leander," she said, squeezing my wrist. "Get a medic up here!"

"They're on their way, Sarge."

A shudder racked my body. Pain and nausea battled for supremacy. I didn't know which was the worse feeling. Both made me want to throw up.

I never thought I'd have this debate ever again. Ten years ago, I swore that part of my life was over. There would never be a need to exsanguinate myself, to add another scar to the multitude. How wrong I was.

"Leander…"

A gloved hand touched my cheek. It smelled like plastic mixed with leather. A swift, hard pat followed the gentleness, just shy of an actual slap.

My eyes shot open, my cheek stinging. I tried to focus on the sergeant's face before it went blurry again.

"Leander, look at me. Keep your eyes on me."

I am fearless, and…

"Hang on just a little bit longer. Help is coming."

———

For more of Leander's story, purchase your copy of THE RATIONALE OF LEANDER WELLES!

Please don't forget to rate/review if you enjoyed the book! Every rating helps indie authors, more than you know.

ABOUT THE AUTHOR

Award-winning dark romance author Ashlyn Drewek has always been a hopeless romantic. She's also fascinated by the dark, macabre things in life (you can blame a love of Halloween and Edgar Allan Poe for that one).

Most of her time is spent making up stories in her head or researching some obscure topic just because she's that much of a nerd. The degree on the wall says she's a historian, but the paycheck says she's a first responder.

Ashlyn lives in Northern Illinois with her patient husband, fearless daughter, and a house full of animals.

For information on news and upcoming releases, check out her website at www.ashlyndrewek.com to sign up for her newsletter, follow her on BookBub, or at any of the social media options below.

ALSO BY ASHLYN DREWEK

The Leander Welles Series:

The Rationale of Leander Welles — a dark, psychological romance about an alleged murder who falls in love with his psychiatrist… or does he?

The Damnation of Leander Welles — a dark, romantic suspense about a cutthroat lawyer and an enigmatic millionaire and what happens when two dark souls join forces. A prequel to Books 1 and 2.

The Wrath of Leander Welles — a dark, romantic suspense about love, revenge, and how a psychopath is willing to go for both.

The Fall of Leander Welles — TBD

The Solnyshko Duet:

The Kidnapping of Roan Sinclair — a dark, MM romance about an American college guy who is kidnapped by a Russian criminal.

The Vengeance of Roan Sinclair — TBD

Other works:

Out of the Dark — A slow-burn paranormal romance about vampires and Chicago cops with commitment issues.

www.ingramcontent.com/pod-product-compliance
Lightning Source LLC
Chambersburg PA
CBHW020809060726
47498CB00017B/1310